WILD AS A WOLF

PAIGE TYLER

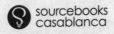

Published by Sourcebooks Casablanca, an imprint of Sourcebooks
P.O. Box 4410, Naperville, Illinois 60567-4410
(630) 961-3900
sourcebooks.com

Printed and bound in the United States of America.
OPM 10 9 8 7 6 5 4 3 2 1

With special thanks to my extremely patient and understanding husband. Without your help and support, I couldn't have pursued my dream job of becoming a writer. You're my sounding board, my idea man, my critique partner, and the absolute best research assistant a girl could ask for. Love you!

Chapter 1

"OFFICER DOWN! REQUESTING IMMEDIATE backup and paramedics," a desperate voice shouted through the radio. "Repeat. Officer down. We have five shooters armed with automatic weapons. Three have already moved inside the nightclub—"

The rest of whatever the officer was going to say got cut off as rapid gunfire echoed over the radio. From where he sat in the rear passenger seat of the SUV listening to the bullets fly, SWAT Officer Hale Delaney cursed. Other voices drifted across the radio as more cops reached the scene only to quickly realize they were outgunned. Hearing them shout for backup and paramedics made Hale's inner werewolf want to break out in the worst way.

"How far are we?" Hale asked, gripping the handle mounted above the seat and holding on for dear life as fellow werewolf Senior Corporal Carter Nelson steered the SWAT vehicle around the next corner, driving way too fast.

"Three miles and closing fast," senior corporal and werewolf Trey Duncan responded calmly from the front passenger seat, his gaze locked on the vehicle's GPS. "We'll be there in a little over two minutes."

Imagining how much damage a handful of people armed with automatic weapons could do in that amount of time, Hale didn't think two minutes was going to be fast enough.

Pushing that thought aside, he did his best to ignore the sounds coming over the radio, focusing instead on counting the number of blocks between them and the nightclub. His efforts were wasted. There was no way to shut out the shouting, gunfire, and screams of terror.

In the front seats, both of his pack mates' eyes glowed yellow-gold, a clear sign that their inner werewolves were trying to slip out as their anxiety built. Hale's own inner wolf felt the same. He only prayed they arrived at the scene in time to do more than help with the wounded and cover up the dead.

"You think we're dealing with the same people who've been terrorizing Dallas the past couple of weeks?" Carter asked, taking another turn so fast the tires of the SUV squawked as they slid across the pavement.

Hale snorted. "Five shooters hitting a nightclub full of people, all heavily armed with assault rifles and multiple-edged weapons. What do you think?"

Carter only grunted in agreement.

This would be their boldest move yet, though. First, there'd been the attack at a large outdoor party near Terrace Grove that ended with a dozen people dead, all of them with ties to the Hillside

Riders, a local gang. Everyone assumed it was the beginning of a new turf war because the MO had fit the narrative. Five shooters, all of them big, muscular, and wearing tactical gear that obscured their faces and protected them from return fire. The way they'd gone straight after the most heavily armed members of the Riders, it made sense they were members of a rival gang.

The second incident had been against a small convenience store. Headquarters hadn't made the connection to the first attack until the description of the same five heavily armed shooters had come through. Then they'd figured out that the store was a front for a gambling establishment run by the Russian Mafia and that all of the dead and injured were inked with known Russian crime tattoos. It was enough to toss the entire gang-war theory out the window and replace it with the thought that this was an even bigger war and that someone was making a move against all the different criminal elements in the city.

If that was true, then the attack on the club tonight made sense. It was a well-known gang hangout and served as neutral ground, where members of twenty or thirty different gangs would frequently gather. If someone wanted to make a dent in the criminal population of the city, that club was the place to do it. But the number of innocent people who would lose their lives as well was more than Hale wanted to think about.

Hale heard gunfire and screaming coming from inside the club even as Carter slid the SUV to a stop half a block short of the front entrance. The second SWAT vehicle carrying their pack mates Senior Corporal Mike Taylor and Officer Connor Malone passed them and came to a stop at an angle in front of the club's doors, serving as a protective barricade.

As Hale shoved open his door and jumped out of the back seat, he realized a barricade wasn't going to be necessary. While the area in front of the club was complete bedlam with people shouting and running everywhere, the shooters had already moved inside.

Hale scanned the area as he started forward, trying to see into every dark corner and alley while also keeping his gaze on all the people fleeing the club. Many of them were bleeding and even more were freaking out. He was pretty sure he saw a handgun or two among the crowd. But this was Texas, so people carrying weapons wasn't exactly uncommon.

He reached the two Dallas Police Department patrol units parked nose to nose up on the curb in front of the club, doors wide-open, lights blazing, shattered glass lying everywhere. There were three injured cops on the ground near the doors. One was groaning in pain from a leg wound, but the other two were unconscious. His keen werewolf hearing picked up heartbeats, but they were both slower than they should have been.

Hale scooped up the cop with the slowest heart rate and sprinted back to the SWAT vehicles. Trey was there already, treating three injured people from the club. As one of the SWAT team's medics, Trey was used to dealing with gunshot wounds, though he was admittedly more experienced with treating werewolves than non-supernaturals. But he simply needed to keep everyone alive until the scene was safe enough for paramedics to move in.

The moment Hale placed the injured cop on the ground, he shouted an alert to Trey that the guy was in bad shape, then he was racing back for the next wounded officer. He passed Connor on the way, carrying the other unconscious cop. When Hale reached the cop with the leg wound, he yanked the man's belt off without preamble and strapped it tightly around the officer's right thigh, then picked him up and ran over to Trey.

There were even more injured people from the club scattered around Trey and his medic bag now, and any other time Hale would have stayed to help. But the shooting and screams inside the club had only gotten worse, and Carter and Mike were in there on their own. It was time to go.

Hale had to urge several terrified people out of the club before he could force his way past the rest of the crowd trying to push their way out. If the area outside the building was pandemonium, inside was chaos beyond his imagination.

The place was dark except for the neon signs illuminating the bar and the strobe lights above the huge dance floor. The darkness didn't keep Hale's keen werewolf sight from seeing as clearly as if it was day, but the spastic lighting made a nightmarish scene all that much worse as people climbed over each other to reach the door. He couldn't blame them, as five big men in heavy tactical gear moved through the still-crowded club shooting in what seemed an indiscriminate fashion.

But then Hale realized the attackers *weren't* merely blazing away at anything that moved. If he didn't know better, he'd think they were only going after the most heavily armed opponents. In this crowd, that left them with a lot of options.

Carter and Mike were on the far side of the club, engaging with three of the black-clad attackers, leaving the other two to roam free through the crowd. Locking his sights on the nearest one, Hale shoved his way through the throng of panicked people. The huge man was pointing an assault rifle at a group of young men crouched down behind a table they'd flipped over—a table that wouldn't come close to stopping the rounds that weapon fired.

Hale itched to pull his Sig Sauer .40 caliber as he moved closer, but in the crowded space he knew that wasn't an option. No matter how accurate he was with the handgun, the risk that he might hit a bystander was too great, considering how many innocents were around the shooter. So instead, Hale put his shoulder down and bulled through the crowd, the muscles of his legs and back beginning to twist and spasm as he partially shifted.

He was less than ten feet away when the guy with the assault rifle somehow picked up on his approach, spinning suddenly and bringing his weapon up and pointing straight at him.

With a growl, Hale launched himself the last few feet, knocking the barrel of the weapon downward just as it went off, bullets ricocheting off the concrete flooring. Praying the stray rounds didn't hit anyone, he slammed into the big man's chest at full speed.

It felt like hitting a brick wall. Hale felt the bones in his shoulder and chest crack as pain surged up and down his spine. Cursing, Hale took the man to the ground in a tangle of arms and legs. He got a grip on the barrel of the assault rifle, ripping it away before another burst of gunfire nearly took his face off. With a heave and a snarl, he slung the weapon across the club, then turned all his attention on his opponent.

The man was back on his feet, circling him with what could only be called a bloodthirsty look in his dark eyes. Hale had studied Muay Thai and Krav Maga since he was seventeen, so he wasn't concerned about engaging in hand-to-hand combat, especially because he was a werewolf, but all it took was one punch from the guy to realize he was dealing with someone inhumanly strong. Even the glancing blow nearly broke his jaw. And when Hale slipped the man's strikes and moved in to slam an elbow into his jaw, the guy barely seemed to notice.

Was he dealing with some kind of supernatural?

For the millionth time, Hale wished that his nose worked as well as all the other werewolves' in the Pack. If it did, he'd have known right away whether the guy was a werewolf or not. But his nose hadn't worked since he was seventeen and some asshole had broken it. Even becoming a werewolf years later hadn't fixed the damage.

The two of them rolled and tumbled across the floor of the club as they fought, smashing through tables and chairs, people screaming as they scrambled away. While Hale couldn't bear to even think about pulling his sidearm in this crowd, his opponent didn't have that problem. In a blur of motion, the man's hand came up with a large-frame automatic handgun.

Hale had no choice but to let the claws on his right hand extend. Hoping the darkness and strobing lights would keep anyone nearby from seeing anything too clearly, he slashed his claws across the guy's forearm. He wasn't aiming to inflict serious damage, but he couldn't let this guy start firing off rounds in the club. Hopefully, he'd be able to explain the claws marks away as a byproduct of all the smashed furniture. It was a risk but worth it to disarm one of these killers.

His claws struck true, digging into the man's forearm. But instead of drawing blood, his claws merely scraped across the skin with a grating sound like nails on an old-school chalkboard.

That didn't make sense. A werewolf's claws could rip through wood, concrete, and even steel in the right situation.

Okay, it was starting to look like this guy definitely *wasn't* human.

The man yanked his arm back a little, glancing down at the scratches Hale's claws had left instead of the bloody gashes Hale had expected. The man lifted his head to regard Hale with an expression that was part anger, part curiosity.

Hale tensed, expecting the guy to put a bullet through his forehead. *That* would be bad. A werewolf could survive damn near any amount of damage, but a bullet to the head or heart would be enough to kill him.

But instead, the man lunged to the side and grabbed the first person within reach—a woman with dark, curly hair who couldn't have been more than twenty-one years old. She screamed as he put a heavily muscled arm around her neck and dragged her in front of him like a shield as he backpedaled, angling toward the back of the club. He was no longer pointing the gun at Hale; he was aiming it at the woman.

Hale bit back a growl and finally drew his own weapon. "Freeze right there! Let the woman go. No one needs to get hurt here."

The guy never slowed, heading for what was most assuredly a rear exit with the woman in front of him as a human shield.

Out of the corner of his eye, Hale saw that Carter and Mike still had their hands full with the other four shooters. There'd be no help coming from that direction.

In the fraction of a second Hale had wasted glancing at his pack mates, the guy with the hostage had moved all the way across the club, regardless of how hard the terrified woman was kicking and struggling. Hale hurried after them, worrying about what would happen to the hostage if he lost sight of them. Being forced to fight his way through the throng of people still in the club looking for a way out slowed him down, and by the time he raced along the dark corridor behind the DJ's booth, the back door was already swinging closed.

Hale slammed through the metal door, darting his head left and right as he found himself in a trash-strewn alley. When he spotted the woman on the ground, his stomach plummeted, but then he picked up her heartbeat.

"Are you okay?" he asked, sliding to his knees besides the woman.

Besides her tousled hair and clothes, she seemed fine. She was definitely dazed though.

She pushed herself upright, nodding and pointing down the alley. "He let me go the moment we got outside. Then he kept running that way. He was so damn fast."

Hale looked in the direction she pointed, expecting the man to be long gone. Which was why he was stunned to see the guy standing at the end of the alley returning Hale's gaze with a look that could only be called challenging. Then he slowly turned and took off.

Any thought Hale might have had about not going after the man disappeared the moment he started running. There was a part of Hale that insisted he was simply doing his job as a cop by chasing a dangerous bad guy. But there was another part—the bigger part—that saw the man running away and couldn't help but think of him as prey.

And as a werewolf, Hale simply couldn't ignore chasing down prey.

Within three blocks of dark, trash-filled alleys, Hale was surer than ever that the man he was chasing was some kind of supernatural. There was no way a human could run this fast, leaping over walls and dumpsters like it was nothing. Hale was one of the faster alpha werewolves in an entire pack of alphas, yet he was still fighting to keep up with the man ahead of him, much less gain any ground.

He must have chased the man for two damn miles, pretty sure the guy was purposely staying just out of reach instead of leaving him in the dust. Hale's gut told him that he was being lured into a trap, but when he finally decided to pull up and end the pursuit, he rounded a corner to find the man standing in the middle of a dimly lit alley, three-story buildings on the left and right, and dumpsters blocking a good portion of the far end.

It was a natural ambush site.

Hale whipped his head around, looking for snipers on the roof and accomplices in the shadows. In all of the previous attacks, there had only been five suspects reported, but there was no reason to think there couldn't be another—or even more than one—waiting for a cop dumb enough to let himself get lured out here to the middle of nowhere, far from backup.

Since he didn't have a nose he could trust, Hale was forced to depend on his eyes and ears. Surprisingly, he neither saw nor heard anything that even suggested there was anyone else out here with them. Only the one silent assailant standing in the dim light coming from a single nearby filth-covered bulb, waiting patiently. Like he was allowing Hale to reach some kind of decision. The guy didn't even have his weapon out.

Having no idea why he did it, Hale holstered his own weapon and began to move forward. He wondered if he should say something about the guy being under arrest but ultimately decided against it. Something told him the man was never going to come peaceably. This was going to come down to who won the fight that was about to start.

The man swung a mind-blurringly fast punch toward Hale's throat, one that would have crushed his larynx if it connected. It didn't. But the next one aimed at his floating ribs sure as hell did; the crack of bones breaking was probably loud enough to hear a block away.

With his martial arts training combined with his werewolf speed and strength, Hale had always thought he was the most dangerous fighter in Texas, but maybe he was wrong. Because now that they were out of the club and free to do whatever they wanted, this guy he was up against was violent AF.

Within sixty seconds, both of them had landed at least a dozen blows each, breaking skin and bones, all in complete silence. The man didn't let out a peep even when Hale broke his collarbone.

Hale hadn't intended to let his inner werewolf make an appearance for this fight. Even if he'd already snuck his claws out in the club, the risk of someone seeing him in his shifted form was too great. It was the one rule the Pack lived by: don't reveal their biggest secret.

But as the man slipped through his defenses again like Hale wasn't even fighting back and aimed a kick at his head that would have crushed his skull, Hale realized he didn't have a choice. This supernatural—whatever he was—was strong enough to kill a werewolf one-on-one. Figuring he'd clean the mess up later, Hale extended his claws and fangs.

The only indication that Hale had caught the man off guard with the sudden shift was a slight narrowing of the eyes. If Hale needed more evidence this guy was supernatural, that was it. Anyone else would have flipped out.

The guy must have decided that claws and fangs justified an upgrade in weapons because, in another flash of motion, one hand came out from behind his back holding a knife with a slightly curved blade about twelve inches long, its razor-sharp edge glinting in the light coming from that one lone bulb.

When the fight began again, this time it was with claws and a blade instead of punches and kicks. Much of Hale's martial arts training—especially Krav Maga—had included defense against people using an edged weapon. But this guy was faster and better trained with the knife than anyone Hale had ever gone up against. Twenty seconds later, Hale already had minor slices across multiple places on his body.

Knowing he would have to take a chance if he

was going to beat this man, Hale stopped blocking some of the strikes, taking several more cuts on purpose to lure the man in closer, letting him think he was slowing down from blood loss. When the man finally became overconfident and overextended himself, Hale struck, going for a blow that would end this fight once and for all.

But just as his claws slammed into the man's exposed throat, Hale saw something that made him wonder if he was seeing things. There along the man's neck, barely visible in the dim light from that naked bulb, were rows upon rows of shimmering, almost-invisible semicircles.

Scales.

The man had frigging scales!

Hale's claws scraped across them with the same nails-on-chalkboard sensation he'd experienced back in the club, sending shivers up and down his spine. The worthless swing did little more than overbalance Hale, leaving him wide-open to a counterstrike in the form of a twelve-inch-long blade being plunged into the right side of his chest.

Hale immediately knew the wound wasn't fatal, since it didn't hit his heart, but it sure as hell hurt. Gritting his teeth to keep from howling in pain, he shoved away from the man to get the blade out, falling to his knees in the process.

For a split second, Hale thought the fact that he wasn't dead would put his opponent off balance enough to allow him to regain his feet and put some distance between them. But in the span of a single heartbeat, the man was moving again, swinging the large blade toward Hale's neck with enough force to take his head off.

Werewolves could handle a lot of damage, but losing a head? Not so much.

Hale tried to fling himself backward, but knew it was too late for that. He was a goner.

The sudden clang of metal on metal was so loud to his sensitive werewolf ears that Hale thought he might actually go deaf, even as the scent of lilac blossoms overwhelmed his nose like nothing he'd ever experienced. Before he could come close to comprehending what had happened, someone shoved him aside and stepped protectively in front of him.

Hale lifted an arm to shield his eyes as bright light lit up the alley, nearly blinding him and casting harsh shadows all over the place. Blinking tears from his eyes, Hale caught sight of someone wearing a long leather duster and swinging a short sword.

A frigging *glowing* short sword!

If Hale was stunned, then the guy with the nearly invisible scales was dumbfounded. Which was probably why he didn't react in time to avoid the spinning back kick delivered by the figure in the leather duster, one that sent Scaly Man flying across the alley to slam into the far building.

Hard.

As in leaving-an-indent-of-his-body-in-the-brick-wall kind of hard. Hale wasn't sure if all the crunching and cracking sounds came from the man or the concrete. Either way, the fight was now officially over.

The figure in the leather duster slowly turned to face Hale, the glowing sword disappearing into thin air. Blinking his eyes several more times, Hale cleared away the last of the light dazzle from his eyes to stare up at his rescuer in disbelief.

The person who'd saved him was a woman. She wore her long, brown hair tied back away from her face in a low ponytail and her green eyes were so bright they reminded him of emeralds.

"Karissa?" he asked softly.

Her stunning eyes widened for a fraction of a second before another bright flash lit up the alley again. His werewolf night vision completely shut down, forcing him to blink his eyes again until they cleared. By the time he could see clearly again, she was gone.

Hale was ready to think it had all been some strange hallucination brought on by his near-death experience. Then he saw the unconscious man slumped against the wall and knew he'd truly seen Karissa Bonifay, the first and only woman he'd ever loved.

Chapter 2

"Only Karissa Bonifay would run away from a big sexy hunk of a man after saving his life," Karissa muttered in exasperation as she walked into the extended-stay hotel she'd been living in for the past few days, fully aware she was talking about herself in the third person and completely fine with that. "Most women would have at least asked for his number. Then again, I suppose I can be forgiven for bailing on the situation since Hale Delaney happens to be the man who ripped out my heart and stomped on it when we were teenagers."

She skipped the elevator, heading for the stairs instead, pausing at the bottom to regain her breath. Her out-of-control breathing had nothing to do with running twenty or so blocks from that dark alley all the way back here to the hotel and everything to do with stumbling across a man she'd never expected to see again for as long as she lived.

"I can't believe you're letting an ex get to you like this," she grumbled to herself as she started up the stairs for the third floor.

She'd been talking to herself like this since middle school as a way to work through difficult problems. Her life had gotten more complicated in high school, so she'd never stopped.

The trek upstairs seemed to take forever as she replayed the past few minutes over and over in her head. She'd damn near lost it when she finally caught up with the SWAT cop chasing that supernatural creature through the back alleys of Dallas, only to realize she'd been following Hale Delaney, the guy she'd dated. Stunned, she'd stood on a nearby rooftop, too overwhelmed to do anything until the supernatural had stabbed her ex in the chest.

Karissa didn't even remember moving, but one moment she was standing on a concrete parapet thirty feet above the dimly lit alley, the next her sword had appeared and she was blocking the blade that would have taken off Hale's head.

The fight against the unknown supernatural hadn't taken long. She'd been so pissed off that her kick had come damn close to killing the guy. Everything was a little fuzzy after that. She'd seen blood on Hale's tactical gear—a lot of it. But the instincts that she'd trusted with her life a hundred times over had insisted that Hale was fine. Functioning on pure adrenaline, she'd cast a dazzling glamour to distract Hale, and then she'd run like a coward.

Karissa did her best to look casual as she reached her room, unlocked the door, and then walked into her suite. Once there, she closed the door and slammed home the dead bolt. Shrugging out of her leather duster, she tossed it on the back of the couch, then did the same with the weapon harness she wore underneath.

With a sigh, she sank down on the couch, laying her head back and trying to get it to stop spinning. That effort proved futile, as every time she closed her eyes, the only thing she saw was Hale getting stabbed. That image, along with the sight of all the blood soaking through his uniform, had her on the verge of hyperventilating. Leaning forward, she put her head between her knees, fighting for a calm that wouldn't come.

"Hale was hurt, and you ran away," she murmured, her voice trembling with some emotion she refused to examine. "What if he's dead?

Deep down, Karissa knew that wasn't a possibility before the thought fully formed in her head. Yes, Hale had been bleeding, but his heartbeat had been strong and his voice steady. Somehow— unbelievably—even after taking a knife to the chest, her ex-boyfriend had been fine. While that answer defied logic, she trusted the instincts that told her it was true.

"Well, he is a coldhearted bastard," she pointed out to herself. "Maybe the blade missed his heart because he doesn't have one. That would explain a lot."

Karissa was on her feet the moment the door to the adjoining suite burst open. She was a microsecond from calling her sword back into existence when she realized it was only her younger brother.

Tall and dark-haired with green eyes a shade darker than her own, Deven stared at her for a moment, his gaze going back and forth between her aggressive posture and fighting gear within reach. He focused on her duster for a moment, his eyes going a little wide, and Karissa wondered what he'd seen. She hoped she hadn't torn her jacket.

"You told me you were only going out for a simple recon of Patterson's hotel," Deven said. "So why are you standing here looking like you're about to attack me, and why is there blood on your duster?"

Blood?

Crap.

It must have gotten on her coat when she shoved Hale behind her.

Sighing, Karissa flopped down onto the couch again. Dominic Patterson was CEO and majority owner of the Patterson Automotive Group and was here in Dallas to oversee the final stages of construction on a new state-of-the-art vehicle assembly plant slated to open its doors in less than a week.

Not that any of that mattered to Karissa. The only reason she even knew the man's name was because he was currently being pursued by a hit man who was almost certainly some kind of supernatural. She and Deven worked for their family's private security firm, which specialized in providing personal protection for high-profile people.

Unfortunately, while she might have been hired to protect the man, it didn't mean he made it easy for her. Patterson was arrogant and stubborn and simply refused to treat the threat against his life seriously. Which explained why she and Deven were staying in a hotel almost a mile away from her client's. And why she'd been forced to recon his hotel covertly in the middle of the night.

She'd been navigating the situation just fine—regardless of the hurdles Patterson had put in front of her—until everything had gone sideways tonight and she'd ended up in the middle of a fight she had nothing to do with, saving a man she hadn't seen in a decade.

"When I headed out, I had every intention of doing a quick security sweep of Patterson's hotel, then coming back here, but I'd barely started looking around when my spidey sense started tingling," she explained. "I got curious, so I followed my instinct across town until I found…well…trouble."

"Why am I not surprised?" Deven asked, sounding much wiser than his eighteen years should allow. "Are you okay?" he added, taking a seat in the matching chair to the right of the couch, his face full of concern. "Do I need to get the first aid kit?"

Karissa smiled, appreciating beyond words that Deven still cared for her as a sister, even if she wasn't quite as normal as everyone else in their family. But her baby brother had never minded that she'd become a Paladin—also known as a filia palladis, or a daughter of Athena—on her sixteenth birthday. To him, she'd always simply been his sister—his cool, if slightly unusual, sister. And that meant everything to her.

"No, we don't need the first aid kit," she said. "I'm fine. Just a few bumps and bruises. No big deal."

"You sure?" He frowned like he thought she might be lying about her injuries. "Because I've never seen you look this shaken up before. What happened? Did the hit man show up?"

Karissa knew why Deven's mind had immediately gone in that direction. There had already been two attempts on Patterson's life, both missing their intended target but ending with innocent people dead anyway.

The first attempt on Patterson's life had happened before Karissa had come on board. Someone had broken into his corporate headquarters and slipped through multiple layers of advanced security, making it all the way to Patterson's office before a security guard stumbled across him. That guard had ended up dead, but the noise had been enough to alert Patterson to the danger in time for him to escape. The ease with which the killer had gotten through security—and the fact that they were dealing with someone who had no compunction when it came to murdering innocents—had scared enough people to convince Patterson to hire her family's security company.

Karissa had interrupted the second murder attempt, this time at Patterson's mansion outside Cincinnati. She hadn't gotten a clear look at the hit man's face but had seen enough to feel confident she was dealing with a man. She was also fairly certain he was a supernatural. There was no other explanation for how fast and silent the killer had been or the disquieting sense of dread that surrounded him. The moment Karissa had gotten close to him, she'd been sure she was going to die in the worst possible way. The premonition had been creepy.

The supernatural—whatever he was—had no problem bypassing the home's extremely elaborate electronic security system and locked doors. Worse, his lack of remorse had shown up again. He'd cut down the two guards outside Patterson's bedroom for no other reason than because he could. If Karissa hadn't been there to chase him off, he would have gotten into the room for sure and Dominic Patterson would have been dead.

And yet, despite all that, Karissa decided she would have preferred going up against a supernatural hit man than whom she'd actually run into tonight. To say that her breakup with Hale had

WILD AS A WOLF   25

been painful was putting it mildly. Truthfully, she'd hoped never to see him again.

"No, it wasn't the hit man," she finally said, abruptly realizing her brother was still waiting for an answer. "Like I mentioned, I was just starting my recon of the hotel's outer perimeter when I picked up something bad happening south of my location. It was impossible to ignore, so I headed that way."

Deven nodded, not even a little surprised that she'd dropped everything because she'd gotten a *feeling*. But these *feelings* were a part of her gifts as a Paladin, and she could no more ignore them than she could the speed, fighting skills, strength, or courage to throw herself into incredibly dangerous situations when innocent lives were at stake.

"I thought it might have something to do with Patterson, even though it was miles away from his hotel," she continued. "Instead, I ended up stumbling across five supernaturals shooting up a nightclub."

"What kind of supernaturals are we talking about?" Deven asked.

"I'm not sure. They looked like your typical mercenaries—big, muscular, and intense. They were also inhumanly strong, superfast, and almost impossible to injure."

"Do you think they're connected to the hit man? Maybe he called them in as backup when he realized he was up against a Paladin?"

She considered that for a moment. "I don't think so. They might have been eager to kill people, but they were about as subtle as a brick to the head. I don't see the hit man working with anybody who would draw so much attention to themselves when he seems to go out of his way to be subtle."

Deven stood and grabbed the shoulder harness she used to carry her throwing blades from the back of the couch. The weapons she couldn't call into and out of existence whenever she needed them. "Maybe. But then again, I could see it playing to the hit man's advantage to have a group of highly visible killers out there running around, drawing law enforcement's attention away from him."

Karissa had to admit she'd hadn't considered that angle, but now that she thought about it, the idea made sense. "I guess it's something worth looking into. It might actually help us figure out who this contract killer is, assuming they've worked together before."

"That's what I was thinking." Sitting back down, he took out the first blade and began cleaning it with a cloth he took from his pocket. "I'm guessing you got into a big fight with one or more of these new players. Is that why you looked so shook up when I came in?"

She sighed. "I did get into it with one of them. It wasn't the fight that was making my head spin."

Deven must have picked up on the fact that

she needed a minute to get her thoughts together because he didn't push. That was her brother. He might be younger than she was, but he was the most patient person in her family.

"I saw someone I know," she said, feeling a weight slipping off her shoulders. "Or at least someone I used to know."

Deven stopped cleaning to look up at her. "Who?"

"Hale Delaney. A guy I dated in high school."

Her brother's eyes widened. "Seriously? Crap."

"Tell me about it," she muttered. "I didn't know it was him at first. I was tracking one of the supernaturals that attacked the club and was shocked to see this SWAT cop in thirty or forty pounds of tactical gear not only chasing after the guy but actually catching up to him. It wasn't until the cop and the supernatural started fighting that I realized it was Hale. I was so stunned that all I could do was stare...until the guy stabbed Hale in the chest."

"Wait. What? Hale's dead?" Deven gasped. "Man, no wonder you were so messed up tonight. I know he was your ex and all, but I'm sorry."

Karissa held up her hands in a placating gesture, trying to prevent her brother from going full-on meltdown. "Deven. Stop! Hale's not dead. At least, I don't think he is. I mean, he was okay when I left."

Just saying those words out loud had Karissa on the verge of hyperventilating all over again. A fact that her very observant brother clearly picked up on. Replacing the four throwing blades he'd cleaned back into the sheath on the shoulder rig, he reached out and took her hand.

"You don't have to talk about it if you don't want to, but I know that you and Hale were close when you were going out in high school," Deven said softly. "I remember you telling me once—more than once, actually—that he was special."

Karissa squeezed Deven's hand, glad that he was on this job with her and not one of her other brothers. None of them would have cared how she felt. Lorenzo, the eldest, especially would have snorted and told her to stop whining so much.

"Yeah, Hale was special," she admitted. "Just between you and me, he was the only man I ever considered giving up my gift for."

Deven did a double take at that. "Why didn't you?"

Karissa shrugged. "Because one day he told me that he loved me, and the next he disappeared out of my life without so much as a word."

Chapter 3

"So, how bad was it?" Hale asked, sipping his coffee as he joined his pack mates at one of the tables in the break room at the North Central Patrol station house.

Since it was the closest division to the site of the shooting at the club, North Central had taken lead on the investigation, at least until headquarters officially tied this shooting to the previous two attacks. The connection seemed obvious to Hale, but the bureaucrats at headquarters liked to take their time with situations like this, especially with all the press coverage it was getting.

"About as bad as you could imagine," Trey murmured from across the room, where he stood gazing out the window at the four a.m. darkness beyond. "Three dead, including one cop. Eighteen injured, a dozen of those in critical condition."

"The numbers would have been higher if we hadn't gotten there when we did," Connor added from where he sat on the other side of the table. "If we'd been ten minutes later, there would have been dozens of additional people in the hospital."

To Hale's right, Carter nodded. His blond-haired pack mate's blue eyes were grim. "Or the morgue."

Hale had missed the rest of the fight in the club but silently agreed. Tonight had been bad, not to mention damn near incomprehensible. Those five supernaturals hadn't been interested in robbing anyone or stealing anything from the club. This hadn't been about claiming territory or sending some kind of message to a potential adversary. No, as far as Hale could tell, what happened tonight had been about nothing more than causing a scene and then waiting for the cops to show up so the bad guys could engage law enforcement along with the gang members in the club. It was like they were looking for a challenge. Which was exactly the same thing the five men had been doing for weeks.

But there was one big difference. This time, they'd arrested one of the supernaturals. While the four who'd remained behind in the club had gotten away, the one Karissa had knocked out cold was currently being held in an interrogation room at the end of the hall. Mike and Gage Dixon, the SWAT team's commander and alpha of their entire pack, were in there right now along with the chief of police and half a dozen other senior officers, trying to get the guy to talk. The fact that Hale had been the one who'd carried the suspect all the way back to the club hadn't gotten him a seat in the room. Of course, Hale hadn't gotten a chance to reveal much in the way of the details when it came to how he'd captured the suspect, so maybe that was the reason he'd been excluded.

Hale took another sip of coffee, grimacing at the acrid taste. Sometimes, he thought cops purposely made the coffee in their station houses taste like crap so no one would drink it. It seemed like an extreme and sadistic measure to go to in order to protect your coffee supply.

As the bitter brew went down, Hale felt a burning in his chest. His hand came up without thought, lightly fingering the fresh scar there. Thanks to his enhanced werewolf healing, the deep wound had sealed up before he'd even gotten back to the club, though it would be tender for another day or so. Still, feeling the wound made it impossible to think about anything but the moment that vicious supernatural had stabbed him. That thought immediately led to Karissa and how she'd appeared out of nowhere and saved his ass. Or, well, his head at least. Even now, hours later, there was a big part of him questioning if any of it had been real. He'd been stabbed in the chest and losing blood by the bucketloads. Maybe he'd been hallucinating.

But as much as he might want it to be so, he knew that wasn't the case. Karissa, the woman he hadn't seen in a decade, had shown up in the middle of that alley and kicked the crap out of a guy who'd given Hale all the fight he could handle. Seriously, Karissa, whom he outweighed by more than a hundred pounds, had nearly put a dangerous supernatural through a wall with one kick.

And she had a sword that could disappear into thin air. What the hell was going on with that?

He was pretty sure he would have noticed a sword if she'd brought it on any of their dates back in high school. Part of him wondered if anything back then had been real or if she'd been lying to him the entire time. Though if he were being honest with himself, he supposed she could have picked up the sword and butt kicking ability at some point over the past ten years. Heaven knew he'd gone through more than a few changes in that time.

Not that it mattered. Hale doubted he'd ever see Karissa and her glowing sword again. An inexplicable weight suddenly crushed his chest, making it difficult to breathe. Damn, he couldn't believe how much that thought hurt. He replayed those few moments with Karissa, wondering if he should have chased after his ex-girlfriend. Then again, she *had* disappeared in a flash of light. Without a functional nose to track her, what could he have done?

Hale was still contemplating that when Mike and Gage walked into the room. Both of his fellow werewolves looked tired and more than a little frustrated.

"Before you guys start bombarding me with questions about the guy Hale brought in, there are a few things you need to know," Gage said when

Hale and his other three pack mates all opened their mouths at the same time. "First off, he isn't talking, not even to ask for a lawyer. Second, we have no idea who he is. He didn't have an ID on him and for reasons no one can explain, it appears that he doesn't have any fingerprints. They've already put his mug shot out there hoping to pick up something with facial recognition, but so far, we've got nothing."

Trey frowned. "If he wasn't talking, what the hell were you and Mike doing in there for two hours?"

"We were hoping to get him to talk," Mike said with a sigh. "But he only sat there the entire time, ignoring the detectives asking the questions and glaring at Gage and me like he wanted to kill us."

"You think he knows that we're werewolves?" Connor asked, curious. "Or is he simply pissed that Hale kicked his ass?"

Hale would have pointed out that he hadn't actually done the ass kicking, but Mike continued before he had a chance to say anything.

"I'm leaning toward the first option," Mike said, moving over to join Hale and the others at the table. "Especially considering the fact that the guy in there is supernatural. I have no idea exactly what he is, but human is definitely off the list."

"How do you know?" Hale asked.

Not that he disagreed. After everything he'd seen earlier that night, there was no doubt in his mind that the guy in the interrogation room was a supernatural. He merely wondered how Mike knew.

"If your nose wasn't so crappy, you would have noticed that the guy smells wrong as hell," Gage answered. "But the real epiphany came when Chief Leclair stepped in the interrogation room, and everyone looked in her direction except him. Instead, he turned and stared at me with hate in his eyes. Then, out of nowhere, he blinked—sideways. He has inner lids like a lizard or something. It was freaky as hell."

"Huh. A supernatural reptile creature," Hale mused, leaning back in his chair. "That's new. Though it explains the shimmery scales I saw while we were fighting."

"You didn't say anything about the guy having scales." Trey crossed his arms over his chest. "But if I'm being honest, until I got a good whiff of those guys, I thought we were dealing with a deranged pack of omega werewolves considering how aggressive and violent they were."

Carter gave him a wry look. "I find that comment personally offensive."

Trey chuckled, as did Hale and the rest of the guys. The Pack was always ribbing Carter about having a little omega in him. Omega werewolves were known for their aggressive tendencies and having control issues when it came to their inner wolf. That wasn't true in Carter's case, of course. As far as Hale was concerned, the guy was pure alpha just like every other member of the SWAT team.

"Speaking of stuff you didn't say anything about," Gage said, pinning Hale with a look, "mind filling us in on exactly what happened after you chased that guy out of the club? Because I couldn't help noticing that you were incredibly light on the details in your report when you first showed up with him slung over your back."

While he'd been more than ready to give Karissa credit for kicking that supernatural's ass a minute ago, now Hale wondered if bringing her up was a good idea. It would only lead to questions he didn't want to answer. But werewolves who'd been werewolves a long time, like Gage, could tell when someone lying, so he didn't have much of a choice.

"When that guy ran out of the club, my inner wolf took over and I chased him, even though I real-ized he was probably trying to lure me away from the rest of you and lead me into an ambush," Hale said. "But instead, he led me down a series of alleys until we were in the middle of nowhere, then he turned around and waited for me to catch up. Like he wanted to find a place to face me one-on-one."

Trey grinned. "So you pulled out all your mad martial arts skills and kicked butt. That's what I'm talking about!"

Hale snorted. "I wish. Whatever kind of super-natural this guy is, he's as fast and strong as we are. He fought me in hand-to-hand combat without breaking a sweat. When I pulled out the claws and fangs, he pulled out a knife and the blade went through my tactical vest like it wasn't even there. Then he yanked it out and took a swing at my head that would have taken it clean off."

Connor and Trey both went wide-eyed in surprise.

"How did you stop him?" Connor asked.

"I didn't," Hale admitted. "Someone else showed up with a sword and blocked the swing before the guy could take off my head."

Gage's brow furrowed. "Someone with a sword?"

Hale nodded. "Yeah. A Greek double-edged short sword called a xiphos."

Everyone stared at him expectantly, though Hale wasn't sure if they were waiting for him to admit how he knew what kind of blade it was or to tell them more about the person who'd saved his life. Something told him it was probably the latter.

"She has to be a supernatural," he admitted softly, almost as if he were talking to himself.

"What makes you think so?" Mike asked.

"For one thing, she could make her sword disappear into thin air," Hale said. "For another, she was damn fast. Not to mention strong. She disarmed the guy, then nearly kicked him through a brick wall. It knocked him out cold."

"I can't believe it's a coincidence she was in that

alley," Gage said. "Did you ask her what she knows about these guys?"

Hale shook his head. "The moment the fight was over, there was a flash of light that nearly blinded me, and by the time my vision came back, she'd disappeared."

Mike sighed. "So we have no way of knowing who this woman is or how to get in contact with her?"

"I wouldn't say that," Hale murmured, still hesitant to reveal the last, most painful, piece of information. But he owed his pack mates the truth, no matter how much it hurt. "I know who she is. Or at least I used to. I'm not sure if I can say I know the person she is now. Her name is Karissa Bonifay. We dated in high school back in Chicago. At the time I thought she was the love of my life…the only woman I would ever love."

"What happened?" Carter asked

"Karissa came from one of Chicago's oldest and most respected cop families," Hale explained. "While I came from…well…let's just say I grew up on the wrong side of the tracks. It would be an understatement to say her family disapproved of us being together, but neither of us cared about that—or at least I thought we didn't. But I must have been wrong because, out of the blue, her three older brothers showed up and told me that she didn't want to see me anymore. When I told them that I didn't believe them and wanted her to tell me to my face, they beat the crap out of me. My family didn't want problems with the cops, so they never reported it. Instead, they moved me to another school on the far side of the city. I never saw Karissa again...until tonight."

Gage seemed to consider that. "Well, at least we have a name. That should help us find her. Though I'm not sure how much good that will do us if she won't talk to you."

"She didn't let that guy kill him," Trey pointed out. "That's got to mean something, right? Maybe she'd be willing to meet with Hale, at least long enough to tell us what we're dealing with."

"Maybe," Gage agreed. "Regardless, I'm going to head back to the compound so I can get some people looking for her and try to find out where she's staying. I'll also talk to STAT about that supernatural we have locked up in a holding cell. Hopefully, they'll be able to give us some idea of what we're dealing with. I'll see if they know anything about Karissa Bonifay as well. There can't be that many supernaturals out there running around with a glowing sword that can appear and disappear on command."

Hale really had no frame of reference to say if Gage was right about that last part, but he agreed that the Special Threat Assessment Team—aka STAT, a covert federal organization set up to quietly deal with scary things that went bump in the night—were the best bet they had in this situation. The Pack had depended on them for help a few times and the organization had always come through for them. While they might be able to help identify those five supernaturals they'd fought tonight, he doubted they'd be able to help him with Karissa. That ship had already sailed and unceremoniously sunk.

He was still thinking about that when Gage said something about Mike staying behind to see if the detectives could convince the supernatural to talk. Hale stood along with his pack mates so they could head back to the compound as well, but Mike stopped him.

"Can I talk to you a minute?" Mike glanced at Carter. "You, too."

Hale exchanged looks with Carter, who seemed as confused as he was. Hale felt like they'd just been called to the principal's office. While Gage was the uncontested leader and top alpha of their team, Mike was the unquestioned second-in-command. He'd been both a cop and a werewolf for a long time and was respected by everyone in the Pack. But if there was one thing certain about Mike, it was that he was always serious—about being a cop *and* about being a member of the SWAT pack. If he wanted to talk to them, it wasn't going to be a casual conversation.

Hoping he didn't look as uncomfortable as he

felt, Hale took a seat at the table again. Carter and Mike did the same.

"You okay?" Mike asked, looking at Hale. "And don't try pretending you weren't shaken up. Your heart was pounding like a drum when you were telling us about Karissa."

Hale hadn't realized that, but it made sense. Hell, hearing Mike say her name was making his heart beat faster right now. "Seeing her was a shock, I'll admit, but I'm okay."

Mike regarded him, his dark eyes thoughtful. "And what if the former love of your life decides to get involved in this situation? Will the Pack be able to depend on you to keep it together?"

Hale wanted to tell Mike that of course they could depend on him. That Karissa was old news, a painful part of his past that he'd let go of a long time ago. But he knew it wouldn't be that simple. Seeing Karissa for those few short seconds had put him into a tailspin he still hadn't completely recovered from. It wouldn't get any easier the next time he saw her. If that ever happened.

"I'll deal with it," he said, not sure what else he could say. "If she shows up, which I doubt. In my experience, Karissa has a history of bailing rather than being around me."

Mike considered that for a moment, and Hale wondered if he believed him or not. Then again, Hale wasn't sure if he believed the words, either.

"So what about you?" Mike asked, turning his attention to Carter. "You completely lost it in that club tonight. I haven't seen your eyes glow blue like that in a long time."

Hale did a double take, not sure he'd heard right. When they shifted, male werewolves had yellow-gold eyes. The only werewolves that had blue eyes were omegas. But that didn't make sense. The Pack might tease Carter for being an omega, but everyone knew he wasn't anymore. Hale had seen his eyes turn yellow-gold hundreds of times.

"I don't know if it was the way those supernaturals smelled or the vicious way they fought, but something about them messed with my head," Carter said quietly. "I'm not even sure when it happened, but one second I was trying to get some people headed toward the exit, and the next I was smashing my way through a wall to get at them."

Hale had definitely missed that part of the fight, so it must have happened after he'd chased that guy out of the club. An alpha's inner werewolf could definitely jump in to take the lead during a fight, especially if he was angry, but it sounded like Carter had gotten so lost in his head that he wasn't even aware of what he was doing. The fact that he couldn't even remember how he'd gotten from one place to another was flat-out terrifying. Maybe Carter truly was an omega.

"I'm sure it was a fluke," Carter added. "It won't happen again."

Mike nodded. "Okay. Just keep up with your mindfulness meditation exercises, and if you feel like you need to talk, come find me."

"I will," Carter promised.

Hale would have asked what all of that meant, but Mike chose that moment to push back his chair. "I'm going to see if they've been able to get that guy to say anything. You two should head home to get some rest."

"Sure you're not going back in there to spend some more time with Chief Leclair?" Hale teased. "Don't think the Pack hasn't noticed the way the two of you are always together. When are you going to ask her out?"

Mike gazed at him, his expression blank. "I'm not interested in dating the chief, or anyone for that matter, so you can tell the Pack to stop betting their hard-earned money on how long it takes me to ask."

He walked out of the room before Hale even thought of a snappy comeback, the door leading to the interrogation room down the hall clanging shut behind him a few moments later.

"I really thought Mike had a thing for the chief," Hale said. He'd caught Mike gazing at Shanette Leclair more than once with an expression that had nothing to do with her outstanding leadership abilities. "But what do I know?"

Carter grunted in reply as they left the room and headed for the exit.

"Hey," Hale said, glancing at Carter as they stepped outside. "I just wanted to echo what Mike said. If you need someone to talk to, about anything, I'm here for you."

Carter didn't say anything, but then, after a moment, gave him a barely perceptible nod.

Hale figured that was the best he was going to get from his pack mate.

Chapter 4

"YOU'RE MR. PATTERSON'S NEW BODYGUARD?" the burly security guard at the front gate of the new assembly plant asked, clearly dubious. "Seriously?"

From where Karissa stood in front of the small guard shack, she watched from the corner of her eye as several other guards stared at her as covertly as they could. They'd obviously heard the rumors that she was the high-priced talent brought in to protect Patterson. Going by the skeptical looks on their faces, they didn't seem to believe it, either.

"Seriously," she told him with a soft laugh. "I prefer personal protection expert, though given the obscenely large amount of money he's paying me, I suppose he can refer to me as his bodyguard if he wants to. Though I'm not sure what he's going to think of paying me all that money just to stand outside the gate of his fancy new assembly plant, staring at the place."

The security guard flushed. "Right. Of course. I have to call the head of security first. You're not on the access list they gave us."

Karissa nodded, not surprised.

She moved a little away from the small building to allow them to do whatever it was they were paid to do. She didn't miss the way most of the men continued to regard her with a mix of curiosity and doubt. She was used to those looks. She was well aware that she didn't exactly fit the mold of the typical bodyguard. While she was fit and toned, she was barely five seven. She came off more as the girl next door than as a kick-ass superhero. Then again, maybe that's why she'd received Athena's gifts when others hadn't.

From where she stood by the perimeter fence, Karissa took in the clean lines of the buildings beyond the immense parking lot of freshly laid asphalt. For a place that should be the definition of utilitarian, Patterson's automotive assembly plant was strangely beautiful, with sweeping architectural features that were there for no other reason than to make the facility look like more than a simple collection of metal boxes. In her limited reading on Patterson, she'd learned that this grand design style was somewhat of a signature for him. He liked to go big.

She'd come here this morning for several reasons. The first was to sit down with the man she was protecting and get him to understand that he couldn't continue to treat this like a joke. Next, she needed to get a feel for the people closest to her employer to see if any of them might be involved in this murder attempt. Lastly, she needed to look into his schedule and make sure she knew where he'd be and when.

Karissa didn't work like a typical bodyguard, staying in her client's hip pocket 24/7. Instead she depended on her Paladin instincts to tell her when her client would be in danger. One look at Patterson's schedule and she'd *know* when the hit man would strike again. She didn't try and understand how that particular gift worked. It simply did, and she trusted it.

Normally, she would have taken care of all this stuff within the first few hours of meeting her client. This job was anything but normal. She'd been in Dallas for three days now and hadn't even met Patterson yet. It bothered the crap out of Karissa that she had to work so hard to get the bare minimum information she needed to do her job. Seriously, if Patterson didn't want her to protect him, why didn't he tell her? She'd gladly leave.

Okay, maybe not, she thought, a spike of anxiety rippling through her at the notion. A supernatural predator was hunting Dominic Patterson. Her gifts wouldn't let her leave before she confronted that threat and dealt with it. The downside of being a Paladin was that sometimes it took on responsibilities that she'd rather have no dealings with.

As five minutes became ten, even the guards in the shack grew bored of gaping at her. While she waited, Karissa found images of Hale popping into her head. She hadn't been able to sleep much last night, her head spinning with mental

GIFs of her encounter with the man she'd known ten years ago.

She couldn't help thinking about how much bigger he'd gotten since high school. Yeah, it had been a decade, but while she remembered her ex-boyfriend being pretty good in the muscle department back then, it was nothing compared to now. He had to be well over six feet tall and was probably two hundred and twenty pounds of pure muscle. And while it didn't seem possible since he'd been super cute back when she'd known him, he was even better looking now. Simply put, he was the most gorgeous man she'd ever seen.

Those thoughts led inevitably to the one area Karissa had been avoiding like the plague—her feelings for him. Willing or not, Deven had dragged a lot of the story out of her last night. He'd wanted to know everything, including how they'd met, how they'd fallen for each other, and then how they'd fallen apart. It was probably an exaggeration, but she swore that last night's convo with her brother had been as painful as the original event. It felt like she'd torn open old wounds that had healed over.

But no matter how painful those memories were, there was no denying the reality that Karissa had been in love with Hale Delaney. Or at least she'd thought it was love in her naive and idealistic teenage mind. Even now, ten years after the fact, she could remember quite clearly how she'd thought the two of them would be together forever. The memories of how badly it had hurt when he'd dumped her still felt like acid pouring through her soul.

Seeing Hale last night, and then talking about him with Deven for hours, had brought back nearly all of those old feelings. The ones she'd thought long gone, buried, and dead. This morning, and even now, her heart was still aching. Part of her desperately wanted to see him again, but there was another part that simply didn't want to put herself through any more pain.

Karissa was relieved when she caught sight of a dark-haired man in a suit walking across the parking lot toward the entry gate. His stride was quick and efficient, with military precision.

"Jerome Guerrero," the man said the moment he stepped through the gate, approaching her with a hand outstretched. "I'm chief of security for the Patterson Group. I'm the one who insisted on bringing you in for the protection detail, along with the boss's son, Glenn. I'm sorry it's taken so long to meet you in person. All I can say in my defense is that the boss is a proud man. Admitting that he needs help is difficult for him. And accepting that help from outsiders isn't his way."

Karissa nodded, shaking his hand, immediately liking the man. She remembered her parents mentioning that Jerome and Glenn were the ones who'd initiated the contract that had brought her to Dallas. While that wasn't necessarily unusual—a lot of her more powerful clients entrusted their staff to handle the contractual details—it was an indicator of possible trouble. Patterson wouldn't be the first extremely wealthy male who had a problem letting someone else protect him. The fact that the person protecting him would be a woman was potentially an added complication.

But her Paladin instincts were telling her that Jerome was someone she could trust. That was one person off her list of suspects.

Jerome signed her in and then got her cleared to enter the plant, complete with a shiny plastic badge that contained an embedded chip that would give her complete access to every locked door in the facility. From the look on the guard's face, she gathered this kind of free access wasn't common.

"I hope you don't take this the wrong way," Jerome said, glancing at her as they walked across the parking lot toward the main building, "but you're exceedingly young for the reputation that comes with your name. I thought you'd be older."

"Don't worry about it. I get that a lot," Karissa said with a laugh. "So you're the one who actually tracked me down for the job?"

Jerome nodded, explaining how he'd used his contacts in the corporate security world to get the name of her family's business. "Once I explained the strange circumstances of how my guards were killed during the second attempt on Mr. Patterson's life, everyone I talked to suggested that you were the person I needed. It seems you have a knack for dealing with difficult and unusual situations."

That was a subtle way of saying that Karissa frequently had to deal with supernatural beings that few people in the world even knew existed. And on those rare occasions when the adversary she faced was a plain old everyday human, they tended to be so malicious and violent that most people would refuse to believe they existed, either.

She could tell that Jerome wanted to ask about her experience with those *unusual situations*, but fortunately their entry into the main building, with its crowds of scurrying construction workers, prevented that conversation.

The place looked even bigger now that she was inside. Two stories tall, with overhead tracks and heavy-duty conveyor belts connecting every part of the facility together. She didn't know anything about automotive manufacturing, but she assumed the plant was designed so that vehicles under assembly could be moved from place to place without ever needing to be touched by human hands. The presence of the high-tech robots mounted all along the production line only reinforced that theory.

But if the substantial number of parts scattered all over the place was any indication—not to mention

the hundreds of workers running around with panicked expressions on their faces—it seemed like
the facility wasn't anywhere near ready to open.

"I should probably warn you that Mr. Patterson
is in a bad mood," Jerome said in a low voice as they
moved through the plant. "The meeting he's in
right now involves last minute preparations for the
opening ceremony. Suffice it to say, it's not going
well."

Jerome led her up a set of stairs to a glass-fronted
conference room overlooking the production floor.
Inside, there were a dozen people, most of them
wearing suits and looking pissed off that they were
the ones tasked with trying to get this place operational in time.

"Jolie Washington is the tall woman in the
power outfit," Jerome whispered, stopping short of
the doorway but close enough to get a good look at
everyone. "She's the lead counsel for the Patterson
Group and is also on the board of directors, which
is what we call our premier investors. We've tried to
keep it quiet, but it's clear they've caught wind that
someone is trying to kill Mr. Patterson. Washington
is concerned the investors will start pulling their
money out if they learn it's more than rumor. I'd
avoid her if you can. She'll try and pin you down
for details when she's not nagging you to keep out
of sight."

Karissa sighed. It was going to be hard enough

keeping an eye on Patterson when the man obviously didn't want her around. Now she had to do it without looking like she was doing it simply so a bunch of rich investors didn't get spooked and run away with their money?

"Tristan Bond is the ancient man on the left side of the table," Jerome added, nodding in that general direction. "He's the chief financial officer and has been since the boss was a kid. One word to describe him would be thrifty. Another word would be cheap. He's been wearing the same dress shoes since the Eisenhower administration. Instead of buying new ones, he keeps paying to have them repaired and resoled every few years."

Karissa was ashamed to admit she had no idea when Eisenhower was in office—well before her time obviously. But then again, she also hadn't realized that people still took their shoes in for repair. So maybe she should have paid more attention in history class.

Jerome opened the door for Karissa, following her inside the conference room. They slipped around to the side of the table, attempting to remain as unobtrusive as possible. It wasn't necessary, since no one even paid attention to them. Instead, everyone was focused on several large monitors mounted on the wall, some displaying complex graphs covered in glaring red lines, others showing columns of equally red dollar figures and dates. Karissa wasn't an expert on this kind of stuff, but she was pretty sure red meant over budget and behind schedule. Which probably explained that bad mood the boss was supposedly in.

Leaning back against the wall, Karissa slowly scanned the room, starting at the head of the table. Dominic Patterson was somewhere in his mid-sixties, though he looked older at the moment. He had dark hair, quickly going gray at the temples, and gray eyes that betrayed the aggravation he seemed to be feeling as he sat there staring at the graphs and figures. She reached out with her gift, trying to read the man she'd been hired to protect.

Karissa had once attempted to explain to Deven how the reading process worked, but it had been a total failure, mostly because she barely understood it herself. It would be nice if she could simply read people's minds, but it was nothing like that. Instead, she picked up on emotions—the stronger the better. So things like hate, love, lust, jealousy, loathing, anger, and greed were easier to pick up on. Beyond that, she simply got *feelings* from people, little bursts of insight that sometimes clued her in on what people were thinking about doing and why. Unfortunately, sometimes she was lucky to get anything more than a general sense of people's emotions. That was part of what made this particular gift so confusing. And why Deven always threw his hands up in the air and walked away whenever she mentioned it.

It turned out that Dominic Patterson was one of those people who was tough to read. Even standing this close to the man, the only sensation she got was one of intense concentration on the task at hand. The fact that there was someone out there trying to kill him didn't even seem to register. Seriously, she'd never seen a man so single-minded.

The younger man standing to Patterson's right was easier to read—and identify. The dark hair and gray eyes marked him as Glenn, the son who'd pushed to bring in outside help to protect his father. Of course, the second Karissa had seen the son's name on the contract for the job, she'd started digging. It turned out that Dominic Patterson was the majority owner of the company, with his son only controlling fifteen percent. Five more minutes of digging revealed that if daddy were murdered, Glenn would get total control of everything. And when *everything* was valued at about ninety billion dollars, it was easy to imagine Glenn being the one who hired the hit man.

But now that she was in the room with him, she wasn't sensing anything that suggested he wanted his father dead. There was some obvious tension between father and son, to be sure, but it was possible she was picking up on the aggravation associated with the delays in opening the new plant. The one thing she could say for sure was that Glenn wasn't motivated by money. He seemed to care nothing for the riches that came with the Patterson name. And judging by the looks he kept throwing toward his father, she'd have to say that Glenn was actually concerned about the older man's health. Maybe he didn't like him getting so upset.

Karissa turned her attention to Tristan Bond next. The man was at least seventy years old and whipcord lean, verging on emaciated, and wearing a frown like it was a permanent part of his wardrobe. But his eyes were sharp, and she got the feeling he could scan a room and affix a price tag on every single thing in the place, commodity and human alike. Based on his current I-just-sucked-on-a-lemon expression, it was like he thought everything around them was either unnecessary, overpriced, or needlessly extravagant. And from the way he glowered at most of the people around the table, he clearly thought the same of them. Karissa could tell that Bond disliked Patterson, though it didn't quite raise to the level of hatred. It seemed he simply didn't care for Patterson's penchant for going over-the-top with everything he touched.

She had no doubt that if Bond had been in charge of constructing this plant, it would have been finished in half the time at half the price, and it would have been twice as profitable. It probably went without saying that it would have been horribly ugly and likely fallen apart in ten years as well.

But being thrifty—as Jerome called it—wasn't necessarily a reason to hire a hit man.

Karissa studied Jolie Washington and the board
members. What she picked up on there wasn't necessarily horrible, but it wasn't good either. It struck
her that Washington and all four of the members
of the board were aware that someone was trying
to kill Patterson. And from the covert glances they
were throwing back and forth between her and
Patterson, it was clear they'd also figured out that
she was here to protect the man. That was to be
expected, since the guards at the gate had already
heard the same rumors.

The disconcerting part of her reading was that
none of the people seemed to care that Patterson's
life might be in danger beyond what it might mean
for their investments. It seemed some were already
planning to reallocate their investments in the
event that the killer was successful. It was cold-
blooded but practical, and once again Karissa was
left thinking that none of these people felt like the
type to hire a killer.

The meeting wrapped up a few minutes later
with everyone agreeing to a plan that focused
on making sure the parts of the plant the press
would see during the ribbon-cutting ceremony
were completed first. Patterson was still pissed the
entire thing wouldn't be completed on time, but at
least it brought the discussion to a close and got

everyone except for her, Jerome, Dominic, and Glenn out of the room.

Karissa watched as father and son argued over a few of the building schematics. She bit her tongue and waited as patiently as she could, but when it became clear Patterson was purposely ignoring her, she decided she'd had enough.

"I stopped by this morning to go over your itinerary, Mr. Patterson, so I can pinpoint times and locations where you'll be the most exposed," she said, stepping closer to the table. "But since it seems clear you're too busy to bother with any of that, why don't we make it official and cancel the contract? You'll forfeit the deposit and three days' worth of expenses, but I'm sure that's a minor amount of money for your company. That way you can focus on whatever you find important—at least until the hit man decides to finish the job."

Patterson fell silent but didn't look at her. Karissa didn't need her Paladin gifts to pick up on the anger rolling off of him. Or to realize she was wasting her time.

"Fine," Karissa said. She hated the idea of walking out like this—especially since her inner Paladin was screaming bloody murder—but she was tired of this nonsense. "If I leave now, I can be at the airport and on a flight back to Chicago by this afternoon."

Giving Jerome a nod, she turned and started for the door.

"There was an understanding when we approached your company," Patterson said suddenly, stopping her. "You were supposed to stay out of sight and be invisible. It was understood that my company could be destroyed if it got out that someone was trying to kill me. Even worse if it were known that I'd hired an outsider to be my bodyguard."

Karissa tried not to snort…and failed. Her parents had a habit of agreeing to all kinds of stipulations and never bothering to tell her about them. Not that she would have paid attention to a ridiculous requirement like that.

She turned back around to face the billionaire and his son, pinning them with a hard look. "Any hope that you could keep this quiet evaporated the second the hit man killed your guards. There isn't a person in your company who's not aware someone is trying to murder you. Those board members who were just in here are already making plans on how to capitalize on your death if it happens. I'm sure some have already started buying stock in your competitors' companies."

Patterson cursed even as his son leaned in and murmured something that sounded suspiciously like "I told you so."

"You can't possibly think the hit man followed us to Dallas from Ohio, can you?" the older man asked.

Beside him, Glenn shook his head, his expression indicating how foolish he thought his father was behaving. Karissa couldn't disagree.

"That's exactly what I think," she said bluntly. "This guy has made two attempts on your life already. He knew exactly where you'd be and when you'd be there both of those times, and if it weren't for a couple of lucky circumstances, he would have succeeded in those attempts. Do you really think a few hours on a plane is enough to make him give up and go away?"

Patterson didn't say anything.

"Okay," Glenn said after a moment. "Let's assume you're right and this hit man is already here in Dallas. What can we possibly do to stop him? We don't even know what he looks like."

"It's true we don't know what he looks like," Karissa agreed. "But we do know exactly where to find him."

"We do?" Patterson looked back and forth between her, Jerome, and Glenn in confusion. "Where?"

"It seems clear that he prefers to make his move at night and in those locations where he knows you'll be alone. In the case of the previous two attempts, your office and your bedroom," Karissa said. "But he also likes to show off and prove he can slip through the tightest security setup. It shouldn't be that difficult to look at your calendar and figure out those times and places where you'll be most vulnerable."

"And then what?" Jerome asked, appearing both doubtful and concerned. "Even ignoring all the supposition and assumptions in your theory, you still haven't said how this helps us, even if you're right."

"If we know where the hit man is likely to strike, it gives us options," she explained. "At the minimum, we can increase your security during those moments and make sure I'm nearby. But it also gives us the opportunity to put an end to this once and for all."

Glenn glared at her. "You mean you want to use my father as bait? It's too dangerous. I won't let you put him at risk."

"Your father is already at risk," she pointed out. "And he'll remain at risk until we catch the person trying to kill him."

It looked like Glenn was ready to keep arguing, but his father cut him off. "Ms. Bonifay is right. I have no idea who wants me dead or why, but I think we can accept that this hit man won't stop until he kills me. So if the best way to stop him is to stick to my routine and lure him into a trap, then so be it."

Karissa lifted a brow. "Does that mean you'll make your schedule available to me and allow me access during those times I think you're at risk?"

If Tristan Bond gave the impression that he'd sucked on a lemon before, Dominic Patterson looked like he was sucking on an entire produce section full of the tart citrus fruit, but in the end, he nodded. "Full access at your discretion."

Karissa breathed a silent sigh of relief before nodding. "Okay, let's get to work then."

Fifteen minutes later, she was walking out of the plant, the notebook in her pocket jammed full of notes on the moments over the next several days when Dominic Patterson would likely be targeted, her instincts humming overtime at all the potential kill points. She'd arranged to be close to him during all of those times, plus several other specific moments at random in case the killer decided to change his MO without tripping her instincts.

Her phone rang as she stepped through the gate, Deven's name showing on the screen. Karissa stopped walking, moving to the side as she took the call. "Please tell me you've finally learned something about the hit man."

Deven and the rest of her family had been working overtime to dig up intel on the hit man ever since they'd been hired. Going up against a killer— especially a supernatural one—without knowing what she was dealing with was basically suicidal. So far they'd found nothing, but since Deven was the company's resident computer expert, she was hoping that had finally changed.

"Oh, I found out something that will interest you but not about the killer," Deven said.

Karissa swore if there was a way to hear someone smiling, it'd be happening right now. She was
pretty sure she wasn't gonna like what her brother
had to say next.

"What are you talking about?" she asked
hesitantly.

"I found an address on your ex-boyfriend,"
Deven said, and then hurriedly kept talking as if
she was going to interrupt. "I know you said you
weren't planning to ever see the guy again, but I
figured you'd like to have an address in case you
wanted to check on how he was doing. You know,
from that stab wound you told me about?"

Karissa's first instinct was to hang up. Between
the hours spent talking about him last night and the
time she'd wasted thinking about him this morning,
Hale had taken up way too much space in her head
already. But before she could even think of moving
her thumb toward that red button on her phone,
her mouth was opening and the words coming out.

"Text me the address."

Chapter 5

HALE LEANED BACK ON THE SECTIONAL COUCH in his living room, watching *SportsCenter* on his wide-screen TV. The commentator—some football Hall of Famer—was breaking down the most recent Cowboys game and attempting to explain what needed to happen to get the season turned around in time to make a serious run for the playoffs. Hale wasn't paying much attention since he'd already heard this same report at least three times over the past several hours.

After getting back from the North Central Patrol station house a little before sunrise, Hale had showered, then put on shorts and a T-shirt, fully intending to jump into bed to get some sleep. But instead, he'd found himself sprawled out on the couch in front of the TV, two boxes of chocolate-covered donuts on the table in front of him for company. He'd told himself that he'd have a quick snack and catch up on the world of sports while he decompressed from the most unsettling evening he'd had in a long time.

That had been five hours ago, and he was no more ready to fall sleep than he had been when he'd gotten back to his apartment. With everything that had happened last night blending together with memories from his high school years, his head was a muddled mess. And unfortunately, damn near all those memories involved Karissa Bonifay.

He'd thought that painful part of his past was gone, the echoes of any residual feelings silenced long ago. Turned out he was wrong about that. His chest hurt all over again, and it had nothing to do with the knife that had been shoved in there last night.

Deciding he should try to get at least an hour of sleep before heading back to the compound, Hale forced himself up off the couch. He reached for what was left of the chocolate donuts, realizing he'd demolished a box and a half of the things, when the doorbell rang.

Wishing for the thousandth time that his nose was good enough to let him know who'd shown up at his apartment, Hale padded barefoot across the carpeted floor of the living room and into the small tiled entryway. He was so used to his nose being pure crap that he'd learned to ignore whatever random scents occasionally popped up. Instead, he trusted his hearing to help him identify people. He had a detailed audio library of everyone in his pack and most of his neighbors, memorizing the tread of their footsteps and the particular way their heart sounded when it beat.

Unfortunately, he didn't recognize any of the

sounds coming from outside the door, which meant it was someone he probably didn't know. Maybe it was someone selling Girl Scout cookies. He could really go for a half dozen boxes of Samoas.

Thoughts of cookies disappeared the moment he opened the door and saw Karissa standing there. Actually, he stopped thinking completely. Total PC shutdown.

"Well, I guess this answers my first question," his unexpected visitor said with an unreadable expression as her gaze roamed up and down his body. "You're still alive after getting stabbed last night."

Hale stared, not sure what to say. Hell, he wasn't sure if he wanted to say anything. There was a part of him that wanted to say "duh," then slam the door in her face. But at the last second, he stopped himself.

Karissa's brown hair was hanging loose, bangs and feathered edges framing her heart-shaped face, the long, curling ends hanging down to brush the swell of her breasts. Those mesmerizing green eyes were even more vivid in the brighter light of the hallway, making it difficult to look at anything but them.

"It was only a glancing blow," he finally managed to say, instinctively coming up with something to rationalize his rapid recovery. "It bled a lot, but there wasn't much damage. The wound closed up within an hour. No stitches or anything."

Karissa lifted a brow like she wanted to call him out on the lie, but she didn't.

He took a step back.

"You coming inside?" he asked, wanting to avoid any more talk of the knife wound. If Karissa insisted on seeing whether he was telling the truth, there'd be hell to pay if she saw that it was completely healed with scar tissue that looked a week old.

Karissa hesitated for a moment and walked through the door, taking a few steps into the living room before stopping to look around. Hale watched as she took in everything, pausing for a long moment on the donuts before finally coming to rest on the framed photos of him with his pack mates mounted on the wall to either side of the TV. She moved closer to the collection of pictures, studying them, particularly the ones of him and his teammates in uniform.

"So you're a cop now," she said, not looking at him. "I have to admit, I never would have pegged you as the type, given the family you grew up in."

The lightly veiled jab stung a little, mostly because it had come from Karissa. Not that Hale would ever admit it. He'd long ago gotten over the fact that he'd grown up in a family of criminals. Apparently, his ex was still hung up on that fact, though.

"Like I never would have pegged you to be running around Dallas in a trench coat, swinging a sword, and playing the vigilante," he responded in a tone as emotionless as hers.

When Karissa turned to shoot him a glare, Hale could tell he'd struck a nerve. But she quickly recovered, any trace of anger disappearing in a flash.

"It's a five-hundred-dollar leather duster, not a trench coat," she corrected, wandering across the living room to the coffee table, gazing down at the donuts. "Not that I'd expect you to know the difference."

"You're right. I don't know the difference. But then again, you always were about the money, weren't you?"

Hale felt a bit of shame at the harsh words coming out of his mouth, but he couldn't seem to stop himself. He might have thought he'd come to accept his past with Karissa, but he'd obviously been wrong about that. The sight of her standing there looking all chill while he was boiling with anger inside was too much.

He braced himself, waiting for the return volley in their game of matching insults, but instead Karissa took a deep breath and slowly let it out. If he wasn't so mad at her, Hale would have smiled. She always had been good when it came to reining in her anger.

"So you're still eating chocolate-covered donuts?" Karissa said.

Hale could tell that she trying hard to keep her

voice casual instead of blasting him in retaliation for his comment about her family having money when his never did.

"Yeah, I still love them." He motioned at the box on the table and the three donuts inside. "You want one, or have you moved on from them, too?"

He regretted his words immediately, not sure why he continued to lash out like that. But it was too late to take them back. So instead, he picked up the box of donuts, holding it out to Karissa, hoping she'd take the delicious olive branch he was offering.

Fortunately, she did, although after hours of sitting out in his living room, the chocolate was soft and smeared all over her fingers. Hale winced. Somehow, she was able to take a bite without making a mess on her face. That was a skill he was still working on.

"What are you doing in Dallas?" he asked as he set the box down on the table again, trying to keep any accusing notes out of the question, even if a part of him wondered if she was here to check up on him. Or was he *hoping* she was here for that?

Karissa didn't say anything as she nibbled on her donut. Hale doubted the delay had anything to do with how good it tasted. She was probably taking her time considering how much she wanted to say—if anything.

"My family runs a private security firm specializing

in personal protection," Karissa finally answered, looking at the donut in her hand instead of at him, almost like she was talking to it. "I'm down here with Deven watching over an industrial magnate named Dominic Patterson who's being targeted by a hit man."

Hale took a moment to unpack all that, trying to figure out what surprised him the most—the fact that Karissa hadn't become a cop like everyone in her family or that she was currently putting herself between a killer and some random rich dude for a paycheck. Not liking the way that second issue made him feel, he decided to find safer ground to walk on.

"Deven?" he said, trying to remember which brother that was. "Isn't he the youngest of the bunch? What is he, like, twelve or something now? Isn't he a little young to be on the job?"

Karissa smirked. "This is going to make you feel old, but Deven is eighteen, almost nineteen. He's good at this security stuff, especially the tech support aspect."

Hale rummaged through his memory bank, trying to recall what he knew about Karissa's baby brother. It wasn't much, but he recalled that Deven wasn't an ass like the three older brothers. At least he hadn't been back when Hale had known him. But then again, Deven had been about eight at that point and juiced up over SpongeBob. How much of an ass can an eight-year-old be?

"Do you have any idea who hired the hit man?" Hale asked.

"Not yet, but we're working on it," she said. "At the moment, I'm more interested in stopping him from murdering my client. He's already tried twice."

As she explained how the would-be killer had slipped past a complex security system both times and come damn close to killing Patterson, Hale couldn't shake the feeling that she was keeping something important from him. Then again, why would he think she'd be completely honest?

He wanted to ask her if the local PD was aware of the threat against Patterson's life but decided the question would be a waste of his time. Of course this guy wouldn't involve the police. Rich people followed different rules than the rest of the world.

"You planning to use Patterson as bait to lure the hit man in?"

The question seemed to catch Karissa a little off balance, but she recovered quickly, her expression hardening. "Considering the killer is going to go after Patterson no matter what I do, I'm not actually using him as bait. But I'll be there to stop him when he makes his move."

"What happens after you apprehend him?" Hale asked, not sure why he was even asking such an obvious question.

She shrugged. "Then it's on to the next job. Somewhere *not* in Dallas."

Even if Hale had known that would be the answer, it still hurt to hear it.

"What about you?" Karissa asked. "Who was that guy with the knife who you chased into that alley all by yourself?"

"I wasn't by myself in that alley," Hale snapped back, telling himself it was none of his damn business when Karissa left Dallas. "Was I?"

"You didn't know I was there, so your point is invalid," Karissa responded. "Just stop avoiding the question and tell me who that guy was."

Hale considered not telling her a thing. It would be totally within his rights to stay quiet about this. It was cop business—*pack* business. But at the same time, she had told him about Patterson. Totally different set of circumstances, but still.

"We don't know who the guy is," he admitted. "He's not talking, and he doesn't have fingerprints so we can't ID him. We're trying for facial recognition, but that takes a while."

She regarded him thoughtfully. "He must be someone dangerous since you were willing to go after him by yourself like that. I grew up in a family of cops, remember? I know you're not supposed to go after dangerous criminals on your own."

Yeah, well, he was a werewolf, so that didn't always apply. But since he couldn't tell her that, he gave her a quick synopsis of the crew's killing spree.

"The guy you chased into that alley was one of

those five men and you decided it was necessary to risk your life by taking him on alone?" she asked.

His first instinct was to deny the allegation, but he couldn't since she'd pretty much hit the nail on the head. Well, she'd left out the part about running prey provoking his inner werewolf into chasing it. But since she didn't know about that, he couldn't hold it against her.

"Yeah," he admitted. "It probably wasn't the smartest thing to do, but I couldn't let the guy get away. Not after he'd already injured all those people."

She sighed. "Okay. I guess I can appreciate the position you were in." She eyed the almost-empty box of donuts like she wanted another one before pinning him with a look. "But you came damn close to dying out there last night. You know that, right?"

Hale thought he glimpsed a flash of concern in her eyes but then dismissed that idea. Why the hell would Karissa care one way or the other what happened to him? She'd made her feelings about him crystal-clear a decade ago.

"Then it's a good thing you happened to be in that alley last night," he said. "Which does bring us to an interesting question. What were you doing in that alley? It couldn't have been a coincidence. And how did you kick that guy so hard he was out cold for twenty minutes? And while we're on the subject of things that shouldn't be possible, maybe you can also explain the disappearing sword?"

Karissa's eyes widened, and Hale couldn't miss the way her heart began to race. But just as she opened her mouth to say something, the ringing of his phone interrupted her.

"You going to get that?" she asked, clearly relieved at the interruption.

Hale didn't want to. He preferred to hear what Karissa might say that would come close to answering all his questions. Unfortunately, with his job, ignoring the phone wasn't an option.

Grabbing his cell from the coffee table, he checked the screen. It was Mike.

"I have to take this," he said, moving to the other side of the living room so he could talk in private. As he thumbed the green button on his phone, he noticed Karissa help herself to another donut. He couldn't help but smile at the furtive way she turned away to eat it, as if he wouldn't notice.

"What's up, Mike?" he asked, keeping a casual eye on Karissa, hoping they had a chance to continue their conversation. Though with all this time available to come up with a good lie, Hale doubted her answers to his questions would count for much.

"I need you at the North Central station house ASAP," Mike said without preamble. "The guy still hasn't talked, and headquarters wants to move him to the North Tower Detention Facility for holding until he can be arraigned. I'm concerned his crew might make a move to break him out during the transfer."

"Seriously?" Hale asked.

He was surprised Mike would even worry about something like that. The guys they'd fought last night were gutsy, but attacking a DPD prison transport? He couldn't imagine anybody being that bold.

"Maybe I'm worrying over nothing," Mike replied. "But there's something that bothers me about that guy. The detectives told him that he might be looking at life in prison and all he did was smile. Like he knows that's not going to happen. Regardless, I want to have people here in case things go sideways during the transfer."

"Okay. I'll be there in thirty minutes."

Hanging up, Hale turned to look at Karissa, opening his mouth to ask if they could continue their conversation later, but she was already heading toward the door.

"I heard," she said, glancing at him over her shoulder. "Be careful. I may not be there the next time some guy tries to take your head off."

"I didn't know you cared," Hale said.

He'd been trying for something clever and snarky but ended up going with the first thing off the top of his head. Even if it probably came out lame and more than a little like wishful thinking.

"Who says I do?" Karissa retorted. "I just don't want someone blaming it on me. You know, considering my weapon of choice is a sword and all."

The door closed behind her before he could

even think of a response to that. Biting back a growl, Hale turned and headed for the bedroom to change clothes.

He was almost all the way across the room when the scent hit him. One of his feet caught on the carpet and he came damn close to face-planting. He barely managed to catch himself, even as he recognized the scent.

He'd smelled it before.

Last night.

When Karissa had blocked the blade that had been going for his neck.

Lilac blossoms.

It was the first real scent Hale could remember smelling in a long, long time. And it had apparently come from Karissa.

He glanced back down the hall to the door of his apartment. Outside it, he could hear her footsteps rapidly receding as she walked downstairs and out the front door of the building.

And yet he could pick up her intoxicating scent.

Crap.

Chapter 6

KARISSA KEPT HER RENTAL VEHICLE TUCKED carefully behind a small moving van as she followed Hale across town. What the heck was she doing?

"Take the next exit and go back to the hotel," she murmured out loud to herself. "Then we can act like this detour into stalker central never happened."

But the next exit on Interstate 635 came and went without Karissa slowing down, regardless of what she'd just said.

"I swear, there must be something wrong with me." She let out a long sigh. "An hour from now, I'll be saying *I told you so.* To myself."

Karissa continued following Hale's bright blue SUV along the interstate and then onto the George Bush Turnpike. A few minutes later, as he pulled into the parking lot of a police station, she once again asked herself what she thought she was doing. But the truth was, the moment she'd learned Hale might be confronting that guy from the alley again, she knew she had to follow him.

Her gift didn't give Karissa superhuman hearing or even close to it, but she'd picked up enough from Hale's phone call earlier to figure out the cops were worried someone would try to break that guy out of custody. Her instincts had taken over at that point. She'd tried to tell herself it was simply because she was concerned about having someone that dangerous loose in the middle of Dallas, but a part of her knew it was something else. Try as she might to ignore the unwanted feelings, she was forced to accept that she was worried about Hale getting hurt if he went up against that guy again.

She'd known well before kicking the man in the chest that he was some kind of supernatural. No one could run that fast.

Hale ran that fast, her inner Karissa pointed out in a little voice.

Karissa chose to ignore that comment, thinking about how dangerous the supernatural was. Her kick had barely damaged the guy. And now Hale—who'd almost been killed by that creature the first time—might be dealing with it again. That bothered her on some instinctive level that almost scared her with its intensity.

Not wanting Hale to see her, Karissa turned and drove around the back side of the parking lot, staying as far away from his blue SUV as possible. Pulling into a space near one of the back corners, she slipped out of her rental car and moved carefully through the lot toward the nearest corner of the station house.

She expected Hale to immediately go inside,

but instead he walked over to meet three other cops in dark blue tactical uniforms like the one he wore, standing near the front wall of the station. It quickly became apparent they weren't moving into the building anytime soon, which gave her a chance to peek around the corner and get an eyeful of the men. All three of them were as tall and muscular as Hale, which should have been impossible because her ex-boyfriend was huge.

"Maybe they just grow them bigger in Texas," she murmured softly to herself, keeping her voice whisper-low, not wanting anyone to overhear and think she was weird because she talked to herself.

As Karissa stood there at the corner, Hale was saying something about hoping he wasn't too late. At least that's what she thought he was saying. Karissa could barely hear his words over the hum of cars moving along the nearby street. Okay, if she was going to eavesdrop on Hale's conversation, she couldn't stay here.

"Wait. Why do you even want to eavesdrop on him anyway?" she asked herself in another whisper. "Do you really think he's telling his cop buddies all about the woman he just spent fifteen minutes hate flirting with?"

The answer to that must have been yes because Karissa was already moving toward the back of the station house before she had a chance to argue with herself about whether she'd been engaging in hate flirting at all. She wanted to say she hadn't but had to admit it was possible.

Two minutes later, she was on the roof of the police station, positioning herself close to the edge, directly above Hale and his three fellow cops.

"STAT came up with an ID on our suspect," one of the men said from below. Karissa couldn't tell which one, although he had a deep voice. "His name is Darijo Tamm and he's from Croatia. Or at least that's what Interpol thinks. Since he appeared out of nowhere about five years ago, they're the first to admit it's probably an assumed name."

"What put this guy on Interpol's radar?" Hale asked.

Karissa realized that Hale's voice was even deeper than the first guy's. Inner Karissa took note and immediately pointed out that men with deep voices were subjectively sexier. Outer Karissa ignored the entire idea, instead focusing on the conversation below her and vaguely wondering who this STAT organization was. She'd never heard of them, which was difficult to believe if they were involved in law enforcement in any way.

"It's more than Interpol actually," the first guy said. "Tamm has also caught the attention of the Department of Defense and the State Department, along with the law enforcement agencies in about twenty different countries around the globe. It seems that Tamm and his four buddies are wanted terrorists for hire. I'd also describe them as simple mercenaries if not for the excess levels of violence they have a reputation for. Regardless, they've shown up in more than a dozen different war-torn countries. If there's fighting going on, they've been there. The strange part is that no one has a clue which side they even support. They show up, cause a lot of hate and discontent, kill a lot of people, and then disappear."

"Anything on the supernatural angle?" yet a third deep voice asked. "Especially the scales?"

Supernatural angle?

Karissa was so stunned she came damn close to falling off the roof. Could Hale and his fellow cops honestly be openly discussing the existence of supernatural creatures like they were talking about the weather? And what the heck was that stuff about scales?

"STAT is still digging," Deep Voice One answered. "If anyone can figure out what these creatures are, it's them."

Now Karissa was really curious about who STAT was. It sounded like they were some kind of federal organization that specialized in supernaturals. But if so, why hadn't her parents ever mentioned them?

She zoned out of the conversation below for a moment, considering the implications of the Dallas PD knowing about supernaturals, not to mention the possibility of there being a federal agency involved as well. A part of her worried about that since it just so happened that she was as much of a supernatural as the man that Hale had fought. If this STAT organization knew something about the guy currently in custody, did they know about her, too?

Karissa was so wrapped up in the idea that STAT might be keeping tabs on her that she almost missed the crashing sound coming from the rear of the station house. Then she heard the sound of thumping boots and risked a glance over the edge of the roof in time to see Hale and his fellow SWAT cops running around the building, heading for the back and the crashing sound that had only gotten louder.

Jumping up, she ran across the rooftop, but before she'd gotten halfway to the other side, the sound of gunfire and people shouting filled the air. Karissa nearly face-planted as her feet froze up in blind panic at the thought of Hale being shot.

"You still care that much about the guy who stomped on your heart?" she said out loud. "That's sad."

She reached the rear edge of the roof to see several large men with weapons climbing into the back of a large cargo van, the man she now knew to be Darijo Tamm with them.

The van squealed away with the back door still swinging open, bursts of automatic weapons coming out, aimed toward the police station. From where she stood on the roof, Karissa couldn't tell if they hit the building or people. She prayed it wasn't the latter.

As the van sped across the parking lot, Karissa was about to jump down from the roof to check for injuries when she caught a blur of movement from the corner of her eye. She turned to see Hale and two of his teammates running after the van. Chasing after a moving vehicle on foot seemed like a supreme waste of time to her—until she saw how fast Hale was moving. The other two SWAT cops easily kept pace with Hale, but Karissa only had eyes for him.

The man was pure power and grace, leaping forward like an Olympic sprinter, only no athlete in the history of sports had ever run this fast. One moment, he was twenty feet from the police station, and the next, he was halfway across the lot and gaining speed.

She stood there on the roof frozen solid as Hale and the other two cops in tactical uniforms disappeared from view. Below her, she could vaguely hear Deep Voice One shouting orders, getting first aid started for the wounded and calling for air support to track the fleeing van.

Karissa knew she should probably go down and try to help. In her line of work, she'd picked up a few first aid tricks of her own. But as the moments passed and she remained standing there like a statue, she realized she was too stunned to even think about moving yet.

Hale and his teammates' acceptance of Darijo Tamm's supernatural background made a lot more sense now—because Hale and the others were supernaturals, too.

Crud.

Her ex-boyfriend—who still seemed to have some kind of emotional hold over her, no matter how much that confused her—was a supernatural like her.

———

"It looks like all five guys on this crew are Eastern European," Carter said from his desk across from Hale's in the SWAT team's bullpen.

Hale silently agreed as he flipped through the police records on the other four members of Darijo Tamm's mercenary team. Each of the men had similar facial features, ruddy skin, and black hair. Each of them had appeared out of nowhere between five and seven years ago.

He and his pack mates had gotten back to the SWAT compound an hour ago and were still doing all the paperwork after Tamm's escape from the North Central police station. They'd also needed to come back to deal with their injuries since they couldn't let one of the dozen paramedics who'd showed up treat them.

The muscles in Hale's left thigh twinged a little as he moved his leg under his desk. He'd taken a bullet there during the fray and Trey had dug it out as soon as they'd gotten to the compound. The wound reminded him how badly they'd all handled the situation at the police station, and he cursed silently.

They'd assumed that if Tamm's crew made a move, it would be during the transfer to the detention facility. To say that he and his pack mates weren't prepared for an assault on the station was an understatement.

Tamm had already been in the van and well on his way to escaping by the time Hale and his pack mates made it around the building. Hale had gone after them out of pure instinct, and Carter and Trey had followed. The chase had been short-lived, though it wasn't so much getting shot that deterred him, even if it had sucked. No, he and his teammates had been forced to break off the chase because it had been too risky to chase after a bunch of trigger-happy people with automatic weapons through the middle of the city.

There'd also been the issue of three big cops running down the street at thirty miles an hour. That probably would have drawn the wrong kind of attention. If it had been nighttime, Hale would have kept going for sure, but in daylight, he couldn't.

"How's the leg?" Mike asked, catching Hale's eye as he walked into the bullpen and over to his desk.

"It's good," Hales said. "What's the word from the North Central station?"

While Hale and his pack mates had immediately come back here, Mike had stayed behind to help deal with the aftermath.

Mike dropped into his chair, swiveling it around so he was facing them. "Eight officers and three support staff personnel ended up in the hospital, but nobody's dead, so I guess we'll take what we can get."

"How the hell did they get all the way down to the holding cells in the basement to get Tamm out without us hearing them?" Carter asked.

Hale would like to know that, too.

"You're going to love this," Mike said with a snort. "We checked the surveillance video for the basement level and saw that at the precise moment that black van pulled into the rear parking lot of the station house, Tamm walked over to the door of his cell and ripped it completely off its hinges."

"Crap," Hale muttered. This had the potential to be even worse. "How many people saw that video?"

"Five people, including Chief Leclair," Mike said. "Fortunately, they seemed to be inclined to blame the damage on poor facility maintenance. I can't say I fault them. What's the alternative? Believing Tamm is a supernatural creature strong enough to tear through steel?"

Hale supposed that made sense. People would

go out of their way to find a reasonable excuse for the unexplainable, no matter how implausible it might be. And once they had that theory, they'd twist themselves into knots in their desire to keep believing it.

Mike filled them in on the rest of the story, including everything that the surveillance cameras had picked up. By the time Mike finished, there was no doubt in Hale's mind that this supernatural crew had been working together for a very long time. That was the only thing that explained how the mercenaries were able to work together so seamlessly without ever saying a word. In fact, it was eerily similar to how the Pack worked together.

"Do you think they'll leave Dallas?" Trey asked, hazel eyes curious.

Mike considered that. "I don't think we're going to get that lucky. Something brought these guys to Dallas, and I get the feeling they're not finished yet."

Trey pushed back his chair. "I'm going to check on the people who got injured this morning."

"I'll go with you," Carter said.

"Me, too," Hale said.

"Actually," Mike said, "I'd like to talk to you about something, Hale."

He paused halfway to his feet, then sat down again. "Sure."

Carter and Trey threw him looks that said *what'd you do now?* before leaving.

Mike leaned back in his chair, regarding him thoughtfully. "What had you so wound up when you got to the station earlier?"

Hale tensed. "I wasn't wound up."

"You weren't?" Mike countered. "Your heart was thumping a mile a minute the whole time we were standing out front talking."

Hale opened his mouth to deny it but then closed it again. Maybe he needed to talk to someone about this whole mess with his ex-girlfriend.

"Karissa Bonifay showed up at my apartment a little while before you called me," he admitted. "I'm not quite sure why, since most of our conversation bordered on hostile."

"Okay." Mike crossed his arms over his chest. "What got you so rattled about her showing up? Do you still have feelings for her?"

Hale sat up so fast his rolling chair almost slid out from under him. "What the hell are you talking about? I don't have feelings for her. She dumped me and I moved on years and years ago."

Mike lifted a brow. "Obviously."

Hale winced. "Okay, maybe there *is* still something there. I'm just not sure what it means." He stared at the DPD logo on his computer screen for a moment before confiding in Mike about what Karissa had told him regarding the job she was on. "I can tell she's hiding something from me about this guy she's protecting. Or maybe the hit man who's after him. I can't explain how I know, but there's something else going on."

"And what does that have to do with whatever you still feel for your ex-girlfriend?"

Once again there was that instinctive urge to lie his ass off, but in the end, Hale decided to throw himself further into the deep water. "There might be a very small, completely unreasonable part of me that can't help but be concerned that Karissa is putting herself between a killer and this Patterson guy. I told myself it's not my concern, but I worry anyway. It's like an involuntary reflex."

Silence greeted that confession, Mike studying him with a knowing look that made Hale want to squirm in his seat.

"Anything else?" Mike asked.

"My nose seems to work around Karissa," Hale admitted, cringing on the inside even as he said the words. "Twice now, I've smelled lilac blossoms. It's the strongest scent I think I've ever smelled. Even when I could smell."

"What do you think that means?" Mike asked casually.

Hale snorted. "You sound like a shrink, you know that?"

"You're avoiding the question."

Maybe he was. But what did Mike expect him to say?

"It sounds to me like Karissa is *The One* for you,"

Mike observed, saying the very thing out loud that had been swirling around Hale's head since she'd walked out of his apartment.

Werewolves had this legend that every wolf had a soul mate somewhere in the world known as *The One*, who would accept them, fangs, claws, and all. Considering it was literally a one in a billion proposition, most werewolves considered it an urban legend. Truthfully, Hale had, too.

Until soul mates started popping up around the Pack like daisies. The next thing they knew, everyone in the Pack had found *The One* for them—except for Hale, Carter, and Mike.

"She can't be my soul mate," Hale said.

His voice was a little harsher than necessary, like he was trying to convince himself as much as Mike.

"Why not?"

Hale cursed. "Because whatever relationship we had fell apart a decade ago. It wasn't even real. We were two teenagers playing a game we didn't know the first thing about."

"I'm pretty sure the soul mate thing doesn't care about any of that," Mike pointed out. "I don't know what brings a werewolf and their mate together, but whatever it is, it doesn't seem concerned about the baggage either party brings to the table. It puts two people together and the magic happens, whether you want it to or not."

Hale couldn't disagree. His pack mates had met

their soul mates in the most impossible ways, and they'd all ended up together against all odds. In those rare situations when one of the aforementioned couples had tried to fight the force that wanted them together, it had gone epically bad.

"Even if you're right," he said, not conceding anything, "it doesn't matter since Karissa clearly despises the very air I breathe."

"You sure about that?" Mike asked, again making Hale think that maybe the man had missed his true calling as a therapist. "What if she feels the same way you do—which I admit seems to be mostly confused?"

"She isn't confused about anything," Hale muttered. "She made it quite clear that she couldn't wait to finish this job so she can get the hell out of Dallas and away from me. I doubt she'll go out of her way to ever see me again."

"Huh." Mike seemed to consider that. "What does Karissa look like?"

"What does she look like?"

"Yeah. Describe her."

Confused why his pack mate would care, Hale nevertheless described Karissa as best he could. "Five seven and slender with long, wavy, brown hair down to the middle of her back. Piercing green eyes, an amazing smile, and dimples."

Hale hadn't realized how far overboard he'd gone with his description until Mike chuckled.

"What's so funny?" he asked almost sullenly.

"Nothing," Mike said, still grinning. "It's just that the woman you insist never wants to see you again was at the station house today watching you."

Hale thought for a minute that Mike was joking, but when his pack mate didn't laugh, he realized his friend wasn't messing with him. He sat up straighter.

"Seriously?"

Mike nodded. "She was on the roof of the station house. I didn't notice her until you, Trey, and Carter had taken off after the van, but I get the sensation she was up there the whole time." He frowned. "I can't believe I didn't smell her. Or hear her, for that matter. But from the look on her face, it was obvious she was worried about you."

Hale did a double take. He opened his mouth to say Mike had to be imagining that but closed it again. While he doubted Karissa was worried about him, he did wonder why she'd been at the police station. Maybe Tamm and his crew were involved with the hit on Patterson. But then why go after gang members, mobsters, and shoot up a club?

"What do you think I should do?" Hale asked. "About Karissa, I mean."

Mike didn't say anything for a long time. Then he reached into the pocket of his uniform cargo pants and pulled out his wallet. Taking out a slip of paper, he stood and walked over to Hale's desk. "All I can tell you is that if Karissa is *The One*, don't waste time screwing around and messing it up or you'll regret it."

It sounded like Mike was speaking from personal experience. But before Hale could ask, Mike tossed the piece of paper on his desk. It was an address.

"This is the hotel where Karissa is staying," he said. "It's one of those big extended-stay places near Market Center. Go talk to her."

Hale picked up the paper, staring at the address as Mike walked out of the bullpen, leaving him alone with his thoughts and the perplexing question of whether he should follow his pack mate's advice or not.

Chapter 7

"CAMERAS AND SENSORS ARE ALL CLEAR," Deven's voice announced over Karissa's earpiece. "I'm not seeing any unexpected movement anywhere along the top four floors."

"Sounds good," Karissa said, slowly scanning the large ballroom and all the expensively dressed people filling the space. "I'm still going to take a walk through the food prep area in the back, and then one floor down to the kitchen and service level. I don't expect the hit man to make a move in a place like this, but if he does, he'll have to come through there."

"You're not getting one of your feelings, are you?" Deven asked, and she could hear the worry in his voice. "Should we get Patterson to the safe room?"

Karissa looked across the ballroom, where Patterson and his son were chatting with several men and women of the wealthy variety. They were chatting and smiling without a care in the world, though she noticed that both he and Glenn would occasionally glance over to make sure she was still nearby.

She shook her head only to remember that her

brother was sitting in a security room all the way down on the first floor of the hotel where tonight's society gala was taking place and therefore obviously couldn't see her.

"No need for that," she said, heading for the nearest exit to the ballroom. "I'm merely being cautious."

Glenn must have caught the move because he immediately looked at her in alarm. She smiled and shook her head again, making a hand gesture she hoped was reassuring. The moment she was out of the ballroom, she turned to one of the plainclothes security guards posted there.

"I'm going to do a security sweep of the service floor. Keep eyes on Mr. Patterson," she told him. "Don't let him leave the ballroom without at least three guards escorting him. Understood?"

The man nodded, then turned his attention back to his area of responsibility, watching the ebb and flow of at least fifty people milling around the grand atrium in front of the ballroom. Karissa slowly made her way through the crowd, bypassing the elevators and the food prep area she'd mentioned to Deven, heading instead for the stairwell in the far southwest corner of the hotel, letting her instincts tell her which direction to go.

Karissa had gotten a strange feeling about the gala the moment she'd seen it on the agenda. She found it difficult to believe the hit man would make a move in a place this crowded, stuffed to the gills with rich, powerful people and their security guards. But something had told her she needed to be here tonight. So here she was, dressed to the nines in a fancy pantsuit, her throwing knives carefully hidden away in little pockets sewn into the jacket, trying to figure out what her instincts were telling her to do.

Reaching the stairwell, Karissa paused for a moment, glancing up toward the steps that led to the roof. The emergency exit up there had been secured, monitored by three different sensors and alarms. If someone had somehow gotten onto the roof without anyone actually seeing them and had tried to come in that way, Deven would have known.

Still, Karissa found her feet taking her that way, heading up the stairs even as she told herself it was a waste of time. Thirty seconds later, she breathed a sigh of relief after confirming that the emergency exit to the roof was still locked tightly, the seal across the door showing no signs of tampering.

"Of course it's still closed," she muttered to herself. "Deven would have told you if there was a problem up here."

Not sure why she'd felt the need to come up here in the first place, Karissa turned and headed back down the stairs, her mind subconsciously drifting to her earlier conversation with Hale. It wasn't the first time she'd replayed it, and she doubted it would be the last.

Karissa had stood at the door of Hale's apartment for what seemed like forever, continuously asking herself what she was even doing there. She'd come damn close to running away, until her hand had reached out and knocked—completely of its own accord, of course. Seeing Hale standing there in nothing but a pair of shorts and an old, worn T-shirt, she'd found herself too mesmerized to form words. Men that perfect shouldn't be allowed.

Since she hadn't completely thought the visit through, Karissa hadn't been sure what to say. And it had shown. The conversation had gotten a little adversarial, sometimes verging on antagonistic. The disconcerting part of the entire confrontation was that she actually felt bad about some of the stuff that had come out of her mouth.

Which didn't make a lot of sense. Given the way Hale Delaney had treated her all those years ago, Karissa had every right to talk to him any way she wanted.

"Why should I feel bad about anything I said to him?"

She'd kept repeating that sentiment to herself throughout the drive over to the police station until she was almost sure she believed it. But when she'd discovered Hale was some kind of supernatural, worries about what she'd said back at his apartment had immediately been moved to the back burner. There were much bigger issues to deal with at the moment.

"It can't be a coincidence that there are so many supernaturals in Dallas at the same time," she muttered as she stepped out of the stairwell and onto the floor the hotel kitchen was on. "Maybe Deven is right, and this is all connected somehow."

Karissa considered that possibility from a dozen different angles, trying to make sense of how it might work. But by the time she'd made it to the kitchen area, she still couldn't see how the hit man and those five killers could be working together. Her brother's theory that they were nothing more than a distraction didn't feel right.

"Hell, Hale is more of a distraction than they are," she said out loud, relieved when she realized there was no one around to hear her. The kitchen staff must have finished cleaning up from dinner already and left for the night.

It was eerie walking through the deserted and dimly lit kitchen. Pots and pans hung from their overhead racks while cooking utensils were arranged in neat rows along the stainless-steel prep tables. Everything was perfect with no one around to use any of it.

She moved out of the kitchens, through several smaller conference rooms, and then into the main concourse, the muted glow of the parking lot lights coming through the floor-to-ceiling windows the only illumination breaking up the heavy shadows that filled every corner.

Karissa was only a few steps into the concourse when she felt a prickling sensation. It quickly built until it seemed like her insides were twisting themselves in knots as feelings of dread and horror threatened to overwhelm her. Knees trembling, she fought the urge to drop to the floor and curl into a tiny ball.

"Oh, crud."

She'd experienced this before. Not as strongly, but it was definitely the same thing she'd sensed in Patterson's mansion outside Cincinnati.

Fighting through the creeping fear threatening to debilitate her, Karissa reached down, feeling the solid, comfortable hilt of her double-edged short sword materialize out of nowhere to suddenly fill her grip.

She turned slowly, letting her instincts guide her, stopping when she spotted a patch of darkness where there should have been light. The edges of the blade in her hand glowed white-hot as she took a step forward, like the sword sensed the evil producing that darkness.

She lifted her hand toward the threat, xiphos blade held high behind her. "No need to keep hiding in the dark. I know you're there."

As if it heard her, the shadow began to churn,

coming alive as something inside pushed its way out. Karissa refused to let it show, but between the swirling darkness and the feeling of dread filling the air around her, she was more than a little off-balance. When a man finally stepped out of the darkness, her hand tightened more on the hilt of her sword, and she had to fight the urge to take a step back.

The man was well over six feet, with broad shoulders and a heavily muscled chest evident under the dark, expensive suit he was wearing. She lifted her gaze, taking in the mane of dark hair framing an angular face with pitch-black eyes.

"Oh, I wasn't hiding," he said in a low, sibilant voice, the sound sending a shiver down her spine. He took another step toward her, his smile freezing her heart in her chest. "I was simply taking the opportunity to watch you and determine if you're truly the young, immature Paladin I suspect you are."

"How could you know I'm a Paladin?" she demanded, not sure she'd actually intended to say that out loud.

"Because you aren't the first Paladin I've faced." He smirked. "In fact, you aren't even the third, fourth, or fifth. Though you are by far the youngest I've encountered in many, many decades."

Karissa started to ask what all that meant, especially the part about him facing other Paladins, which implied he was much older than he appeared. But before she had the chance, the man took another step forward. As he moved, his clothing began to shimmer and shift, like thick ink flowing over glass. Before her eyes, the suit he wore transformed, replaced with multiple layers of gleaming leather armor. A thud on the floor drew her attention to a pair of scuffed boots covered with dark stains that could only be blood.

The man reached behind his back with both hands, slowly coming out with two single-edged swords. Karissa immediately recognized the wickedly curved style of the Greek kopis blades as cousins to the weapon she carried.

"It's unfortunate to see how young you really are," he said as he approached her, the two blades twirling in front of his emotionless face in a blur of motion. "I was looking forward to a true challenge."

Karissa barely had time to get her weapon up to stop the blade coming toward her neck. The impact of steel on steel vibrated through her arm all the way down to her toes, numbing her fingers so much she could barely feel the leather-wrapped hilt under her palm.

She had to stagger backward to avoid the next sword swing. Whatever the man was, he was stronger and faster than she would ever be. Before she could even finish the thought, she was on the verge of falling, and doing everything she could to keep those blades away from her.

"Yes, you're definitely a new Paladin," the man said, coming after her relentlessly. "Or maybe Athena made a mistake choosing you. She does that every time, making her decision based on her champion's heart instead of their fighting ability. I keep hoping that will change someday. But it hasn't happened yet in hundreds of years."

Karissa was too busy avoiding his vicious attack to pay much attention to what he was saying. Finally giving in to the inevitable, she threw herself to the carpet-covered floor and then rolled several feet to the side to get a moment to catch her breath. When she came to her feet, she banished her sword, reaching for one of the throwing knives hidden under the bolero jacket she'd worn to help blend in with the rich crowd.

She was already reaching for the second blade before the first one reached its target. She threw hard. She threw fast. She'd never missed a target since accepting her gifts as a teenager and she watched in disbelief as the man stepped quickly to the side so that the first blade barely nicked the side of his neck. The second blade, on the other hand, thudded solidly right into the center of his chest.

For a moment, she foolishly thought it was over, but then he yanked the knife out of the heavy leather armor, casually glancing at the bloody tip for a moment before casting the weapon aside. Then he moved after her again, ignoring the trickle of blood running down the side of his neck.

"Is that the best you have, Paladin?" He snorted. "I find it hard to believe Patterson is paying you to keep him safe when you can't even save yourself."

The man swung one of his curved blades, aiming a blow that would have taken off her head if she hadn't recalled her own sword. Even then, she had to scramble yet again to avoid getting hit. She'd never come close to losing a fight since taking up the mantle of Paladin and now she was forced to accept that this man could easily kill her. It was a humbling epiphany, to say the least.

She considered calling Deven and asking for backup, but the thought of this cold-blooded monster going after her brother sent chills down her spine.

Still, refusing to give up, Karissa fought back, shifting her fighting style and trying to depend more on speed and deception than the brute force advantage she was used to having. At the same time, she pulled one of her last two knives and held it in her left hand, not to throw but to block those swings that made it past her first line of defense.

The change in tactical approach slowed down her opponent, at least enough to allow Karissa to get in a few offensive swipes of her own. None reached home, and even as her opponent was

forced to defend himself, she couldn't help thinking he was toying with her. The constant smile on
his face did nothing to alleviate that suspicion. He
was enjoying this.

That snide smile slipped a bit when she landed
a solid kick to the center of his chest, sending him
tumbling twenty feet down the concourse and
bouncing off one of the floor-to-ceiling windows.
Too bad he didn't go through it.

"My, my, my," he murmured, returning casually
to his feet as if amused by the fact that she'd put
him on his ass. "Perhaps there's more to you than it
seems. I almost felt that last blow. That hasn't happened in a very long time. Could it be that Athena
got it right for once?"

The words were barely out of his mouth when
one of his blades slipped past her defenses, the
razor-sharp tip slicing a line across her midsection. Karissa didn't feel anything, but with a blade
as sharp as the one he wielded, that didn't mean a
thing. Refusing to look down to see how badly she
was injured, she instead threw herself backward,
knowing the next swing of his sword would probably kill her immediately.

She hit the ground rolling, coming up on one
knee to cast a dazzle glamour in the man's face,
immediately followed by both of her remaining
knives. Having learned her lesson the first time,
she didn't bother aiming for the upper body. This

time, she threw one straight at the man's crotch, the other for the section of thigh left exposed by the leather armor pieces hanging down from his torso. With the glamour blinding him, he should only be able to block one at best, but she needed to hurt him enough to make him back off a bit.

Even temporarily blinded as he was, the man was able to deflect the first blade. But the *thunk* as the second knife sank deep into his thigh was immensely satisfying.

Karissa came up holding her sword to parry the next attack, only to find the man casually waving away her dazzle glamour. Then he reached down to pluck the knife out of his leg like it was nothing more than a splinter.

"Perhaps there's more fight in you than I expected," he said as he tossed the bloody knife aside, his eyes so dark now they were practically sucking the available light out of the concourse. "But as much fun as this has all been, I'm done playing. Don't worry, before I kill Patterson, I'll be sure to tell him you earned every penny of your fee."

As he spoke, the two swords he'd been using faded away in that dark, inky cloud that had preceded the change in the man's clothes. In the next instant, another weapon appeared. This one was a six-foot-long spear with a flat, leaf-shaped metal head on one end and a blunted spike on the other.

The man came toward her, twirling and spinning

the spear around his arms and body in a blurring pattern that was so fast she could hear the sharpened tip whistling through the air.

Karissa took an involuntary step backward. Having never fought anyone holding this kind of weapon, she knew she was in way over her head. But if she turned and tried to run, he'd put the thing through her back.

Taking a deep breath, Karissa pushed down the ever-present sense of dread and took a step forward to meet him, blade held high above her.

But as the man closed the last few yards separating them, there was a clatter of noise behind her. Karissa threw herself to the side as the sound of gunfire filled the concourse.

She snapped her head around to see Deven and several other members of Patterson's security detail standing in the open doorway of the kitchen, every one of them firing toward the man wielding the spear.

The man cursed and Karissa turned to see an expression of rage on his face like nothing she'd ever seen before. It was as if he was trying to kill them all with nothing but his anger.

He spun his spear so fast now it created a wall of dark color in front of him as he deflected the bullets. With another snarl of fury, he backed toward the windows behind him, those inky shadows she'd seen earlier coalescing into existence and quickly enveloping him.

"This isn't over, Paladin," he hissed before he disappeared completely.

A second later, the black smoke faded, leaving nothing behind but a bullet-riddled window and a group of stunned and rattled security guards.

"What the hell?" one of them murmured, only for Deven to cut him off in a firm tone not to be ignored—which was pretty impressive considering he was only eighteen.

"Go check on Patterson," her brother ordered. "I want a dozen men around him at all times until he's ready to leave and then a fully secured motorcade back to his hotel. And don't tell anyone about what you just saw."

None of the men argued, though Karissa didn't miss the terrified glances they gave to the place recently occupied by the black shadow.

A moment later, Deven was at her side, though it took a second for her to realize he was focused on her injury. A cool breeze let her know he'd pulled the hem of her silky blouse up enough to expose the wound. Whatever he saw made him inhale sharply.

"That can't be good," she murmured.

Glancing down, she saw that the wound wasn't as bad as it could have been. Thanks to her fast healing, it was now little more than a thin line across her stomach, two inches above her belly button, no deeper than a paper cut. Honestly, it stung more than hurt.

Deven freaked out nonetheless. He quickly took a first aid kit out of his pocket to start cleaning the wound.

"Okay, now it hurts," Karissa hissed as the antiseptic hit.

"What the hell was that thing?" Deven asked as he worked. "How was he able to disappear like that? And why didn't you stop him?"

"Don't know. Don't know. And I couldn't," she admitted before giving her brother a complete rundown on her fight with the man. "All I can say for sure is that he knows I'm a Paladin, and that he carries weapons very similar to mine. There's also the fact that I'm damn lucky to be alive."

That answer seemed to hit her brother hard, and he didn't say anything for a little while as he put the first aid stuff back in its bag. "What are we going to do?"

"We need to find out who that guy is and how to stop him," Karissa said, tugging her blouse back down, her mind already turning to how she could find answers to those questions. One particular solution immediately popped into her head, even though she didn't like it.

"I'll update Mom and Dad with everything you told me about this guy, but I'm not holding out much hope," Deven said. "It's not like they have many sources when it comes to supernaturals."

"I might have an idea where I could get the

information we're after," she said, wondering if she could really do this. "I don't like it, but I don't see any other option."

Her brother looked at her curiously. "Okay, that sounds suitably mysterious. You want me to come with you?"

Karissa shook her head. "Thanks, but no. I think this is one I'm going to need to handle on my own."

Chapter 8

KARISSA WAS DISAPPOINTED WHEN SHE couldn't find Hale at his apartment, but instead of waiting for him to come home, she got back in her car and headed for her hotel. She'd try again in the morning, and if that didn't work, she'd go see him at the SWAT compound. Either way, she was done for the night and more than ready for bed.

She was so wrapped up in thoughts of the supernatural she'd fought less than an hour ago that she didn't see Hale waiting for her outside her room until she was practically on top of him. His dark-blond hair was shorter than it had been in high school, and it looked like his nose had been broken badly at some point, but that certainly wasn't the biggest change he'd gone through since she'd seen him last.

"Wow. You're really tall," she thought to herself only to realize a moment later that she'd actually said it out loud when Hale lifted a brow and gave her a questioning look. "How did you know I was staying here?" she asked quickly, deciding to act like that previous line hadn't just come out of her mouth. "Are you stalking me or something?"

"This coming from the woman who showed up at my apartment this morning and then followed me to the police station." Hale snorted. "But no, I'm not stalking you. We need to talk, and as a cop, it wasn't that difficult for me to figure out which hotel you were staying at."

The thought that Hale had been looking for her made her feel warm all over, even though she was irked he'd spotted her at the police station.

"What do you want to talk about?" she asked, quite proud at how casual the question sounded.

Hale didn't say anything, his crystal-clear blue gaze focused on her midriff and the tear in her blouse that was completely covered by the bolero jacket. If she didn't know better, she'd think he knew she'd gotten injured earlier.

"I thought maybe we could talk in your room," Hale said, his gaze lingering for a bit longer on her jacket before he lifted it to meet hers. "Unless you really want to discuss your supernatural abilities out here in the hallway."

Karissa had known this conversation would happen at some point. They were both hiding secrets, and the other one knew it. But that didn't keep a knot of worry from developing in her stomach. Up until now, the only people who knew about her abilities were her family. That was all about to change.

"Yeah, I guess we should take this inside."

Taking out her key card, she unlocked her door, then led the way into her suite.

"I'm going to change clothes," she said. "The fridge is stocked if you want something to eat or drink."

Not looking to see if he took her up on the offer, Karissa walked into the bedroom and shut the door, then quickly changed into the pajama pants and T-shirt she always slept in. It was more about making sure Hale didn't catch a glimpse of the rip in her blouse than the desire to be more comfortable, although the PJs were definitely that. For some reason, she didn't like the idea of coming across as weak or incapable in front of him.

"That is completely stupid," Karissa whispered to herself as she paused at the door for a second to settle her nerves. "Why do I care what he thinks about me?"

She found Hale standing over by the living room's small desk, looking at the file she had on Dominic Patterson, his son, and his company.

"Nosy much?" Karissa commented as she walked into the small kitchen and opened the fridge to grab a bottle of Powerade. The moment might call for something alcoholic, but it was late, and she was already dehydrated from the fight with that supernatural tonight. Since Hale hadn't helped himself to her stash, she pulled out another bottle for him.

"Sorry," he said, not looking sorry at all as he

opened the sports drink. "But the file was lying open on your desk, and I couldn't help but be curious."

Her first instinct was to berate him for snooping in her stuff, but she curtailed the urge, remembering why she'd gone looking for Hale tonight in the first place. If she expected him to help her figure out what kind of supernatural the hit man was, she couldn't start the conversation by yelling at him.

"Even if I really want to," she murmured.

Karissa almost choked on her drink when Hale gave her a grin. The man was too damn sexy for his own good.

"I see you're still talking out loud to yourself all the time," he said with a soft chuckle before glancing down at the photos of Patterson. "So this is your billionaire client?"

"Yeah, that's him." She moved closer to study the pictures with him. "And that's his son, Glenn, the one I'd initially pegged as a possible suspect for hiring the hit man."

"Initially?" Hale repeated, glancing over at her curiously as he took another long sip of his drink. "You don't think so now?"

"He certainly has the motive." She shrugged. "If his father dies, Glenn gets total control of the company, which is worth billions upon billions. But I get the sensation he genuinely cares about his father. I mean, if it weren't for Glenn, I would never have been hired. He's also the one who makes sure I get access to his father when the man is doing his best to keep me pushed to the outside of everything."

"Maybe he's simply a good actor," Hale murmured, looking through the other photos in the folder, including Jerome Guerrero and the other key players in Patterson's organization. The rest of the pics were of the security guards who'd been killed.

"Damn," Hale said, turning the photos to get a better look at them, taking in the guards' broken and torn bodies. "Whoever did this must be incredibly strong. Vicious, too."

"You could definitely say that," Karissa agreed, remembering the fight she'd barely survived.

She took another sip of her drink so she wouldn't have to look at the pictures anymore. She didn't want to imagine herself—or Deven—ending up like that.

Hale glanced at her, his eyes dipping down toward her midriff for a quick second. "You fought with the hit man recently, didn't you?"

Again, the instinct to lie and keep everything secret from the man who'd hurt her so badly all those years ago was difficult to resist. But this was why she'd gone looking for Hale in the first place. She needed to tell him everything if she expected his help.

"A few hours ago," she admitted. "Patterson was

attending a private gala across town. The top five floors of the hotel had been completely locked down, with guards, cameras, sensors, and alarms everywhere. There should have been no way for the hit man to get anywhere even close to him."

"But he did."

Karissa nodded. "I was doing a security check of the service floor one level down from the ballroom. I didn't honestly expect to find anything, but then he just appeared out of nowhere, right in the middle of the concourse that runs along the front of the meeting rooms."

Hale set his Powerade down on the desk beside the file folder, his expression curious. "Appeared out of nowhere? What do you mean by that?"

"Just that. He simply appeared. Out of nowhere."

Karissa walked over to the couch and sat down. The move made the wound on her stomach twinge a little, but she did a decent job hiding it. At least, she thought she had until she looked up and saw him gazing at her midriff again. Like he somehow knew exactly where it hurt.

"Maybe you should start at the beginning," Hale said, coming over to sit in an armchair. "Tell me exactly what happened tonight."

And just that easily, she did. Starting from the moment she'd walked out of the kitchen area, Karissa told him everything in detail, focusing on the hit man's appearance and the sense of dread that filled her in his presence. Hale remained quiet for the most part, occasionally stopping her to ask a question here and there. Pointed, insightful questions, she had to admit.

"So this guy can appear in a swirl of dark smoke?" he asked, looking more alarmed than suspicious. "And then disappear just as easily?"

She considered that. "I'm not sure I'd call it smoke. There's no smell and it doesn't billow and roll the way you think of smoke from a fire doing. This is more like he's somehow captured pure darkness and wraps it around himself. Like a shroud."

"That's not creepy at all," Hale said, making a face. Karissa silently agreed. "Are the swords he uses like yours? Can he can make them appear and disappear like you do?"

"They're single-edged blades instead of double, but they're definitely Greek in design. And yeah, he can pull them out of thin air like I do."

Hale seemed to think about that for a moment. "Have you ever considered this guy might be the same as you? Whatever kind of…person…you are, I mean."

"Well, I suppose I deserved that," she murmured, more to herself than him. "But at least you didn't call me a *thing*."

Her oldest brother, Lorenzo, had done that once and she still hadn't forgiven him.

"I'd never do that," Hale said softly, and Karissa

couldn't help but wonder if he was talking to her or himself.

"The gifts I have are only given to one person at a time, so there's no way the hit man can be like me," she finally managed to say. "Still, it's terrifying that he possesses some of the same abilities I have, which is why I'm hoping that maybe you— or this STAT organization I overheard you talking about—might be able to help me figure out what this guy is and how to stop him."

"So you really *were* up on the roof at the police station?" Hale said, making Karissa realize what she'd let slip. "You heard us talking about that supernatural crew and that STAT is working on identifying them, and you thought they could help you ID this man you're up against. That's the only reason you invited me into your hotel room, isn't it?"

Karissa didn't miss the hurt in his voice, even though she had no idea where it came from. Why would he care if she only wanted to use him to get information? A part of her wanted to tell him that she'd followed him to that police station because she was worried about him, but she simply couldn't force the words out. She had too much pride to ever admit to that in front of him.

"Yes, I was on the roof," she said, fighting to keep the confusion and heat out of her voice. "And yes, I heard you talking about STAT and how you thought they could get information on supernaturals. But no, there was no elaborate scheme to lure you in here to help me. If you remember, you're the one who showed up at my door, which kind of blows that theory out of the water."

She didn't mention she'd gone to his apartment barely thirty minutes ago for the express purpose of asking him for help. That would mean admitting he was right in his accusations, which was never going to happen.

"You might not have invited me in with the intention of using me as a way to get to STAT, but you certainly jumped on the opportunity when it presented itself," he pointed out.

Even if that were all completely true, Karissa couldn't stop the anger rushing through her. It hurt knowing how little he truly cared about her.

"Okay, yeah, I was hoping that you or these people from STAT could help identify the hit man," she gritted out. "I know whatever we used to have is long gone, but silly me for thinking you might still care more about my life than keeping score on an old grudge. I see how it is, though, so feel free to take the Powerade with you when you leave."

Ignoring Hale, she jumped up from the couch, her stomach twinging harder this time. Refusing to let it show, she moved over to the fridge again and dug around until she came out with a Snickers. It was hard as a rock from being so cold, but that was the way she liked them.

Karissa ripped open the wrapper and stood there as she ate, refusing to turn around as she gnawed on the cold candy bar. She wasn't moving an inch until she heard Hale leave.

Unfortunately, by the time she'd finished the Snickers and savored all that chocolate and pea-nutty deliciousness, she hadn't heard a single sound from behind her, much less the door open and close. Deciding that a second candy bar was out of the question, she finally turned around to see Hale still sitting there with an expression on his face that was hard to describe. She wanted to call it contrite but wasn't quite sure if that was correct.

"I'm sorry," he said before she could even think about what she might say to him. "I'm not sure where all of that even came from or why I said it, but all I can say is that I'm sorry."

Part of Karissa—a really big spiteful part— wanted to refuse the apology and tell Hale that he could take his sorry and stuff it where the sun didn't shine. Because he might not know where all those words had come from, but she did. It was his feelings for her. Or the lack of them, she supposed would be a better way to put it.

Karissa kept those thoughts to herself. Nothing she said would change anything for the better anyway. She needed Hale's help identifying Patterson's would-be hit man, so she'd have to bite her tongue for a while longer.

"Then you'll help me?" she asked. "You'll talk to these friends of yours and see if they've ever heard of this supernatural I'm up against who wants to kill Patterson—and now me, apparently?"

Hale winced a little at that, the low blow bringing Karissa more satisfaction than it probably should have. But he finally nodded, which was a win as far as she was concerned.

"Of course I'll help you," he said quickly, like he was trying to make up for his earlier words. "But before we contact STAT about whether they can ID this supernatural, I'd like to talk to you about something else first."

"What's that?" Karissa asked warily, suddenly wondering if she should be worried.

"When I asked if this killer might be like you, you said something about the gifts you have only being given to one person at a time. What did you mean by that? What kind of gifts were you given and when?"

Karissa sighed. She'd known that asking Hale for help would almost certainly end with her secret coming out. Considering how similar her abilities were to the hit man's, it was practically a given. But she was willing to tell him if it led her to learning what she wanted to know. At some point in the future, she expected Hale to return the favor when it came to spilling personal secrets, though. And she had no doubt that he was keeping a lot of them.

"I became a Paladin on my sixteenth birthday," Karissa said, leaning back against the counter. "That means I've been gifted with the powers of a filia palladis—a Daughter of Athena. Those gifts— which include many of the things you've seen me do—are only given to one person at a time. After me, someone else in the world will be selected to carry the gift. And considering the fact that this thing I fought tonight has apparently killed multiple Paladins in his life, the next person might not have to wait very long."

"A Paladin?" Hale whispered softly, looking completely baffled. "Um, maybe you should back up and start from the beginning because I don't have any idea what you're talking about."

Chapter 9

ATHENA WAS REAL?

Hale's head spun at a hundred miles an hour as he wondered whether Karissa was simply messing with him. Not that it wouldn't be called for. He had been acting like an a-hole just now.

"You remember how crappy I felt that night of my sixteenth birthday party?" Karissa was asking, dragging his attention back to the conversation at hand and the woman who'd had him completely off-balance since the moment he'd seen her coming toward him in the hallway.

"Vaguely," he said, trying to recall those memories, digging into the far reaches of his hard drive. "We chalked it up to you eating too much red velvet cake, right?"

"Yeah," Karissa murmured, her lips curving in a small smile. "That was what we thought even though I'd only had one piece. It was a big piece no doubt, but not big enough to make me sick. I went to bed a few minutes after you left the party but woke up a little while later to find my whole body glowing, my muscles twitching out of control, and a sword that kept appearing out of nowhere every time I put my hand out. As you can imagine, my parents completely freaked out."

"Wow," Hale whispered, remembering back to those days right after his body had started going through the changes that would end with him being a werewolf. It had been hellish, but at least he'd never had to worry about glowing in the dark. "Weren't you scared?"

"Of course," she admitted. "My parents got me into the car, ready to take me to the hospital, but the symptoms disappeared before we even got to the end of the driveway. No matter how scared I was, there was a part of me completely fine with not going. I wasn't exactly thrilled at the idea of a bunch of doctors poking and prodding me like some kind of science project. Ultimately, the symptoms came back, but every time we'd even consider going to the hospital, they'd disappear again. It was nerve-racking."

"So what did you do?"

Hale completely understood not wanting strangers getting that close to him. He'd refused to go to the hospital himself, even when his fangs had come out in the middle of a nightmare.

"Honestly? I hid." She gave him a sheepish shrug. "It wasn't my bravest moment, I admit, but I was a sixteen-year-old kid and confused and terrified. I stayed in my bedroom for days, refusing to let anyone see me. Until the priest showed up."

Hale did a double take. He wasn't sure what he'd been expecting, but it definitely wasn't this. "Wait a minute. A priest?"

Karissa nodded. "Yeah. This old guy in dark robes walked right up to the house and rang the doorbell. Then he asked for me by name, saying he needed to talk to me about my gift," she said, and from the distracted expression on her face, it was obvious she was replaying the memory in her head. "My parents weren't too thrilled about letting him in, but the man—Nicos—wouldn't take no for an answer. Nicos said he was from a religious order that still revered the old gods, and that I was a Paladin. As you can imagine, that only confused me more than I'd already been before."

Hale remembered the perplexing time right after Karissa's sixteenth birthday party, as well as the weird weeks that had followed it. Karissa had claimed she was dealing with family stuff, but he'd felt her pulling away from him more and more. In the wake of their breakup, he'd looked back and assumed she'd found someone else.

But now it seemed clear it hadn't been that at all.

"Okay, you're a Paladin, a daughter of Athena," he said, almost laughing at himself for saying those words out loud. "But what the heck does that even mean? What did this Nicos guy tell you? And how did he teach you everything?"

"Let me start with the second question first, since it's the easiest," Karissa said with a sigh. "The rest of it is definitely complicated."

"Now I'm even more curious," he said.

Her lips curved into a wry smile. "Unfortunately, Nicos was far from forthcoming with the details, so some of this is stuff I've picked up on my own over the years. It turns out that only one Paladin exists at a time. When one dies, another is created automatically. My name and location appeared in an ancient book maintained by this religious order that Nicos is part of. He was selected to come and give me the welcome-to-the-team speech, explain the basics of my job description, and then promptly leave. It was infuriating."

Hale frowned. "He didn't give you a way to get in touch with him or this order of his?" Rupert Giles would never have left Buffy in the lurch like that. "You know, in case of emergency?"

"He gave me a card with a phone number on it," Karissa said. "But on the few occasions that I've tried to reach him, the calls go to voicemail. Nicos hasn't exactly been good about getting back to me. According to him, being a Paladin is my calling and it's up to me to figure out how to deal with it."

"That sucks," Hale murmured. "But back to my original question. What does it mean to be a Paladin?"

"Well, according to Nicos, beyond being associated with wisdom, handicraft, and warfare, Athena was also known as the patron goddess of heroic endeavor," Karissa told him, as if that explained everything. "That's where my gifts come in. I help with those heroic endeavors."

When he only continued to stare at her, Karissa kept going.

"Heroic endeavors as in working for my father's private security firm," she said with a rueful laugh "Besides my fighting abilities, the most important gift I received from Athena is an overwhelming need to protect others and a knack for fighting evil—human and otherwise. It sort of goes hand in hand with being a supernatural bodyguard."

If Hale had thought his head was spinning before when Karissa had talked about Nicos showing up at her door, it was nothing compared to what it was doing now. Seriously, it was like the room was starting to blur.

"So you're, like, some kind of superhero now?" he asked, even as he realized how ridiculous those words sounded. "You run around saving people from evil villains? With an unhelpful mentor who doesn't return your calls?"

Karissa laughed again and Hale told himself that the beautiful sound had no effect on him whatsoever, even as he felt his heart thump a little bit harder.

"I don't really run around saving people," she explained. "I work for my parents, which means I go where the job takes me. Their company gets hired to protect high-profile people all around the world and they send me out on the jobs that are deemed the most high-risk."

"High-risk meaning that someone's actually trying to kill their clients?" Hale said, getting a sinking sensation in his gut.

He'd never liked Karissa's parents, especially her father. Sure, part of that was because the guy was so cop that he bled PD blue, which hadn't meshed well with Hale's particular family background. But more so, it was because her father had always struck him as the kind of jerk who viewed everyone in the world as someone to be stepped on to get where he wanted to be. Hale couldn't help but worry now that Karissa's parents were using her gifts to get what they valued most—money. Why else would they send her out on all the most dangerous jobs?

While his mind had been wandering, Karissa had been telling him about some of the clients she'd protected, and Hale quickly realized she hadn't been exaggerating about the supernaturals she'd gone up against. It sounded like she'd faced more supernatural threats than the Pack had—and that was saying something.

"So you're fast, strong, good with weapons, and can make a sword appear out of thin air," he said as Karissa finished a story about facing a half-demented shape-shifter who was trying to kill a client. "What other gifts has Athena given you?"

"Those are pretty much the highlights." Karissa shrugged. "Other than that, I guess you could say I'm pretty good at reading people. Not like I'm a walking lie detector or anything, but my instincts will usually tell me if someone is trying to play me. Those instincts are also exceptionally good at alerting me when something really bad is about to happen."

That admission struck a chord and answered a question he'd been meaning to ask for a while now. "Are those instincts the reason you showed up in that alley in the middle of nowhere in time to save my life?"

"Pretty much," she said, almost seeming shy about it. "I'd been planning to do a sweep of Patterson's hotel, but my instincts led me across town to that club instead. I saw you running out after one of the shooters and I followed. I didn't have a choice. My instincts demanded I go after you. You know the rest of the story."

Hale sat there, replaying the conversation through his head over and over. He didn't doubt these instincts Karissa had described were real— werewolves were all about trusting their instincts— but he couldn't ignore the little voice in the back of his head whispering that this was yet another sign of fate taking a hand in his life and making sure he and Karissa crossed paths again.

As if she truly was *The One* for him.

"Okay, I've told you all about my gifts," Karissa said, coming into the living room to sit on the arm of the nearby couch. "Maybe now you can tell me about these STAT people and how they might be able to help me figure out who this hit man is."

"No chance you might be able to just call up Nicos and get him to help you?" Hale asked, pretty sure he already knew the answer.

"He would never help me with something like this," Karissa said with a shake of her head. "Not when this is clearly shaping up to be a situation of me against whoever the lone hit man might be. Nicos would probably see any assistance on his part as providing an unfair advantage."

Hale winced. He hated to think about how many times her request for help had been ignored for her to become this cynical. "I'm pretty sure I shouldn't be doing this, but I'm going to do it anyway. STAT stands for Special Threat Assessment Team. They're a covert federal organization that specializes in dealing with supernaturals that are beyond the capabilities of other forms of law enforcement. As you can imagine, they like their secrets, so keep everything I tell you to yourself, okay?"

When Karissa nodded, Hale then explained how the Dallas SWAT team had stumbled across the aforementioned agency, discovering in the process that it was difficult telling the story of the Pack getting in a fight with vampires in Los Angeles without revealing that they were all werewolves. From there he told her about all the other times STAT had helped them out with supernatural situations.

"Wait a minute," Karissa said, holding up a hand. "Back up a bit. Are you telling me that vampires exist? That can't be possible."

"Says the woman who carries a sword given to her by an ancient Greek goddess." He chuckled. "Trust me, the world is far stranger than even you know."

Karissa seemed to consider that for a moment before giving him a shrug. "Okay. So how do I get this secret government agency to help me?"

"You don't—I do."

Hale had no doubt that he could get Gage to act as a go-between with STAT, especially once his boss learned there was a supernatural hit man in Dallas in addition to Tamm and his crew.

"Are there any other details you can give me on this contract killer?" he asked. "Anything at all that might give STAT a lead they can use to ID this guy?"

They went over the entire fight between Karissa and the hit man again, both of them focusing on any little thing STAT might be able to use. It was when they were talking about how the guy had used those swords of his that she let slip a detail Hale was sure she'd purposely left out before.

"What do you mean he cut you?" Hale said, surprised at the surge of alarm that reared up inside him at the mere thought of Karissa being hurt.

"It's not that big of a deal," she insisted, her voice casual even as her hand came up to rest on her stomach in a move that was probably subconscious. "Just a little scrape."

"Can I see?" he said, immediately cringing at the creepy way that sounded. "I mean, if that's cool with you. I just want to make sure you're okay and that the wound isn't…um…infected."

He had to stop talking—like, right now. Because his excuses were getting lamer by the second and he knew it. But at that moment, he was about thirty seconds away from a complete and total meltdown as his inner wolf fought to slip out, demanding to know how badly Karissa had been hurt.

He fully expected her to tell him to go to hell. He wouldn't have blamed her a bit if she did. So he was stunned when she slowly lifted the bottom of her T-shirt just enough for him to see from her midriff to the top of her pajama bottoms.

His first thought was that swinging a sword must be really good for the core because his ex had some nicely defined abs. As distracting as the thought was, it faded quickly when he saw the cut incised horizontally across her stomach above her belly button.

Before he realized what he was doing, Hale reached out to gently trace along the cut with his finger. All he could do was stare, his mind filled with nothing but white noise. Feeling the warmth of her skin under his touch, he found himself reeling at the thought that someone had hurt her. That she could have died.

Part of him realized that the wound wasn't as bad as he'd first feared. In fact, now that he was looking more closely, he saw that the cut had closed up already. Not healed as much as a werewolf's would have been at this point but much further along than any non-supernatural would have been. Still, seeing the little dots of dried blood along it rattled the hell out of him, the coppery scent of it overwhelming.

It hit him then that he could smell her blood. It probably wouldn't have been that big of a deal for any other werewolf, but given that his nose hadn't worked well enough to pick up any scent in over ten years, this was a rather momentous occasion. Then something else filtered through his fuzzy head, and he realized he'd been smelling the blood since meeting Karissa in the hallway. That must have been why his attention had been drawn to her stomach over and over while they'd talked. On some level, he must have been aware she was hurt.

More evidence that the two of them were soul mates.

As if he needed any.

But how the hell was he supposed to bring the subject up to Karissa when she obviously had no interest in hearing it?

I know you dumped me ten years ago and that you clearly feel nothing for me and can't wait to finish this job so you can get the hell out of Dallas, but would you reconsider all that now since we're soul mates?

Hale knew that wasn't feasible, at least not until he and Karissa were able to spend enough time together for him to figure out if they had any shot at all. Fortunately, now that he'd agreed to help her with getting information on this hit man, maybe he'd have that time. He hoped.

He was still carefully tracing a finger along Karissa's bare stomach, a part of him surprised that she didn't seem to mind, when the connecting door to the adjoining suite suddenly opened and a young man stepped into the room. The guy immediately froze when he caught sight of them.

Karissa shoved her shirt down at the same moment Hale jerked his hand back, feeling like he'd just been caught making out in the school hallway by the principal. If the principal looked like a kid who wouldn't grow facial hair for another five years.

"Um…Deven," Karissa said, quickly jumping up. "You're here. Great. This is Hale Delaney. He was checking my injury."

The young man, who looked kind of familiar now that Hale had heard his name, stepped forward to shake hands. "Checking your injury, huh? I never heard it called that, but you do you."

Karissa smacked her brother on the arm. "Very funny. I'm being serious. Hale and I were talking about him using some of his law enforcement resources to track down info on the hit man, but when I mentioned the fight I had earlier this evening, he was worried about my wound and concerned that I might…get an infection."

"Sure, whatever you say," Deven murmured with a lifted brow that all but confirmed he wasn't buying anything his sister was trying to sell. He looked at Hale. "Good to hear you're planning to help out. Karissa said something about you being a SWAT cop. She also went to great lengths to tell me how fast you could run while wearing all that heavy tactical gear. My sister seemed quite impressed, though I'm sure she's already told you that."

Now it was Hale's turn to lift a brow, cocking his head to look in Karissa's direction even as a stupid warm sensation crept up through his chest. "Yes, I'm part of the Dallas SWAT team, but no, your sister never got around to mentioning her admiration for my physical prowess. It must have slipped her mind."

Karissa stood there looking like she wasn't sure if she wanted to smack her brother again or dig a hole in the floor and crawl in. Hale thought she might actually be blushing. Then again, it could simply be anger.

"If you're here, I assume that means everything is taken care of with Patterson?" Karissa said to her brother. "He's canceling some of his more ill-conceived appearances, now that he has a healthier appreciation for how dangerous this hit man really is, right?"

Hale's confusion must have shown on his face because Karissa turned his way. "After the fight was over and we'd gotten Patterson and his son safely locked down in his penthouse suite with guards in every room, I sat down and tried to get him to realize exactly how dangerous this guy is without revealing too much of the supernatural stuff. I needed him to cut back on all these huge social events making it damn near impossible for me to protect him."

"How did he take that conversation?" Hale asked.

He'd never met Dominic Patterson so he couldn't say for sure, but something told him that a man like that wouldn't like anyone trying to tell him what he could and couldn't do.

"I don't know," Karissa admitted. "I ended up leaving to come find you before I could get an answer out of him. Which is why I'm hoping my brother has something good to tell me."

Hale turned to look in Deven's direction, even as his mind replayed what Karissa had said. She'd been trying to find him. He assumed it was in regard to trying get STAT's help identifying the hit man, but why hadn't she said anything about it?

"There's some good news but probably not exactly what you were hoping for," Deven said with a slight wince. "After I stressed the fact that the hit man could show up anywhere he wants, Patterson agreed to curtail most of the larger social events he had planned over the next week or so before the grand opening of his plant. But he insists on going on with several smaller, more personal events, including dinner with the governor and several key investors at the Monarch restaurant. It's tomorrow night and Patterson wants you at one of the nearby tables so you blend in but are still close enough to keep an eye on him."

Hale could immediately tell from the expression on her face that Karissa wasn't thrilled about that plan.

"I don't have anything to wear to a fancy restaurant like that," she said. "I'm going to be up half the night shopping online and hoping I can get a dress delivered by tomorrow."

"No need. Patterson had his assistant, Peggy, order something for you. It'll be here in the morning," Deven said. "I think he assumed that I'd be going with you as your date—which is all kinds of weird—but now that Hale has agreed to help, he can go instead." Deven looked at him. "Do you have a suit, or do I need to get one for you?"

Karissa started sputtering and stammering about how he was far too busy to go on a *date* with her tomorrow night. Hale had to bite his lip to keep from chuckling. Damn, she looked adorable as hell all discombobulated as she tried to figure out what to say next.

"I have a suit," Hale said, locking eyes with Karissa for a second before looking at Deven. "We have to do formal functions for the mayor and chief of police occasionally. They like us to look nice."

"It's all settled then," Deven said, giving them a broad grin. "The two of you can have a nice dinner together—paid for by Patterson, of course—while still being close enough to protect him, and I get to stay behind the scenes in the security room watching the monitors and sensor feeds, where I can do what I'm best at."

Karissa still looked rather dazed, but Hale got the feeling she wasn't too upset about having dinner with him at a fancy restaurant. At least he hoped not. He was definitely looking forward to tomorrow evening. He'd wanted to have a chance to spend some time with her to see if there was still anything between them. This *date* would give him that chance.

Chapter 10

KARISSA STOOD IN THE LOBBY OF THE HOTEL off Elm Street, waiting for Hale to arrive, feeling more than a little self-conscious in the dress she was wearing. Not that she didn't wear nice clothes as part of her protective details, but truthfully, she'd never worn anything remotely like this.

She'd thought Patterson's assistant was sending over something ordered at an upscale department store, but the gown that had shown up at her suite looked like a designer original that probably cost more than she wanted to think about. While the emerald-green silk with the tiny gemstones sewn in here and there on the bodice fit perfectly, there was no place to hide her throwing knives. Worse, the heels that had come with it were ridiculously high. It made her feel like she was walking on stilts. And yet, the only thing she could focus on at the moment was what Hale was going to think when he saw her in the dress.

Which was absolutely bonkers since she shouldn't give two hoots about his opinions. But at the same time, she did. It was bizarre, unsettling, and all-around confounding. It was as though he continued to have this hold on her ten years after he'd dumped her.

She was about to go check in with Deven so she'd stop obsessing over her ex when she caught sight of Hale walking into the hotel, looking incredibly attractive in a dark suit that almost certainly didn't come off the rack. The jacket was perfectly tailored to hug his broad shoulders and emphasize his powerful chest while the pants showed off his trim waist and muscular legs. Her pulse skipped a beat at the sight of him.

"Well, thank you," Hale said as he stopped in front of her, a sexy smile tugging at his mouth. "I try never to miss leg day."

It took about five seconds to realize she'd said at least a portion of her thoughts out loud. Possibly all of them. She seriously needed to stop that. She was considering doing that aforementioned check in with Deven before she embarrassed herself any further when she saw that Hale's eyes had suddenly gone from their usual baby blue to bright gold.

If she didn't know better, she'd think it was a trick of the light coming from the crystal chandeliers high above them.

But she *did* know better.

She'd realized there was something different about him that first night, given the way he'd fought the creature in the alley and then again when she'd seen how fast he'd been able to run after the van at the police station. On some level, she supposed she'd accepted he might be a supernatural. She had no idea what kind, and truthfully, she'd been avoiding having to think about it. But the glowing eyes were making that rather difficult now.

"Don't you both look amazing," a voice said from off to her right, making Karissa jump even though she knew it was Deven. "From the way you were getting lost in each other, I'd almost think you guys were on a real date."

Karissa glared at her brother. "What are you doing out of the security room? Who's got eyes on Patterson if you're here being a nuisance?"

"There are a dozen discreetly dressed but heavily armed guards already on the restaurant terrace, all within a few strides of our client and his son," Deven said, motioning them toward the elevators. "There are more in the main part of the restaurant and in the kitchen. As far as why I'm down here being a nuisance, it's to make sure you arrive in time for your dinner reservation. Can't have the two of you losing the perfect location to watch Patterson *and* enjoy the romantic Dallas skyline."

Karissa would have glowered at her brother again, but he was already walking ahead of them toward the elevators, motioning for them to keep up. She started to follow, but a warm hand on her arm stopped her. Glancing down, she saw Hale's long, exquisitely shaped fingers draped casually around her wrist. When she looked up, she noticed the gold glow had disappeared from his gaze. But the heat was still there.

"I didn't get a chance to say it before your brother showed up," he murmured softly, leaning in so close that she could feel his breath on her cheek. "You look absolutely stunning in that dress. Even now, it's hard to find the words to tell you."

The compliment shouldn't have meant a thing to her—not with all the history between them—but Karissa had to admit that it affected her anyway as heat swirled in her middle, then spread throughout her body.

"Jerome will meet you on the forty-ninth floor," Deven said, leaning into one of the elevators to swipe a key card and push a button before stepping back out so Karissa and Hale could step inside. Before the doors could close, he reached out and handed them two tiny earbuds. "These will let you monitor the security comm channel, but no one will be able to eavesdrop on your conversation until you double-tap the bud. In case you want to have a little *personal time.*"

As the elevator doors slid closed, her brother winked at them. Seriously. He actually winked!

"Deven has more personality than I remember," Hale remarked as the elevator quickly rose. "He used to be so quiet."

"Well, he *was* only eight years old at the time," she pointed out. "And rather focused on video games. So unless you could pontificate for hours on the intricacies of Sonic the Hedgehog, I don't think he was very interested in anything you had to say."

Hale nodded. "That makes sense. He definitely seems to be taking to this whole private security gig, considering that he's only eighteen. I get the feeling he knows what he's doing when it comes to the tech support side of things."

Karissa found herself smiling, feeling a silly sense of pride. "He *is* really good at it. To the point that I like being in the field with Deven way more than with any of my other brothers. We work well together, and I like spending time with him."

The elevator door opened before Hale could say anything and then Jerome Guerrero was there to meet them. As she and Hale stepped out, Karissa made the introductions.

"Glad to meet you," the chief of security said, leading the two of them across the main section of the restaurant that clearly took up a good portion of this level of the building. "When Deven mentioned who would be joining you this evening, I took the liberty of doing a background check. You have an impressive résumé, especially given your family history. Good to have you on the team."

Hale didn't respond as they continued moving across the restaurant. Karissa knew about Hale's family and their dodgy history and could only assume that's what Jerome was talking about. Still, she felt a little embarrassed for her former boy-friend. She knew what it was like to be completely defined by one's family—for good or ill.

The Monarch was a beautiful establishment, with a tray ceiling, graceful chandeliers, and small lamps providing an intimate ambiance to the well-spaced booths and tables. In almost every direc-tion, the large floor-to-ceiling windows presented a stunning view of the downtown Dallas skyline, which was currently being lit up in warm orange and pink as the sun began to set. The view was as incredible and perfect as the restaurant itself.

"We thought this booth would allow you to be close enough to Patterson's table to be there if needed, but far enough away so the boss doesn't feel like you're crowding him," Jerome said, covertly motioning with his head in the direction of a big table near the center of this section of the restau-rant. Karissa didn't recognize most of the people there, but she knew money when she saw it.

"This table is perfect," she murmured, scanning the rest of the people around them, immediately spotting the other members of Patterson's security team. Some were dressed as waitstaff, but most were sitting at tables like her and Hale, playing the part of customers. "We'll take it from here."

Jerome nodded and handed them a set of menus Karissa hadn't even noticed he was carrying, then walked away like he was simply another maître d' at the expensive restaurant.

"You honestly think we need to worry about the hit man making a move in a place this public?" Hale asked as he reviewed the menu.

"Probably not," she admitted. "But I'd rather not take any chances. Especially since we don't know that much about the man. And by the way, don't worry about the prices. Dinner is on my client, so order whatever you want."

"While I like the sound of that, having someone else pay for dinner kind of ruins the first-date mystique," he said. "It seems ungentlemanly."

Karissa snorted out a laugh. "Who says this is a date? And even if it is, since when did we ever worry about who paid? I tend to remember both of us having to raid our piggy banks to come up with enough cash the first time we went out together."

Hale smiled at the memory, the expression bringing an inexplicable burst of warmth to her chest, and for a moment, Karissa almost believed they truly were out on a date like that night more than a decade ago when they'd slipped away to be together.

"We ended up having to go to Dairy Queen because it was the only place close enough to get to on our bikes," he said with a soft chuckle. "And if I remember correctly, we shared a basket of chicken strips and fries so we'd have enough money for each of us to get a Blizzard."

Karissa told herself it was ancient history, that none of it mattered. But that didn't keep snapshots of that night from flashing through her head and making her smile.

"We ate those Blizzards so fast I thought my brain would freeze," she said, remembering the pain fondly. "And then we ended up staying at that table outside for hours talking. We didn't leave until they chased us off at midnight, remember?"

"Oh, I remember. Your parents were so pissed at me when we rolled up in your front yard," Hale said, his grin slipping a little. "I thought your dad was going to shoot me."

"Well, I *was* only a freshman in high school, and twelve thirty was way past my curfew," Karissa said with a laugh, but then stopped when she realized Hale probably hadn't been kidding about that last part. "Dad really wouldn't have shot you. You know that, right?"

"I'm not so sure about that," he said softly, turning his attention back to the menu. "He never thought much of me from day one and taking his daughter out on a date without him knowing about it was just another strike against me."

"I told him it was my idea," she insisted.

Her father hadn't cared about that, though. Her opinion hadn't counted for much back then. Actually, it didn't count for much now.

They were interrupted before they could do any

introspection about their first date by the arrival of their server, forcing Karissa to take a quick scan of the menu she hadn't even perused yet.

"Hmm, no chicken strips with fries so I guess we'll have to make do with whatever they have." Hale glanced at her. "Ladies first?"

Karissa looked at the menu again, deciding to go with the Caesar salad, wood-grilled chicken, and a side of summer squash. It sounded relatively tame to her sensible ear, but the fact that her simple meal alone was going to cost Patterson almost sixty dollars—more with the wine the waiter recommended to go along with the chicken—still made her squirm a little. She didn't mind spending some-one else's money, but truthfully, given a choice, she'd rather be back at DQ with a basket of finger food.

Hale ordered a ridiculously expensive piece of Texas Wagyu striploin steak with two sides of garlic whipped potatoes.

"Meat and potatoes. I should have known," Karissa muttered with a laugh, earning a chuckle from Hale.

"When am I ever going to get another chance to eat a piece of Wagyu that costs this much? And besides fries, there's absolutely nothing that goes better with a good steak than mashed potatoes."

Unable to come up with anything to refute that, Karissa took a moment to throw a covert glance toward Patterson's table. While the man sat there looking completely relaxed as he chatted casually with the governor and several of those closest to him, his son was obviously tense. Glenn was constantly turning his head to look around him, like he thought the hit man would pop up in the middle of dinner.

"Did you have a chance to talk to your STAT contact about the hit man yet?" she asked, turning her attention back to her dinner date. "Not that I'm trying to rush you or anything, but there are lives on the line—mine included."

Their server interrupted before Hale could answer, bringing glasses of water and a basket of warm bread, along with their wine, which he made a show of pouring. Karissa wondered if Hale would use the distraction to avoid answering the question.

"Gage and I talked to STAT's resident expert on supernaturals, Davina DeMirci, this morning," he said, ignoring his wine and instead taking a sip of water. "She's a witch who runs a club for supernaturals out in LA. She's helped us more than a few times over the past year or so when we ran into supernaturals we didn't know how to handle. Davina promised to give this request her full attention. I'm hoping she has something soon."

Karissa wondered what it said about her life that the idea of a witch providing intel for the feds and the Dallas SWAT team barely got a rise out of her.

Just another day at the office, she supposed. She was about to ask just why a SWAT team was getting mixed up so much with supernaturals, but Hale interrupted her with his own question.

"So what was it like growing up as a Paladin? I mean, it can't have been easy going to bed as a typical teenage girl and then waking up as someone so completely different. It seems like a pretty big responsibility for a sixteen-year-old in high school to take on."

Karissa started to answer but then stopped when she realized that no one had ever asked her what being a Paladin was like. Of course, no one but her family *knew* what she was in the first place, but it wasn't like any of them had ever openly wondered what all of this meant for her life. Not even Deven.

"It was great," she said.

When Hale sat there regarding her with a dubious look on his face, she sighed.

"Okay, parts of it were great, but there were a lot of aspects of the gift that…well…they kind of sucked."

Karissa paused to try her wine, deciding the citrus and apple notes of the chardonnay really were as delicious as the server claimed.

"It was really cool at first," she finally said. "I went from the little baby sister that nobody in my family looked at twice to a kick-ass superhero overnight. My brothers didn't know how to deal when

I started kickboxing with them without breaking a sweat."

Hale held out the basket of bread to her. "But?"

She took a small piece of pumpernickel, absently spreading butter on it. "But then one day I was walking down the street and found myself following a man I'd never met before," she whispered, remembering that moment like it was only yesterday. "I couldn't have said why I did it. I simply knew that I had to follow him."

Hale didn't say anything, instead giving Karissa time to collect her thoughts and decide exactly how much she wanted to tell him. She nibbled on the bread, savoring the creamy taste of the butter. Surprisingly, she found herself feeling extraordinarily open at the moment.

"I followed the man halfway across the South Side of Chicago, sure I was losing my grip on reality," she said, sipping more wine. "Until he slipped through a fence around an abandoned power station and led me to a room full of teenage girls he'd left tied up in there. They were half starved to death and terrified."

"What did you do?" Hale asked.

Karissa got the feeling he already knew the answer to that and wasn't judging her at all. That felt strangely nice.

"My sword appeared in my hand," she said, her mind going back to that moment, when she'd yearned for a way to make that horribly evil man regret every life choice he'd ever made, only to suddenly feel a leather-wrapped hilt under her fingers. "And I discovered my new purpose in life—protecting the innocent and destroying evil."

"So you went to work for your parents' security company to protect the innocent and destroy evil?"

She winced a little at that, recognizing what Hale was implying with the otherwise-innocent question. But only because she'd changed from the girl she'd been back at sixteen years old.

"My parents' company was just getting off the ground back then," Karissa murmured. "With my three oldest brothers helping, they'd picked up quite a few local clients but were always complaining about not being able to pull the bigger corporate jobs that would take the company to the next level."

"And then you and your gifts came along," Hale said, pausing as their server appeared with their dinner.

Karissa glanced at Hale's steak, surprised that the chef had been able to cook it so fast. Until she realized the thing was still practically mooing. Well, Hale had asked for it very rare.

"Exactly," Karissa said, picking up her knife and fork. "The original plan was that I'd join the Chicago PD for a few years to gain experience like my three older brothers did and then work for my parents doing support stuff. But when Dad realized what I could do, the plan changed. It wasn't very long before he started putting me on protective details with my brothers."

"At sixteen?" Hale asked, looking at her in surprise as he cut his steak. "I know your dad was a cop for twenty years or something, but how the hell did he pull that off?"

"Fake ID," she said with a shrug, glancing over to make sure everything was still good with Patterson before cutting into her chicken and taking a bite, picking up the thyme and lemon as soon as it hit her tongue. "I didn't care. I liked the idea of being involved because it finally made me feel like an important part of the family. And I was important, because with me around, it wasn't long before Mom and Dad's company started growing by leaps and bounds, first across the U.S. and then around the globe. To this day, I'm still shocked I was even able to finish high school."

"Is all of the work like what you're doing for Patterson?" Hale asked, taking another bite of steak and chewing with carnivorous pleasure. "Personal bodyguard to the rich and famous, I mean."

She tasted the squash, trying to figure out what they'd spiced it with. Definitely Parmesan cheese and maybe a little rosemary. "I do a little industrial counterespionage, helping big companies keep their crap from being stolen, too. But yeah, mostly it's the personal protection stuff. I think you'd be surprised at how often people want to kill the rich and powerful."

"Probably not that surprised," he said with a snort before digging into a ridiculous mound of mashed potatoes. "So you mentioned there were aspects of Athena's gifts that sucked. What did you mean by that?"

"It's not so much the gifts that suck," she corrected, squirming a little at the way Hale had posed the question. According to Nicos, Athena no longer existed in a form that could be offended. The spirit of the goddess carried on but only in the form of her Paladins. Still, it seemed wrong to act…unappreciative…of the gifts she'd been given. "But how my life has changed since I've gained them."

Hale nodded but didn't push for more, apparently content to enjoy his dinner and let her explain as much or as little as she wanted to.

"I don't really have a life," she finally said, pushing her Caesar salad around with her fork before eating some of it. "I go from one assignment to another, usually back-to-back without a break. When I do make it home to Chicago, I sleep in my old bedroom at my parents' house. I don't have a car and everything I own can fit in a single suitcase."

"Wow. That does meet the definition of suck," Hale said. "Have you ever thought of taking a break? Or is that even a decision you're allowed to make?"

She frowned. "I'm not sure. I know my parents are using me and my gifts to make themselves incredibly rich. I know that my brothers—outside of Deven—don't really care about me. Worse, I know that I'm frequently ignoring where my Paladin instincts are telling me to go thanks to my family's desire to make money. But they're family, so what the hell am I supposed to do?"

He let out a rueful laugh. "I don't know. It's not like I have much experience with family. But maybe you can start by telling them you're getting your own place and then go on a two-week vacation somewhere with no phone and no internet."

"You make it sound so easy," she said, wondering if she'd truly ever have the courage to do something like that. She'd spent so long accepting her parents' guidance when it came to her gifts that she wasn't sure if she'd know what to do on her own.

As they ate, they talked about where Karissa would go on vacation if she could go anywhere. It was a surprisingly difficult decision. It turned out that while she'd been to many countries for work, she'd seen very little of those places while she'd been there. In fact, she remembered the airports more than anything else. Which was kind of sad.

When their server came to take their empty plates and ask if they had room for dessert a little while later, Karissa almost declined, but when the man described their specialty, a chocolate cake with peanut butter, banana mousse, and vanilla ice cream, she couldn't resist.

It was while they were waiting for their cake and coffee that she sensed a change in Hale's demeanor. Karissa wasn't sure if it was her Paladin instincts, but she could definitely feel the tension in the air.

"Can I ask you something?" he said suddenly, before she could question if there was anything wrong. "It's something I've wanted to ask you for the past ten years."

The way Hale spoke—like the words were being forced out under duress—combined with the tightness along his jaw told her this probably wasn't anything she wanted to hear. But she nodded nonetheless.

He took a deep breath. "First, I want you to understand that I get it. I really do. You're given these amazing gifts, your life is completely changed overnight, and there was simply no place for me in it anymore. But why couldn't you have told me that instead of dumping me the way you did?"

In the space between one heartbeat and the next, it was like the entire world around her froze. There was no movement, no sound. Well, except for her ragged breath whooshing in and out of her lungs. Confusion warred with anger as she attempted to make sense of what Hale had just said.

"What are you talking about?" she demanded, the words coming out almost in a hiss as the anger began to win out. "I didn't dump you—you dumped me. That Friday before spring break we talked about hanging out the entire vacation, but you never called like you said you would. And you didn't return the messages I left for you either. Then when we got back to school, I find out that you'd moved away without telling me. So how is that me dumping you?"

Chapter 11

HALE STARED AT KARISSA WERE SHE SAT ON THE other side of the table, feeling like they were suddenly speaking different languages. That would at least explain why he was so damn confused right now. And why she was suddenly so angry at him.

"Karissa," he said slowly. "You might have used your three brothers to deliver the message, but it was still you breaking up with me that Friday night before spring break."

Anger drained from her face, replaced by an expression of complete confusion. Which only baffled him all the more. He was sure he was missing something important here. Only he wasn't sure what.

"I'm going to ask this again. What the hell are you talking about?" Karissa said, her voice trembling a little, like she was fighting to retain some semblance of control. "I didn't tell my brothers to give you any kind of message. And I sure as hell never wanted to break up with you."

Breathing became difficult then as a two-ton weight settled on his chest, the invisible force trying to crush the life out of him.

"But Lorenzo and your other two brothers..."

Hale trailed off, stumbling and feeling like he didn't have enough breath in his lungs to form the words. "They showed up at our apartment right before I was getting ready to go over to your house. They told me that you didn't want to see me anymore. That you decided we were too different for it to ever work out. That you wanted to be with someone more like you."

Karissa recoiled like someone had slapped her. "I never said any of that. I would never say any of that. How could you believe them?"

Time continued to slow until Hale swore he could feel every thump of his heart within his chest. "Because everything they said was true. They told me that my family's criminal background defined me. That I would never escape it and was doomed to end up in that life eventually. That I would never be good enough for you."

Across from him, Karissa looked like she was going to be sick. "And you took Lorenzo's word that I had given up on us all of a sudden? Just like that? You didn't think I'd have the courage to say it to your face?"

Hale opened his mouth to answer but closed it again as their server appeared with two slices of cake and two cups of coffee. If the man was looking for some kind of enthusiastic response at the sight of all the gooey goodness, he left disappointed. Neither of them said a word.

"I wanted to talk to you," Hale said, deciding now would be a good time to stare at that cake. It was the most delicious-looking chocolate cake he'd ever seen in his life, and right now, it was wasted on him. "But when I headed for the door, intending to go to your house, they stopped me."

"What did they do?" she asked, the fingers of her right hand wrapped around her dessert fork so tightly he thought she might bend the thing.

He clenched his jaw. "To put it bluntly, they beat the crap out of me."

Karissa's eyes went wide. "What?"

"I put up a good fight, but there were three of them, and they were all older than me and out-weighed me by at least twenty-five pounds." He gestured to his crooked nose. "I have Lorenzo to thank for this. He kicked me in the face so many times the doctor couldn't even properly set it."

She swallowed hard, going pale. "You were seventeen years old."

"And Lorenzo was twenty-eight at the time, but he didn't seem to care about that."

"Why didn't you tell me what they'd done right away?" Karissa asked, looking so devastated that it took his breath away.

"You mean beyond the fact that I had believed them when they said you didn't want to ever see me again?" Hale said with a wry smile before slowly taking a bite of cake.

He supposed the combination of moist chocolate cake filled with layers of creamy peanut butter and banana mousse was delicious, but at the moment it could just as well have been dirt. He was too focused on all the lies and everything he'd lost to worry about the taste of a meaningless dessert.

"In addition to that, I spent three days in the hospital in a semiconscious daze dealing with a concussion, broken ribs, and a smashed face. And if that wasn't enough, there was the threat Lorenzo whispered in my ear right before he and your other brothers left."

"What did he say?" she asked softly.

"That your dad had enough evidence on my family to put my father and brother in prison for life if I even thought about talking to you again."

On the other side of the table, Karissa stopped trying to mutilate her fork and instead used it to slice off a corner of the cake on her plate.

Hale turned his attention back to his own dessert, taking his time eating, even remembering to take a sip of coffee now and then. Other than the silence, they probably looked like a normal couple on a normal date to those around them. Then again, maybe everyone would write off the silence because the cake was so delicious, which made a lot of sense. It *was* very decadent.

"When you didn't call me that weekend, I started

to get really worried. I was afraid something had happened to you," Karissa said, her gaze still locked on her cake, which she was doing an excellent job of demolishing. "That's when Dad and Lorenzo told me that you'd left Chicago. That your family had gotten on the wrong side of some other criminals and decided to move. They said that you'd chosen them over me and that you never wanted to see me again."

"And you believed them?" Hale asked softly, cup of coffee halfway to his mouth. He could barely smell the rich roast compared to Karissa's enticing lilac blossom scent that filled the air around him. "Just like that?"

"Not at first," she admitted quietly, her eyes full of sadness. "But when I got back to school after spring break and you weren't there..." She shrugged. "Then yeah, I guess I did believe it. You were always talking about your dad's habit of getting on the bad side of some of the other crime families in Chicago. Plus I knew your father never liked me. It was like he thought I'd wear a wire when you and I were together or something."

Hale considered that. When she put it that way, he could understand why she might believe he'd bailed on her. His father especially had been a train wreck back then. He'd seemingly been on the verge of going to prison or being offed by a rival at least once a week and twice on Sunday. And it was true that nobody in his family had liked the fact that Hale was dating the daughter of a cop.

"When I told my father about the threat to send him and my brother to prison, my life as I knew it was over," Hale said, cutting into his cake again but not eating the piece yet. "He shipped me off to a school out past Schaumburg. I had to live with an uncle who hated me for disrupting his bachelor lifestyle."

Karissa reached across the table to take his hand. "I'm so sorry."

Hale was so focused on what it felt like to have Karissa touch him again after so many years that he couldn't even speak. The warmth of her skin was incredible, and her hand seemed so tiny compared to his, but more than that was the sense of connection he felt to her. He couldn't describe what it felt like to know that she didn't abhor the idea of touching him.

"It wasn't your fault," he finally said, his voice sounding rough to his own ears.

"No, but I'm still sorry about what they did to you," she clarified. "My family broke us up. They purposely interfered in our lives and destroyed what we had, making me believe you didn't want me anymore."

His inner wolf howled at the realization that her family had tried to get in the way of their soul mate bond. Part of him wondered if that had been their intent when they'd come between him and Karissa, but he immediately dismissed the idea. He hadn't been a werewolf back then, and there was no way her family could have known he would become one.

"Why did they do it?" he pondered out loud, as much to himself as her. "I mean, I knew they never thought I was good enough for you, but to go as far as they did seems extreme, don't you think?"

Karissa didn't say anything for a long time, using her free hand to toy with her cake, pushing the chocolate and banana mousse around with her fork. When she finally looked up, her eyes were practically blazing with fury.

"This all happened right after my run-in with that guy who'd kidnapped those girls," she said. "I told my dad that I wanted to tell you about my new gifts, but he didn't want me to say anything to anyone. I pushed back on that idea, saying I was going to tell you regardless of what they wanted, but in the end, they finally talked me into waiting until after spring break to talk to you about it."

"Which was when your brothers beat me up," Hale said. "Doesn't sound like a coincidence."

"I'm sure it wasn't. My dad sent them to make sure I didn't get the chance to tell you about being a Paladin." Her mouth tightened. "My parents sabo-taged our relationship because they didn't want me focusing on anything or anyone else except being a Paladin. They looked at my gifts and saw dollar signs right from the start."

And that greed had ruined everything he and Karissa had.

"What do we do now?" he asked, realizing only after the fact that he'd intended to ask what *she* was going to do. But he didn't bother attempting to correct himself.

"I suppose that's up to you," Karissa said softly, gazing back down at her cake again. "Part of me wants to try and fix what my family broke. But there's another part that can't help but wonder if it's too late for that."

Hale almost jumped to his feet, his inner wolf ready to tell her it definitely wasn't too late—that it would never be too late for them—but Karissa interrupted him before he could get the words out.

"Of course, if I'm being honest, there's yet another part of me that wants to board the next plane to Chicago, kick in Lorenzo's front door, and give him a piece of my mind, then do the same to my dad."

"Maybe you can wait on that," Hale said with a chuckle, even though he wouldn't mind joining her. "I'd prefer to focus on the part about trying to fix what your family broke."

She continued to study her cake, her hand still holding his. When she finally lifted her head to look at him, her gaze was full of hope. "I want to focus on that, too, but how do we even do that?"

"I'm not sure," he admitted, wanting desperately to tell her about the soul mate thing but knowing now wasn't the time or the place. "What do you say we start with finishing our dessert and then take it from there?"

Karissa seemed to consider that for a moment, then smiled. "I'd like that."

Chapter 12

"How did dinner go?" Deven asked as he walked through the door from his adjoining suite. "Did you and Hale have a pleasant evening?"

Karissa looked up from the bottle of water she was opening to see that while she'd changed into her comfortable T-shirt and pajama pants after getting back to the hotel, her brother was still wearing his suit. It made him look older than he really was, which was why he probably liked to wear one as much as possible.

"Pleasant evening?" Karissa said with a snort of laughter, taking a sip of water. "What are you, eighty?"

Deven chuckled as he walked around the peninsula-style counter and over to the fridge to dig through her stash of junk food. A moment later, he reemerged with a bottle of water and three packs of Reese's Peanut Butter Cups. That was her entire supply. Good thing he was her favorite brother or she might be tempted to pull her sword on him.

"I wasn't listening in on your dinner conversation. Promise," her brother said, taking a seat on the couch and tearing open the first package. "But I checked out the video feed every now and then.

It looked like you and Hale were having a pretty intense discussion. I wanted to make sure everything was okay."

Karissa grabbed a Snickers, then joined Deven on the couch, sitting back with a sigh. She'd loved how the designer dress and killer heels had made her look, but she was glad to be out of both after the long evening. Dinner hadn't been that bad since she was sitting the whole time, but then Patterson had decided to move his business event back to his penthouse suite, which meant organizing a secure motorcade on the fly, then standing around in sky-high heels for three hours while her client schmoozed a roomful of the rich and powerful.

"It actually went well," she said. "I mean, I found out a few very disturbing facts, but it all worked out in the end."

Deven gave her a curious look, peanut butter cup halfway to his mouth. "Disturbing facts? That sounds kind of ominous."

"Yeah," she said. "Things about why Hale and I broke up."

Karissa bit her tongue the moment the words were out. She shouldn't have told Deven about that. What she and Hale talked about wasn't going to paint their brothers—or their parents—in a very good light. But Deven wasn't only her favorite brother. He was also her best friend. If she couldn't talk to him about this, who could she talk to?

"And?" he prompted, looking even more inter-ested now.

Sighing, she told him about Lorenzo and their other two brothers beating Hale so severely he'd ended up in the hospital, then threatening to send his father and brother to prison for life. On the far end of the couch, Deven sat there looking totally stunned.

"Do you really think Mom and Dad told our brothers to do something like that?" Deven asked, the disappointment on his face making it clear he already knew the answer to that question.

Karissa unwrapped her candy bar and took a small bite, hoping she didn't regret consuming so much sugar at this time of night. "Can you hon-estly imagine Lorenzo coming up with something like that on his own? The senseless violence part, I guess. But blackmail definitely isn't his style. Mom and Dad were behind all of it."

Deven shook his head. "That's seriously messed up."

"Tell me about it," she muttered.

She couldn't think about what her family had done without it making her blood boil. Every time she thought about what Lorenzo, in particular, had done to Hale, she wanted to cry.

"Should we confront Mom and Dad now or wait until this job is over?" he asked. "I'd be lying if I said I can't wait to watch you trounce all three of our dumbass brothers at once."

Karissa sagged with relief. She'd been relatively sure that her youngest brother would take her side, but it was still nice to hear him say it out loud.

"After," she said firmly.

He nodded. "Okay. So where does that leave you and Hale?"

"We've agreed to try and reconnect," she said.

"Something tells me there's a *but* coming."

"There is." She ran her hand through her hair with a sigh, then pulled up one leg to rest her foot on the couch. "Deven, it's been ten years since we were together. I don't know how this could even work."

Her brother frowned. "Why not? You still like him, right?"

"Yeah—a lot," she said. "More than I would ever have thought possible, considering we haven't seen each other in a decade. At dinner tonight, it was almost like we'd never been apart. It's so easy being with him."

"Then why are you even hesitating?" Deven asked.

"Because it's more complicated than that," she said, eating the last of her Snickers and wishing everything could be as simple as her eighteen-year-old brother seemed to think. "Regardless of the chemistry, Hale and I aren't the same people we were a decade ago. I'm a Paladin with all the issues that come with that. And Hale…well…I'm not sure what he…"

"What he…?" Deven prompted when she stopped, realizing how close she'd come to revealing a secret that wasn't hers to reveal. That Hale was some kind of supernatural.

"I was going to say that Hale is on the Dallas SWAT team," she said, feeling bad for lying to her brother, if only by omission. "He has a life here while mine is wherever the job takes me. I'm never in one place for more than a few weeks. How could anything ever work between us?"

She hadn't been able to make things work with any guy since she'd become a Paladin. Why would this be any different?

Deven offered her one of the last two peanut butter cups. "I know I'm only eighteen and don't exactly have a whole lot of experience when it comes to this romance stuff—okay, I don't actually have any experience at all—but it seems like you should spend less time worrying about the happily ever after and more time on trying to reconnect first. Once you figure that out, then you can worry about the logistics of making it work. For right now, don't overthink it."

Karissa took a bite of her peanut butter cup, her mind running laps. It wasn't long ago that her brother was a little kid hunched over a controller, playing video games for twelve-hour stretches while surrounded by empty bags of chips. Now, he was sitting here giving her advice on her love life.

And that advice wasn't too shabby. It made her wonder when her brother had grown up so much and how she'd missed it.

"When did you go and get so wise on me?" she asked with a smile, fighting the urge to lean over and ruffle his hair like she used to do when he was younger. It was time to accept that her brother was too old for that now.

He laughed. "I was always like this. You were simply too busy to notice. Now, stop trying to distract me with the compliments and tell me that you're going to try and get back together with Hale."

Karissa had already made a mental list of reasons why anything involving Hale was doomed to failure. Even now, she could come up with another half dozen. And yet, at the same time, the thought of leaving Dallas after this job was over and never seeing Hale again made it hard to breathe. The dichotomy made no sense.

She let out a sigh. "I'm probably going to regret this, but yeah, I'm going to try getting back together with him."

"Cool." Her brother stood. "Now you just have to figure out how you're going to find time to reconnect with your ex-boyfriend while still keeping Patterson alive and catching this supernatural killer we don't know anything about yet."

She didn't say anything as Deven disappeared into his suite, closing the door behind him.

Yeah, finding time to hang out with Hale would definitely be tricky, but she was going to get back what she'd lost all those years ago, whatever she had to do. Because the thought of losing Hale again was too painful to think about.

Chapter 13

HALE PRESSED THE SUV'S ACCELERATOR TO THE floor, watching the needle on the speedometer edge past ninety miles an hour. He would have gone faster, but the traffic along US 80 heading east was starting to build up as the late-day commuters got out of work and began to leave the city.

"We're less than five minutes out from the hunting preserve," Carter said from the passenger seat. "State Highway 205 is coming up in about a mile. Head north."

Hale nodded, glancing in the rearview mirror to see Trey in the back seat talking on his cell phone, his face pinched with worry.

"It's all five of them," Trey announced, hanging up. "Local law enforcement tried to move into the preserve but were pushed back under heavy fire. Multiple bodies were recovered as the police were forced out, and there are at least a dozen other people unaccounted for somewhere on the property."

"Damn, how large is this hunting preserve?" Carter asked, looking up from the GPS.

"Saying it's big is an understatement," Trey said as Hale turned onto State Highway 205, moving so fast the vehicle almost went up on two wheels. "We're talking about twelve hundred acres, most of it heavily wooded or covered with brush."

"What the hell made these guys attack all the way out here?" Carter added, holding on to the door handle as Hale weaved in and out of traffic. "Their MO is getting weirder by the day."

Hale couldn't even hazard a guess. In the four days since the attack on the nightclub, the Gang of Five—that's what the local media had started calling them—had attacked three more groups. There'd been strikes against a known crime boss and his large security detail, then a drug-manufacturing warehouse guarded by twenty men carrying automatic weapons, and finally an underground fight club with hundreds of thousands of dollars passing hands from betting and every person there carrying a weapon.

The media couldn't seem to decide if the Gang of Five were violent criminals who should be stopped or dark vigilantes who should be cheered, even as the body count continued to climb.

When Hale pulled off the road onto the hunting preserve, he found three police cruisers there— all of which had sustained considerable damage from gunfire. One of the officers stood near his car, bleeding heavily from a head wound. He waved them frantically through the gate, motioning toward a group of buildings at the end of a long gravel driveway. Hale didn't want to think where the cops who'd come in the other cars were.

They found a dozen other damaged cars and trucks closer to the main hunting lodge, injured people lying all over the place. As soon as Hale brought the SWAT SUV to a halt, a sheriff's deputy came stumbling toward them, name tag torn off his blood-soaked uniform. A tall woman in a cowboy hat walked beside him, helping the man stay upright. Far off in the distance, Hale heard the sounds of gunfire.

"Please tell me there are more of you on the way," the deputy said as Hale stepped out of the truck. "There are five confirmed shooters out there in the woods somewhere, heavily armed and vicious as hell. We have multiple deputies and officers down, along with an unknown number of civilians. It's like they're being hunted."

The irony of people who'd paid to come to this place to hunt now being hunted wasn't lost on Hale.

"We have more on the way," Carter said, walking around the back of the vehicle with Hale's M4 carbine and his tactical vest. "They'll be here in less than fifteen minutes."

"But we won't be waiting for them," Hale said, shrugging into his vest as an extra-long burst of automatic weapon fire echoed through the nearby woods. "The three of us will go in now and try to save as many people as we can, while hopefully pinning down the location of the five…hunters."

The deputy eyed Hale like there was something seriously wrong with him but then slowly nodded. "Okay, I'll round up as many of my fellow deputies who can at least walk, and we'll go in with you."

"No," Hale said firmly. He didn't need to hear the man's labored breathing to know the guy wouldn't make it through another trip into those woods. A quick glance around the gravel parking lot revealed that the other deputies and local cops weren't in any better shape. "Stay here and coordinate the medevac for the injured. When the rest of the SWAT team gets here, let them know which way we've gone."

The deputy's expression slowly morphed from anger to shame before finally settling on acceptance. "Okay, I'll handle it."

Hale paused long enough to glance at the woman, giving her a meaningful look he prayed she'd understand. Someone needed to keep an eye on the deputy so his pride wouldn't cause him to bleed out. Apparently the woman understood because she gave Hale a slight nod as she moved a little closer to the man.

Turning, Hale ran toward the tree line. Ahead of him, Carter and Trey were already disappearing into the sparse woods. Over the radio, he could hear them softly announcing their intentions as far as which direction they were heading.

"I'll be playing it by ear like I usually do," Hale told them. "Be careful, you two."

Receiving soft words of confirmation, he ran deeper into the woods, slipping a thirty-round magazine into his weapon as he went, then pulling the charging handle of the M4 to the rear and letting it go, loading the first round before stopping where he was. Once again, he wished his nose weren't such utter crap. If it worked like his pack mates' did, he'd be able to get a track on almost everyone in the area. Since it didn't, he'd have to make do with his enhanced hearing and hope for the best.

Closing his eyes, Hale focused on the sounds around him. The tidal wave of noise almost overwhelmed him, from the pop of gunfire to the crashing of heavy underbrush and the wheeze of labored breathing. Even the rapid-fire thud of adrenaline-fueled heartbeats. With so many overlapping sounds, it was tough to distinguish direction and distance, but at least he managed to get a sense of where the majority of the crap was going down, and that was good enough.

Turning in that direction, Hale started running at full speed, weaving among the trees, ducking under low-hanging branches, and jumping over fallen logs. Off to his right, he picked up the sound of two sets of steady, crunching strides—Trey and Carter. They were some distance away but moving in the same general direction he was.

A flash of movement to his left had Hale throwing himself to the side, tumbling across the rough ground before he brought his M4 up, ready to shoot. He froze when he saw it was a large white-tailed deer, the rack on the buck more than three feet across and at least a dozen points. The animal stood there in the middle of a shoulder-high nest of thickets, beautiful eyes wide in terror. Hale had no idea whether it was all the shooting going on or the fact that he smelled like a wolf, but either way, the poor deer looked ready to lose his mind.

Another burst of gunfire echoed in the air, startling the deer so much the animal jumped ten feet—sideways. Before Hale could even think about whether he should move, the deer bounded away through the brush, moving like he couldn't get away fast enough.

Hale shook off the surprise, berating himself for allowing a deer to distract him. But he'd barely made it another fifty feet before something else slowed him down. There, on the far side of a fallen tree trunk, was a body.

He'd been so focused on trying to reacquire a track on the sounds around him that he almost didn't notice it until he nearly landed on it. The man, wearing an orange hunting vest, wasn't breathing. The three bloody holes in the back of the man's vest were obvious evidence of what had happened.

"Confirmed civilian fatality about six hundred meters in," Hale whispered into his radio mic. "There's nothing I can do for him."

"Copy that," Trey murmured back. "I'm pretty sure he won't be the only one we find. I'm smelling blood all over the place."

Hale didn't say anything as he continued to move through the woods, trusting his ears to lead him toward the closest fight. Within seconds, he could hear shouts and soft cries of pain.

Cursing, he ran faster.

A sudden thrum of noise overhead jerked him to a sliding stop, dead leaves flying everywhere as he dropped to a knee and jerked his M4 upward, in the direction of the noise, forefinger moving toward the trigger.

At the last second he backed off, realizing the noise was a helicopter coming in so low its skids were actually hitting the tops of some of the trees. He thought it was a police chopper coming in to provide air support, but then he saw some kook leaning out the side door of the bird with a big camera on his shoulder.

Crap.

Newsies.

A burst of automatic gunfire rattled from somewhere nearby, with at least one of those rounds slamming into the helicopter. The bird veered to the left suddenly, tipping so hard the cameraman would have probably tumbled out the door if he hadn't been strapped in. Hale supposed that meant he wasn't the only person in these woods not overly fond of reporters. Especially those that flew a heli-copter into the middle of what felt like a war zone.

Hale sprinted through the forest, following the sounds of fighting to a clearing where the trees and underbrush thinned enough to allow him to get a good look at what was going on ahead of him.

Four people were pinned down behind the minimal shelter provided by two relatively small trees that had fallen against each other at some point before collapsing to the ground in a condition that was more rot than solid wood. Even as he watched, automatic weapon fire from deeper in the forest began to chew into the tree trunks, blasting big chunks of the wood away, drawing shouts and curses from the people trapped there.

It took Hale way too long to find the two shoot-ers. He'd been looking for the dark tactical gear they'd been wearing during the attack on the club, but instead it was a mix of browns and greens that blended in with the forest background. The two supernaturals were wearing camouflage clothing and gear. If it wasn't for the muzzle flashes from their assault rifles, he might have completely missed them, even with his enhanced vision.

Charging forward, Hale dropped down and slid to a stop behind the fallen trees and the four people hiding there. Bringing his weapon up to his shoul-der, he fired a quick three-round burst at each of the supernaturals. He'd hoped to make them duck for cover, maybe even back off a little, but neither one did more than flinch.

Growling in frustration, Hale glanced at the four people he was trying to save. One was a sheriff's deputy, bleeding heavily from a wound in his right shoulder and another from a through-and-through shot in the left thigh. Someone had wrapped a belt around the man's leg as a tourniquet, which was probably the only reason he was still alive.

The three civilians were faring better, but not by much. There was an older man and two boys that barely looked out of their teens. The man had a laceration across the forehead and blood soaking through his jeans while one boy was cradling his left arm to his side like his shoulder was dislocated. The other boy appeared uninjured but was glassy eyed as he absently stared down at the blood smeared here and there across the orange hunting vest he wore.

Hale popped off a few more shots at the supernaturals, hoping to keep them at bay. Providing cover so the four people with him could escape wasn't going to work. The deputy would have to be carried, and while the older man might be able to walk, he was going to need some help. That left one kid with a bum arm and his traumatized brother to handle the deputy.

Not good.

"Trey. Carter," he said into his radio. "I need

backup ASAP! I'm pinned down by two of the bad guys with four injured people we need to get out of these woods."

"Sorry, but I've got two bad guys of my own to deal with and half a dozen walking wounded," Trey said.

"What about you, Carter?" Hale asked, pausing as one of the supernaturals darted closer to take cover behind a tree. Hale cursed silently as he recognized the man.

Darijo Tamm.

"Um…Carter has left the building," Trey said. "He got into hand-to-hand combat with one of the bad guys. His eyes went blue, and he completely lost it. He disappeared a few minutes ago, apparently planning to chase down bad guy number five and dismember him one body part at a time."

Hale cursed again, this time out loud. Whatever was going on with Carter, it was getting worse. And with Trey busy, there'd be no help coming anytime soon. He was on his own when it came to facing Tamm and the other supernatural, not to mention saving these people.

Another blur of movement caught his eye, and Hale jerked his head up to see Tamm's buddy moving to the right, probably trying to get around to their flank and pin them down in crossfire.

Hale didn't pause to think. He simply stood up and snapped his carbine in that direction, firing a three-round burst at the moving target. The first round missed, but the second and third struck true, one in the supernatural's exposed bicep and the other right in the side of his neck. He went down hard, his forward momentum causing him to tumble head over heels until he slammed into the base of a thick pine, the impact jarring loose a shower of needles.

Hale thought for sure the supernatural wouldn't be getting up after that, but he did. The man staggered to his feet, a faint trail of blood running down his upper arm and neck. He shook his head hard—like someone trying clear the cobwebs after getting punched—then he turned and stared at Hale with the most vicious expression he'd ever seen.

"What the hell is that thing?" a soft voice murmured, and Hale turned to see the kid with the bum arm staring wide-eyed at the supernatural he'd just shot. "Why isn't it dead?"

Hale didn't have an answer. At least not one that would make sense.

More bullets suddenly came his way, forcing him to duck and reminding him that they didn't have much time to find a way out of here.

"If I distract them, can you and your brother carry the deputy?" Hale asked, looking at the kid.

The boy cast a terrified look at the older man, who bore enough resemblance to the kids to make Hale think the man must be their grandfather.

"I can take of myself, Brody," the gray-haired man said firmly, clearly picking up on his grandson's concern. "You get the deputy and your brother out of here. I'll be right behind you."

Brody didn't look so sure, but he nodded and grabbed his brother's shoulder, desperately shoving him toward the injured deputy.

"What are you going to do to distract them?" the man asked Hale. "I'm not very fast at the best of times, and I'll be slower now. If they chase us, I won't make it very far."

"They won't be chasing you. I promise," Hale said.

"How do you know?" the man asked.

"Because they'll be more interested in me," Hale told him.

The man regarded Hale dubiously for a moment, then looked at his grandkids, who were crouching there with the deputy's arms draped over their shoulders.

"Okay," Hale said, yanking another magazine out of his vest so he'd be ready to reload. "When I make my move, wait a couple of seconds, and then get away from here as fast as you can. You should be out of the woods in less than a mile."

Hale didn't wait for a reply but simply gave them a nod, then jumped up and ran straight toward Tamm and his buddy. The news helicopter zipped overhead again even as he pulled the trigger on his

M4, alternating back and forth between the two supernaturals, aiming in different locations with every shot, hoping to find a weak spot.

He didn't find any.

While the rounds definitely knocked the supernaturals backward a little bit—and apparently hurt like hell if the grunts of pain were any indication—none of them did much damage. Even a head shot seemed to bounce off of them.

On the bright side, the four people he was trying to protect were already on their way out of the area. He simply had to give them more time.

As if reading his mind, Tamm and the other supernatural split off, like they both intended to go after the kids, their grandfather, and the deputy, forcing Hale to make a choice on which one of them he'd have to stop.

Dropping the near-empty magazine, Hale loaded a fresh one and then turned to the second supernatural, firing the entire thirty rounds into the man's chest at almost point-blank range. The supernatural flew backward with a roar that was unlike anything Hale had ever heard, the eerie sound echoing through the forest.

Hale didn't wait to see how much of an effect it had on the man but instead spun around and charged straight at Tamm, raising his now-empty weapon like a club. It was dangerous—and probably stupid—but it was all he could think to do at the moment. He needed to give the four people behind him a little more time.

Tamm definitely wasn't ready for an all-out physical attack, but he recovered quickly, getting off a few shots before Hale closed the distance between them. One of the bullets missed, but the other got him in the stomach. The pain was like a white-hot poker as it tore through him, but then it was out, and the pain immediately began to recede.

Growling, Hale attempted to bring the butt of his M4 up to smash it into Tamm's face, only to have the guy grab the weapon out of his hands and throw it across the clearing. Before he could even think about reaching for his sidearm, Tamm planted his large foot in his chest, sending Hale flying backward through the air.

A second later, Hale smashed through a dense, scrubby tree covered in smokey-pink flowers, the thick branches crunching and cracking under his weight. He'd barely come to a stop, a snapped off limb digging painfully into his back, before Tamm was charging toward him, clearly planning to finish him off.

Going for the nearest thing that could be used as a weapon, Hale scrambled to his feet, scooping up a three-foot length of tree branch and swinging it at Tamm's face with all his might. He didn't expect much, so he was surprised when the supernatural reared back from the impact, roaring in agony, blood running down his chin.

Huh. Apparently bludgeoning these guys with a stick worked better than shooting them, Hale thought.

Overhead, the helicopter flew by again, momentarily distracting both of them.

Tamm recovered first, ripping the branch out of Hale's hands and chucking it so high in the air it almost seemed like it was going to hit the helicopter. The pilot swerved to the side before moving back into position so the cameraman could keep filming the action.

Tamm kicked Hale in the chest again, shoving him backward to put some distance between them, then bringing up his weapon, finger on the trigger. The man snarled something, and Hale swore he heard the word *lupine*. That couldn't be good.

Hale dove to the side, barely avoiding the burst of automatic weapon fire aimed at his head. Rolling on the ground, he came up with a roundhouse kick, snapping his right foot at Tamm's weapon and sending it flying into the bushes. The urge to shift was hard to ignore, even though he already knew that claws wouldn't hurt the guy. Then again, his handgun probably wouldn't either.

Of course, wolfing out with a news helicopter hovering overhead would probably be frowned upon by Gage and the rest of the Pack. So with his trusty tree branch out of reach, that left his handgun as the only option.

Hale had just reached it when a crashing sound to the left reminded him that he and Tamm weren't the only two supernaturals in the clearing. He jerked his head around in time to see the second guy barreling toward him, weapon in hand.

From the corner of his eye, Hale saw Tamm drawing his own handgun, and he knew he was screwed before the first round was even fired. He'd barely been able to handle one of these supernaturals, even with his M4. Facing two with a handgun and unable to shift? This part of the fight would be over before it started.

Then a blur of movement crossed the clearing, intercepting Tamm's buddy. The supernatural tumbled to the ground as a vivid flash of light lit up the surrounding trees, immediately followed by the shrieking sound of metal being torn apart. It took Hale a second to figure out that something had sliced the man's assault rifle in half. A moment later, the air filled with the scent of lilac blossoms.

Karissa is here?

Then he saw her, standing among the trees behind Tamm, a wicked smile on her face, her long leather duster fanned out around her in the breeze.

"Funny meeting you here," she said, looking at Hale. "Need some help? Again?"

Before he could come up with something witty to say in return, Tamm turned toward Karissa, lifting his pistol in her direction.

Hale was halfway across the clearing before he even realized he was moving. He slammed into the supernatural so hard that he could hear bones crack. Hale ignored the pain in his shoulder, focusing on getting the gun out of Tamm's hands and stopping him from ever hurting the woman that he was sure now was his soul mate. Even if she didn't know it yet.

Once the handgun was out of the equation, the fight degraded into a savage bare-knuckle brawl, Hale punching Tamm over and over again as hard as he could. The supernatural barely seemed fazed by anything Hale was doing, returning as good as he got. It probably didn't help that Hale kept trying to look over his shoulder to see what Karissa was doing, more worried about her getting hurt than anything Tamm might do to him. His lack of focus earned him a broken nose, but it was worth it.

Hale's battle with Tamm carried him back and forth across the clearing, the helicopter overhead keeping them in view. He had no idea how long he was going to be able to keep this up, since it seemed clear that Tamm was getting the upper hand. Werewolves could take a lot of punishment, but they could be severely hurt—unlike Tamm, who seemed impervious to anything Hale tried outside of that one time he'd slammed a branch into the guy's face. Hale even tried to replicate the attack with another tree branch. But for some reason, it didn't do a damn thing this time.

From the corner of his eye, Hale could tell that Karissa's glowing sword seemed to be doing a lot more damage. But while the hunter she was fighting was bleeding from more than a dozen wounds, he wasn't slowing down a bit. It was like he enjoyed the pain.

And then, like a silent alarm had gone off, the two supernaturals abruptly disengaged from the fight at the exact same time. Then, just as suddenly, they both turned and bolted off through the forest, moving fast.

"Should we go after them?" Karissa asked from beside Hale, looking like she'd been having way too much fun.

"Why bother?" he said. "Even if we caught up with them, all we'd be able to do is fight them to another stalemate. Unless you have another one of those swords hidden somewhere on you that I can use."

"Afraid not," she said.

Karissa turned to look at him, her eyes going wide in alarm as she got a look at his freshly broken nose and the lacerations on his face. She reached out like she was going to cup his jaw only to pull back as the helicopter buzzed in even lower, the wind from the rotors swishing the branches of the pine trees, showering them with needles.

"Maybe we should get out of here before they end up crashing on us," Karissa said, turning and darting into the heavier part of the woods, where the helicopter wouldn't be able to see them.

Hale followed, finding himself wondering what it would have felt like if she'd actually touched him.

Chapter 14

"Is there any more sausage and pepperoni left?" one of the big, brawny SWAT officers asked from the far end of the row of tables where Karissa was sitting with Hale and several other members of the Dallas SWAT team.

Hale had introduced her to everyone, but there were so many that the names had started to blur after the first three or four. Karissa knew that the guy sitting on her right was Trey, and that the dark-haired guy across from her was Mike. Then there was Carter, who was sitting slightly off by himself near the back of the training classroom they were currently in for this late-night pizza party.

She'd come to the SWAT compound with Hale because he said that their STAT contact was supposed to call in with some information on the hit man trying to kill Patterson. But so far, all she'd seen were a lot of really muscular cops—and even more pizza.

"Sausage and pepperoni coming your way," someone said, passing two boxes down the table toward that side of the room.

Karissa watched as the big guy who'd asked for the double meat opened the top box and practically inhaled the first slice. A second slice followed just as fast. She tried not to gawk, but she couldn't help it. Hale and his SWAT teammates were serious about eating. They'd already gone through about twenty boxes of pizza along with enough soda and beer to fill a small swimming pool.

"So," Hale said from beside her. "Were you planning to tell me how you managed to show up in the middle of that forest just in time to save my bacon? Again?"

Karissa took a few seconds to finish chewing her bite of cheese pizza, taking the opportunity to glance over at Hale, trying not to gawk at him. When they'd left the hunting preserve, Hale's nose was broken, and he had cuts on his face and what had looked like a serious gunshot wound to the stomach. Now, a few hours later, everything looked completely healed.

She looked at the other SWAT officers around them, laughing and eating, talking about what had happened earlier that day, none of them the least bit shocked that Hale had already healed from wounds that should have put him in a hospital for a few days at least. While Karissa had already accepted Hale was supernatural, she couldn't help but wonder what *kind* of supernatural could possibly heal that fast. How many other members of the SWAT team were like him? All of them? Was that even possible?

"Remember those instincts we talked about?"

she said, turning her attention back to him. "Well, I had just gotten out of a meeting with Patterson and his chief of security when I got this sense that something terrible was about to happen. I immediately jumped in my rental car and followed my instincts until I ended up at a hunting preserve outside of a tiny town I'd never heard of. Then I got out of my car and ran until I found you."

"Well, I guess I owe my life to those instincts," Hale said with an expression that turned Karissa's insides all gooey. "Because if you hadn't shown up when you did, I'm not sure I would have made it out of those woods."

And just that fast, the warm sensation she'd been experiencing disappeared in a flash, an ice-cold wave of worry taking its place. The idea that Hale could have been killed threatened to steal every bit of breath from her lungs and she had to fight not to hyperventilate.

"Hey, you okay?" Hale asked softly, his blue eyes clouded with concern.

"What?" she mumbled, lifting her hand to tuck the few strands of hair that had escaped from her ponytail behind her ear. "Yeah, I'm fine."

Hale didn't look like he believed that, but before he could press her on the subject, Trey spoke.

"Is it true that you have a sword that glows like a lightsaber?" he asked in a lighthearted tone, almost as if he could somehow tell there was something wrong. "Hale mentioned it, but none of us were really sure what he meant."

"Oh," Karissa said. "Um, yeah."

Reaching over her shoulder, she pulled her sword out of the air close to her back. She could have pulled it from anywhere but decided it looked cooler when she did it like that. Kind of like it was in an invisible sheath.

"I've always thought of it as more like Sting from *Lord of the Rings* than a lightsaber," she said, tilting the glowing sword this way and that.

"No, it's definitely more like the Darksaber from *The Mandalorian*," Carter said, perking up a little at the sight of the short sword. "Do you know where the light comes from? What the power source is, I mean?"

Karissa considered that as she finished her pizza. "I'm pretty sure it's powered by dork magic. I've never seen it this bright, though." She grinned. "That must mean there are a lot of dorks in this room."

"Very funny," Hale said dryly, putting a fresh slice on her plate.

"What happens if someone else holds the sword?" Mike asked. "Does it stay lit up like that?"

Karissa flipped the short sword around, holding it by the blade and offering the leather-wrapped hilt to Hale's teammate. The moment Mike took the sword, it disappeared with a barely audible pop, making nearly everyone in the room jump a little.

She reached behind her back and pulled the blade out again before letting it disappear into thin air.

"I'm the only one who can touch the sword," she explained, picking up her bottle of water and taking a sip. "Anyone else tries and…well…you saw the results."

"Hey, guys, y'all are going to want to see this," Rachel, Hale's tall, blond teammate, said with a slight Southern accent as she walked in the door, interrupting whatever anyone was about to say next about Karissa's disappearing sword.

Picking up the remote control on the table, Rachel turned on the room's overhead projector. She pushed a few more buttons and a moment later, the local news popped up on the screen, a broad expanse of a pine forest visible behind a solemn-faced reporter.

"Oh crud," Hale whispered. "I was hoping to have at least one night of peace before this footage hit the air."

"If you're just tuning in," the man said in that concerned voice that all reporters must learn at some point, "it's been confirmed that the Gang of Five has struck again, this time at a hunting preserve outside of Terrell. There are reports of numerous casualties, including five members of local law enforcement."

The feed on the screen flipped to gurneys being loaded into ambulances lined up near the preserve's main building like cabs at a taxi stand. Thankfully, the news was respectful enough to not show any of the fatalities. Karissa didn't know how many there'd been but was sure it was too many.

"While the Gang of Five were able to once again evade capture, the outcome of today's horrible attack could have been even worse if not for the valiant efforts of local law enforcement and three members of the Dallas SWAT team who raced into the middle of the melee to rescue over twenty people from the woods."

The video flipped back to the overhead view of the forest, clearly showing Hale down there fighting the two supernaturals. The wind from the helicopter rotors was pushing the treetops around enough to hide some of the more incredible aspects of the battle, but it was clear that Hale was in a fight for his life against two cold-blooded killers. The reporter pointed out that Hale's weapons had no effect due to the amount of body armor the attackers had been wearing.

Karissa understood why the media had jumped on the body armor angle. How else were they supposed to explain why the bullets Hale had fired had caused so little damage? When all else fails, people will go with the only rational explanation available, even if the visible evidence doesn't quite support that conclusion.

Cheers rang out through the training room

when a picture of Hale popped up on the screen, obviously taken during some kind of DPD award ceremony, the photo showing him in his dress blues getting a metal pinned on his rather broad chest.

"Don't you look handsome," Karissa thought, only to realize she'd actually said it out loud.

That drew extra catcalls from nearly everyone in the room—even Carter. The man was actually grinning along with the rest of them.

"But even an officer as dedicated as Hale Delaney needs a little help now and then," the reporter added in a tone that was almost playful. "As seen when a local cosplay performer showed up in a black duster, swinging a sword. Now we certainly don't advocate civilians getting involved in dangerous shootouts like this one, but in this case, I'd like to think that Officer Delaney appreciated the assist from the sword-wielding Good Samaritan."

Karissa watched the video playing in the background behind the reporter, wondering what was making her feel so strange. It took a few moments for her to realize it was simply the fact that she'd never seen herself fight. It was weird. Like she was watching a movie of someone else down there under the trees, twisting, slashing, and fighting for their life.

"You do look pretty kick-ass in that long leather coat," Hale said softly, nudging her shoulder with his as the pine-tree-forest footage ended and the

reporter transitioned seamlessly into a piece on the
rising cost of produce at the local markets, the guy's
voice never changing inflection from the previous
story of death and destruction. "But at least they
couldn't see your face, so that's good."

Karissa agreed with a nod. The last thing she
needed was for her face—immediately followed
by her name—to get splashed all over the news. It
would make doing her job impossible, not to mention the fact that her parents would have lost their
collective minds.

Around her, everyone went back to laughing and
talking. Karissa was surprised at how seamlessly
she slipped into the conversation. It was funny:
In some ways, she felt more welcome and relaxed
here than she did with her own family—or at least
anyone in her family outside of Deven.

After a while, Hale's teammates finished up
eating and left, either to head home or take care
of the calls that continued to come in. There were
plenty of threats facing Dallas beyond the Gang
of Five. Within a few minutes, it was only her and
Hale, along with Trey, Mike, and Carter.

Karissa was about to ask Hale if their STAT contact might call soon when another SWAT officer
walked in. He headed straight for the front of the
room and the remote control that Rachel had left
there after turning off the news. Hale had pointed
the big man out earlier, saying something about

the man being his boss. Gabriel…Gary…or maybe Gage? She should have paid more attention.

"It's Gage," Hale said with a soft chuckle. "You just said all of that out loud. And yes, everyone heard."

She shrugged, not the least bit embarrassed. Maybe because she felt so comfortable around Hale and his friends.

"Davina just called," Gage said, throwing Karissa an amused look before turning on the overhead projector again, flipping through the input sources until he pulled up the room's computer and connecting to Zoom. "She said with the information from this latest attack, she's got an ID on Tamm and the other supernaturals."

On the screen, the Zoom app popped up, a pretty woman with shoulder-length electric-blue hair displayed larger than life there.

"Hey, everybody," she said, giving them a wave. "Sorry it took me so long to set up this call, but it's getting harder and harder to magically encrypt our conversations. Damn online security systems view my magic as a malware attack and keep booting me out."

Karissa blinked in amazement at the implications that a witch was hexing the internet. Was that even a thing?

"Davina DeMirci," Hale said, mouth twitching at her look of wonder. *Unless she'd thought out loud again*? "This is Karissa Bonifay. I've mentioned the two of you to each other already, so assume the basics are out of the way."

"Nice to meet you, Davina," Karissa said with a smile. "When Hale told me that you and STAT might be able to help me, I was thrilled."

"You might not be as thrilled when I tell you my thoughts about this supernatural hit man you're dealing with," Davina said. "But before we get to him, let's talk about this Gang of Five crap. By the way, I saw the video footage of that fight in the woods. Consider me impressed."

Karissa did a double take. "The video is showing all the way out in California?"

She cringed at the thought of her parents seeing it. They hadn't given her name, and no one could see her face in the video, but how many women ran around in a duster with a sword? Hopefully, her family was too busy with other cases to watch the news, at least before some other world event caught everyone's attention.

"Hale, I have to give you credit for helping me track down these five supernaturals," Davina said. "When you described these guys as hunters, it tripped something in my head and sent me scrambling for my old Romanian references."

"Romanian?" Trey repeated, sitting up straighter in his chair.

Davina nodded. "Back in the height of the

Roman Empire, there was a small population of supernaturals isolated in the Carpathian Mountains of Dacia, a province of what we now call Romania. When they were first discovered, the group possessed very little in the way of supernatural abilities. In fact, they only had slightly above-average strength and some accelerated healing. But the people responsible for finding entertainment for the Coliseum didn't care. They razed the village to the ground and dragged the survivors back to Rome."

"Okay, hold on a second," Mike said with a frown. "Are you trying to tell us that the supernaturals we've been fighting are ancient Roman gladiators?"

"Not quite," Davina said. "While many of those original villagers were thrown into the gladiatorial ring to fight for their lives, others were used for another purpose—being bred with other supernaturals the Romans had captured in order to produce the perfect fighter for the games. I have no idea how they did it or how long it took, but at some point prior to the fall of Rome, they created the Balauri, also known as the dragons of Rome. They're strong, fast, and aggressive, and they have nearly impervious skin."

"Dragons?" Hale echoed. "You mean the scales we could barely make out on these guys come from real dragons?"

"If you mean a *Game of Thrones* kind of dragon,

probably not," Davina said. "But there are several vaguely humanoid dragon-like creatures out there with scales. Any of them could have been involved in the breeding. Regardless, when Rome collapsed, the surviving Balauri scattered. They quickly learned that while there was no one around to force them to fight any longer, the instincts bred into them—mainly that overwhelming need to hunt and kill—couldn't be ignored. Apparently those same instincts still exist in their descendants to this day, along with their other supernatural abilities."

Gage crossed his arms over his chest. "So you're saying these Balauri band together and travel the world looking for a good fight?"

Davina shrugged. "Pretty much. Even after all these centuries, the training instilled in their ancestors remains strong in the current generation. They yearn for the thrill of the gladiatorial game and are driven to look for worthy opponents. That explains all the mercenary work they've done. They're searching for something to give their life meaning—the more dangerous the challenge, the better."

"Crap," Hale muttered. "This might sound out there, but what if that's why Tamm and his buddies came to Dallas in the first place? For a band of killers looking for a good fight, we'd be too good of a target to pass up."

Karissa considered that. Was Hale saying that he and his teammates were all supernaturals and would therefore be able to give the Balauri the competition they were looking for? She longed to ask, but now wasn't the time.

"That would explain why there's no rhyme or reason to their attacks," Mike said. "They don't care about all the people they've been going after. They're trying to get our attention and arrange opportunities to force a confrontation."

Trey leaned back in his chair with a groan. "Okay, assuming you're right about these guys, we need to figure out a better way to fight them. You might not have gotten the memo, Davina, but we were lucky to break even the last time we faced these dudes."

"Do you know if they have any weaknesses?" Hale asked her.

The blue-haired witch let out a sigh. "No idea. I mean, they were bred to be invulnerable, you know? That's why your claws don't have an effect on them."

Claws?

Wait. What?

Everyone kept asking questions about how to deal with the threat, but unfortunately, Davina didn't have much more information for them than that.

"Since I've given you everything I have on the Balauri," she said, "why don't we turn our attention to Karissa so we can talk about what kind of supernatural she's up against?"

"Good idea," Gage said, pushing back his chair, then glancing at Karissa. "We'll give you and Davina some privacy."

Karissa wouldn't have minded if they stayed, but everyone was already getting to their feet—including Hale. She was so used to hiding everything about her life that her first instinct was to do the same here.

But did she really want to do this on her own?

Chapter 15

As much as Hale wanted to stay, he stood to leave along with the rest of the guys. He was both surprised and relieved when Karissa grabbed his arm.

"I'd like you to stay," she said, her green eyes imploring. "Please."

He couldn't deny the sensation of warmth that crept up through his stomach to settle deep into his chest at the request. As if he would ever say no to her.

"Of course," he said, giving her a smile.

Hale caught Karissa glancing at him out of the corner of her eye as he sat down. She'd been doing that a lot since they'd gotten back to the SWAT compound, and it wasn't that hard to understand why. He knew she'd been freaked out after seeing how injured he'd been in that fight earlier and couldn't understand why he wouldn't go to the hospital when she urged him to.

Her concern had faded over the past few hours, however, replaced by confusion as she'd watched his wounds heal right in front of her eyes. She hadn't remarked on it or even asked him about it but, instead, continued to regard him with wonder. Even if she tried to hide it.

"Can you see the photo I'm sharing?" Davina asked, her image replaced on the big screen by a large portrait of a British guy dressed in a red military uniform. It looked like one of those fancy oil paintings in a museum from the time of the Revolutionary War.

"That's him!" Karissa said, her hand coming up to grab Hale's, squeezing tight. "That's the guy I fought the other night who nearly killed me."

Hale flinched. Nope. He still didn't like hearing her say those words out loud.

Another portrait popped up on the screen, this time of a man in a dark jacket and a white shirt with the collar tips just showing above an equally dark ascot. It took a moment for Hale to realize that the man in the two paintings was the same guy. Not only that, but he appeared to be the exact same age even though the paintings had to be at least forty years apart—Revolutionary War and the Regency period.

"Oh, fudge," Karissa murmured. "I don't think I like where this is going."

Two more paintings appeared on the screen. One was of their mysterious guy sitting in a fancy upholstered chair with a shotgun in one arm, his free hand resting on the head of a hunting dog. The other showed the man in another military uniform, this time from World War I. The man's face hadn't changed a bit, even though nearly a hundred and fifty years had passed.

Photos took the place of oil paintings for the next few images. There was a black-and-white picture of the man in an officer's uniform on the deck of a large warship, and then another black-and-white of him leaning against a wall in front of a castle. The last one, in full color, showed him dressed in a suit, sitting in a boardroom.

"I couldn't find any other images after the one in the suit," Davina said, reappearing on the screen. "I'm assuming that with the advent of computers, he realized it would be too easy to catch on to him. Since the mid-eighties, he's gone to much greater lengths to hide his existence."

"Okay, you've definitely got our attention," Karissa said. "Who the heck is this guy?"

"His name is Thomas Bagley and he was born in England in 1750, which means he's over two hundred and seventy years old," Davina told them. "He's been around that long because he's the living embodiment of the Greek god Deimos, much in the same way you're the embodiment of Athena."

"Deimos?" Hale repeated, glancing at Karissa as he dug through the few remaining memories from his high school Western Civilization class. "I've never heard of him."

"Deimos was the son of Ares and Aphrodite," Davina said. "He was the god of dread and terror. In fact, his name literally means *dread*. He frequently fought beside his father in battle, where he would cripple the enemy with the feelings of dread that emanate from him."

"That's exactly what I experienced when I was fighting him," Karissa admitted softly. "I felt terrified merely being in the same room with him."

Davina nodded. "Being the son of Ares meant that Deimos was extremely gifted in all forms of combat with nearly any weapon. There was also some kind of connection to Hades, which is where Deimos got the ability to move with those shadows that you described to Hale. Essentially, he's moving through the Underworld when he does that. Regardless, all of those abilities now reside in Bagley, and he's been honing them for a very long time."

Hale considered all those paintings and photos of Bagley in military uniforms. The man could do a lot of honing over two centuries of war and fighting.

"Okay, so this Thomas Bagley/Deimos guy is all stabby-killy. I get that part," Karissa said. "But what I don't understand is how he's been able to live so long. Nicos, the Greek priest who did such a bang-up job of informing me of my Paladin responsibilities, went out of his way to let me know that I won't live any longer than a normal human. So why has this guy been alive for almost three hundred years and I'm simply normal old me?"

Hale couldn't imagine living that long. The

thought of outliving everyone you loved and cared about was awful to think about.

"I'm surprised this mentor of yours never told you any of this," Davina said with a disappointed expression. "I mean, Greek and Roman avatars are fairly common, so this kind of information is readily available to anyone who studies the supernatural community. But regardless, the differences in an avatar's lifespan basically comes down to what's being asked of you. In this case, what Athena is asking of you versus what Deimos expects from Bagley."

"I'm not sure what any of that means," Karissa said.

"Athena's gifts are given to those who are both unselfish and courageous, and all that's asked in return is that you use them to protect those in danger. In this exchange, you remain the same person you have always been but with supernatural abilities."

"And Bagley?" Hale prompted, wondering where Davina was going with this. "What makes his exchange so different that the spirit of Deimos granted him such a long life?"

"Deimos is drawn to those who possess a violent and cruel nature," Davina said, her smile disappearing completely. "Those who glory in war and pain, and want power and control over others and are willing to do anything to get it."

"So Thomas Bagley was basically a prick before

he ran into Deimos," Hale said. "But I still don't see what he's sacrificing."

"To put it bluntly, Bagley is sacrificing his free will," Davina said. "Those who accept Deimos's gifts allow the majority of their personality and soul to be subsumed by his spirit. Bagley gets the power, money, the thrill of killing, and the extra-long life, but in return, he's essentially shoved in the back seat for the most part. He's a passenger in his own life."

"Seems like a crap deal if you ask me," Karissa muttered. "So this move against Patterson is only for money then?"

"Deimos—and now Bagley—glories in violence, pain, conquest, and control." Davina shrugged. "What better way to do that than to track someone down and kill them while getting paid for it? For someone like Thomas Bagley, it would be the ulti-mate expression of total conquest."

"Okay, that's sick and demented," Karissa said. "What I don't understand is why Patterson isn't dead already. I mean, my ego would like it if it were me keeping Bagley away, but after my first real run-in with the guy, I can admit he's probably not that worried about me. Truthfully, with that Underworld teleportation trick, he could have popped in whenever Patterson was alone whenever he wanted and off him in a flash."

"And what fun would that be for the god of

dread?" Davina countered with a frown. "I swear, this Nicos guy should be sued for mentoring mal-practice. This is Bad Guy 101 stuff. Looking into his past, it wasn't hard to figure out that Bagley tends to play with his victims, pushing them to the edge of insanity before he finishes them. There's some indication he's paid extra for the suffering he puts his victims through."

"Okay, now that's even more sick and demented," Hale said. "I don't suppose you have intel on who hired him for this particular job?"

"I'm afraid not," Davina said with a look of dis-appointment. "STAT is working on it, but appar-ently the list of people who would want Patterson gone is rather long. But on the bright side—if you could call it that—there's a good chance Bagley might have put your client on the back burner for the time being."

Karissa exchanged surprised looks with Hale before turning her attention back to Davina. "He's going after someone else instead?"

"Yes," Davina said solemnly. "You."

Beside him, Karissa froze, her face going pale. "What do you mean?"

Davina sighed. "The stories say that a long time ago, Athena got into some kind of fight with Ares and kicked his ass. Apparently, it must have been a monumental mud-hole stomping because Ares never got over it. Anyway, it resulted in the Greek god equivalent of a blood feud. Ares handed that feud—and hatred—down to his son, and now Deimos continues the fight by tracking down and killing Athena's Paladins. I was able to confirm that this current embodiment of Deimos has fought and murdered five Paladins in his life. It seems to bring him an incredible amount of pleasure to kill them. Now that he's identified you as a Paladin, I can't imagine him doing anything but going after you."

Hale clenched his free hand so tightly that his knuckles cracked. It was only when Karissa squeezed his other hand that he relaxed a little. But as his fist unclenched, he couldn't miss the four spots of blood in the middle of his palm—or the flash of his extended claws.

He only hoped Karissa hadn't seen them.

"What can Karissa and I do about Deimos—or Bagley or whatever the hell his name is?" Hale asked in a voice so low it was almost a growl. "How can we defeat him?"

"All I know about this subject is what I read in my books," Davina said with a grimace. "But being a Paladin, I imagine Karissa is brave and clever, fast and strong, and willing to risk anything to protect the innocent, as well as those she cares about."

Hale couldn't be sure, but from the way Davina was looking at him when she said that last part, it made him wonder if she knew that he and Karissa were soul mates.

"But Thomas Bagley is a killing machine," Davina continued. "Because of his deeper connection to Deimos, he'll be more powerful than you, Karissa. He's faster and has more endurance, too. His centuries of combat experience—especially against other Paladins—combined with his complete lack of concern for any living creature will give him an incredible advantage over you. He's remorseless and will use your hesitation to let innocents get hurt against you. He'll turn your compassion for others into your greatest weakness. While I'm sure you're an amazing Paladin, you simply aren't on par with a supernatural who's been around for as long as Bagley has—or one who has fought in as many wars as he has."

Karissa's hand tightened on Hale's, her heart beating faster. "Are you saying I have no chance against him?"

"I would suggest you talk to Nicos and see if he has any suggestions," Davina said before shaking her head. "But on your own, I don't think you have much of a chance."

Hale squeezed Karissa's hand in return. "Good thing she won't be alone, then."

Chapter 16

"THERE'S ONLY THE ONE BEDROOM," HALE SAID as he unlocked the door to his apartment and stepped back so Karissa could walk in ahead of him. "So I'll take the couch."

Karissa did a quick scan of the open-concept living room/kitchen, taking in the sectional couch, big screen TV, and collection of photos on the wall around it that she'd have to take a closer look at later, before turning to face him.

"You don't have to do that," she said. "I don't mind sleeping on the couch."

Hale set her weekender—which they'd picked up from her hotel—down on the floor by the couch. "You don't really think I'd let you sleep on the couch when I invited you to stay here, do you?"

She didn't answer. Instead, she watched as Hale walked into the kitchen and opened the fridge. Surely he couldn't want any more food tonight. He'd eaten a pizza and a half all by himself!

Karissa had been caught off guard when Hale asked her to stay at his apartment. Her first instinct was to say no, even as Hale explained he was worried about Bagley showing up at her place in the middle of the night. But when she'd felt a burst of warmth flooding her chest, she realized exactly how long it had been since anyone but Deven had demonstrated that kind of concern for her well-being. It had damn near melted her heart.

"You know I'm a Paladin and can take care of myself, right?" she'd asked, feeling a smile curve her lips.

"Yeah, I know you can," he'd told her. "But you heard what Davina said. Thomas Bagley has killed other Paladins and is almost certainly going to be coming after you. There's no way I can let you go back to your hotel room, not on your own."

"So, what, you plan on keeping me at your side continuously until we figure out how to stop him?" she'd asked, really wanting to know if he'd thought this out.

"Would you have a problem with that if I said yes?" Hale had asked softly. "I want to do everything I can to keep you safe."

Karissa let that question settle in for a moment before trying to answer it. She'd spent the last ten years being the one who had to keep everyone safe. The idea that there might be someone who would stand up to be the one to keep *her* safe—to say it was an unfamiliar concept was putting it mildly.

But in the end she'd decided she kind of liked it. So she'd agreed to stay at his place…at least for a night or two.

Now that they were at Hale's apartment and she

was watching him putter around in his kitchen, digging for whatever he was looking for, Karissa was glad she'd accepted his invitation. As bizarre as it was, it felt like this was where she was supposed to be. Then again, as a Paladin, she'd spent the entirety of her adult life following her instincts, so was this honestly any different?

"What do you want to drink with your popcorn?" Hale asked, head still stuck in the fridge. "Soda or beer?"

"Popcorn?" Karissa asked with a laugh. "How can you want to eat any more food after all that pizza?"

Hale pulled his head out to look at her. "First, that pizza was more than an hour ago. Second, popcorn isn't a food. It's a snack. That means it doesn't count."

She shook her head with another laugh, opting for the beer. While Hale microwaved the popcorn, she took the opportunity to send a text to Deven about where she'd be spending the night. She didn't want him freaking out and calling her parents, thinking Bagley had grabbed her or something.

The response back was typical Deven. Have fun but make good choices.

As Hale dumped the popcorn into a large wooden bowl and started to add butter and some kind of cheese powder, Karissa sent more texts to her brother, bringing him up to speed on Thomas

Bagley/Deimos and the fact that he would almost certainly be coming after her.

Then it's a good thing you're staying with Hale, Deven wrote back. Watch out for yourself. I can keep an eye on our client in the interim. I've already been doing some digging on who may have hired the hit man. I think I'm getting close.

Karissa wanted to immediately tell him to stop digging and not put himself at risk. But she kept her thumbs under control and realized she had to let her brother do this. He'd been wanting to take a more active role in their cases and now he had his chance. There was no way she could stand in his way, even if she was terrified he'd get hurt.

Be careful, she finally texted back. And don't even think of putting yourself in a bad situation without calling me first for backup.

Putting her phone away, Karissa grabbed her bag and moved it into the bedroom, setting it on the floor beside the door and taking a moment to look around. Hale's was a typical bachelor's room, complete with sand-colored walls and a dark-blue comforter on the bed. There wasn't a duvet or throw pillow in sight, but there was an expensive treadmill against one wall, along with a bunch of work-related pictures he'd put up with thumbtacks.

With a jolt she realized that, with the exception of the treadmill and pictures, the bedroom looked similar to Hale's when he was in high school. Only back then he had posters of bands and muscle cars. At least his current bed looked more comfortable than the rock-hard twin-size thing he had then. Not that she'd ever had a chance to do more than sit on it for a few minutes at a time. His parents hadn't liked her hanging around their apartment, especially not if she was anywhere they couldn't keep an eye on her. They'd probably been worried she was going to plant a bug or something.

With one more glance at the big, comfy-looking bed, Karissa turned and headed back into the living room, finding Hale already sitting on the couch, a bottle of beer in his hand and the bowl of popcorn on the table in front of him. She sat down beside him, her mind absently recognizing once again how much bigger he was than her. Even after spending nearly a week with him, it was still difficult to get used to how much he'd changed.

Hale reached for the other bottle on the table and offered it to her, then grabbed the bowl of popcorn, resting it in his lap as he scooped up a handful. It was then that she got a good look at his palm and the four crescent-shaped scars located there.

Unbidden, her mind immediately turned to their earlier conversation with Davina, the one when the witch had mentioned *claws* and then later Hale had clenched his fist so tightly that his knuckles had turned white. Karissa thought she'd seen some blood but told herself that was silly. Maybe that thought hadn't been so silly after all?

Karissa opened her mouth to ask, afraid that if she didn't, the question would pop out on its own anyway, as was her habit. But then she hesitated, not sure she had the right to even ask him something like that.

Sure, she'd told Hale about being a Paladin. But truthfully, other than the whole pulling-a-sword-out-of-thin-air thing, her supernatural nature was rather tame. She realized that his might not be. What if he didn't want her to know about his *claws*?

Maybe she should put a pin in the subject of his supernatural secrets for now and revisit it at a better time.

"Were you going to tell me about the claws?" Karissa asked, the words slipping out regardless of what she'd just decided.

Hale froze, his hand halfway to his mouth, a few pieces of popcorn falling back into the bowl as he stared at her, his eyes wide.

"How did you…?" he asked, panic on his face.

"Davina let it slip earlier when she was telling us about the Balauri." Karissa tried to keep her voice casual, hoping it would calm him down. Though she wasn't quite sure what had made him so upset about her knowing he had claws. "I didn't know for sure until I saw the palm of your hand just now."

Hale looked down, the rest of the popcorn falling out of his hand and back into the bowl as he stared at the tiny scars there. They were so faint it was difficult to believe they weren't weeks old.

"Um…it's…complicated," he finally said, watching in a daze as she slipped a hand past his to snag some of the popcorn.

"Yeah, I would imagine having claws would complicate any situation," she said in agreement, nibbling on a piece of popcorn. It was perfectly buttery with just the right amount of salt. "Do the claws have anything to do with you surviving that knife through the chest and being able to run down a speeding van?"

Hale didn't say anything, simply went back to eating his popcorn. He was silent for so long that she thought he might not answer her, but then he spoke.

"I'm a werewolf," Hale said softly, hesitantly.

As if he thought he was delivering a death sentence.

Or maybe he thought she'd freak out. Which was silly. Wolves were gorgeous animals. She should probably keep that to herself. Hopefully, she hadn't said it out loud. Since Hale didn't react one way or another, she felt it was safe to believe she hadn't.

"I can't really say I saw that one coming," she admitted, drawing up one leg and resting her forearm on the back of the couch as she half turned toward him. "Did you get bitten by another were-wolf? Was it someone else on the SWAT team?"

That earned her another frown of confusion.

She waved her hand. "I saw you, Trey, and Carter all running after the van at the police station, so I assume they must be like you. I also heard you guys talking about supernaturals in a way that implied you're used to the subject. If you're a werewolf, it's not much of a leap to assume at least some of your teammates are as well."

Hale shook his head in amazement. "That's actually shockingly reasonable." He regarded her thoughtfully. "You're taking this way better than I thought you would."

She gave him a small smile. "I guess it's been that kind of day. After learning about Romanian gladiators with impervious dragon skin and a Greek god of dread who wants me dead, werewolves seem almost chill."

"When you put it that way," he said.

Karissa sipped her beer. "So…did you get bitten by another werewolf or not?"

"Not," Hale said, taking a sip of his own beer. "That isn't how werewolves are created. That's only a fairy tale."

"Don't hold it against me," Karissa said with a laugh. "Up until a few minutes ago, I thought were-wolves were a fairy tale, too. So if it isn't from a bite, how did you turn into one?"

His brows drew together as he regarded the bowl of popcorn in his lap. After a moment, he lifted his gaze to meet hers.

"I was working as muscle for one of the organized crime families in Chicago," he said quietly. "I was pulling security at this underground fight club they ran when—"

"Whoa…wait…back up a second," she said, holding up her hand. "You can't just drop that on me and not expect me to interrupt with a bunch of questions. How did you end up working for the mob when you promised you'd never get mixed up in that world?"

Hale shrugged and took a long drink of beer. She hoped he was stalling because he was searching for the right words, because he had *promised*.

"I know we talked about getting out of Chicago and going to college together, but after we…well, reality came crashing back down on me," he said so softly she could barely hear him. "It wasn't like my parents were going to pay for school anyway, and even if they'd wanted to, I barely made it through my senior year. Going into the family business was the only option I had. Or at least the only option I thought I had."

Even if their breakup couldn't be laid directly at her feet, Karissa still couldn't help feeling like she carried some of the blame for Hale ending up in the family business. He'd once told her that it was her unflagging optimism about his future that gave him the strength not to get sucked into that world. She guessed that after the split, he'd given up on all of that. But there was no changing the past.

"Did you start working for this mobster right out of high school or…?" she asked.

"Pretty much," he said. "My dad had visions of me working my way up to enforcer or even one of the guy's lieutenants."

She did a double take. "Wow."

"Yeah, I know. Admittedly, it's not something I ever thought I'd see myself doing, but with my martial arts training, he figured I'd be a natural, I guess."

She remembered seeing Hale fight that first night in the alley, then again at the hunting preserve, and thinking how skilled he was. "Wait a minute. You didn't learn martial arts after becoming a cop?"

He shook his head, giving her a wry smile. "After your brothers beat me up, I swore that I'd never again be in a situation where I couldn't defend myself, so as soon as I moved in with my uncle, I started taking martial arts classes."

Karissa nodded. "So before I interrupted, you were saying something about being in an underground fight club. I didn't even know there was a place like that in Chicago."

"I'd be surprised if you *had* heard of the place, considering that's the whole purpose of the *underground* part," Hale said. "There were probably a thousand people crammed into a space made for about half of that, and most of them were drunk off their asses."

"I can already see where this is heading," Karissa muttered.

Drunk people and confined spaces rarely mixed well.

"The long shot won the fight that night, so a lot of people lost obscene amounts of money," Hale continued. "The crowd, which was already worked up from watching the fight and being crammed into a tight, windowless space like a bunch of sardines, got pissed really fast. To this day I'm still not sure what happened, but one minute there was a bunch of pushing, shoving, and shouting, and the next people pulled guns and started shooting."

She didn't even want to imagine how horrible that must have been. "I'm surprised they let people have weapons in there."

Hale let out a snort. "It wasn't the kind of crowd who willingly turns over their weapons. Not that it would have mattered. Something bad was going down after that fight no matter what. Bullets flying and people trampling each other to get out of there was bad enough, but then a fire broke out behind the bar. The damn thing spread like crazy."

She shuddered. Being trapped in a tight underground place filled with flames was like a nightmare come to life. "What did you do?"

Hale's eyes were distant as he relived the memory. "I got my boss and his people out, taking a round in the leg in the process. By then, the whole building was on fire. Even once I got outside, I could hear the roar of the flames and terrified screams of everyone who was still trapped in the building. I couldn't just leave them there, so I went back in to save them."

"You went back into a burning building?" she asked incredulously.

"I had to," he said, still lost in thought. "The idea of leaving them down there like that never even entered my mind."

Karissa leaned forward, holding her breath as she waited for whatever was coming next. She still didn't understand how all of this was connected to Hale becoming a werewolf and was almost afraid to find out.

"I don't know how many times I ran down into that burning pit of hell, but it seemed like no matter how many people I pulled out, there were always more," he said.

"Wasn't anyone else helping you?" she asked, even though she already knew the answer. How many people in the world, outside of a firefighter, would purposely run into a burning building to save someone they didn't know?

He shook his head. "No. And if that wasn't bad enough, there were still people shooting at each other in the middle of a fire. They were more concerned with the money they'd lost than the threat of the ceiling collapsing on their heads."

Karissa tried to wrap her mind around that level of foolishness and failed. Even though she'd seen humanity at its worst since becoming a Paladin, the situation Hale described still defied logic.

"By the time it was over, I'd been shot two more times, burned in more places than I could count, and had half my ribs caved in by a falling support beam," he said softly. "I lay there on the sidewalk outside the building, certain I was going to die and strangely okay with that because I'd saved a lot of people."

Hearing the finality in Hale words, it was all she could do to keep from crying. Once again, there was a voice whispering in the back of her head that said this was all her fault. That if she hadn't left him, then none of this would have happened.

"I didn't die, of course," Hale added with a soft, self-deprecating laugh. "Obviously. Instead, I woke up in a hospital room a few days later being told I was some kind of modern miracle because according to the doctor, I should have died from blood loss and multiple lacerations to my lungs and kidneys from the broken ribs. I didn't really know how I'd lived through all of that or what was going on with me until a few months later when Gage—who's the alpha of our pack as well as the SWAT commander—tracked me down and explained what happened."

Alpha?

Pack?

Karissa's head started to swim. She obviously recognized those terms in relation to wolves but was starting to think this werewolf thing was more complicated than she'd thought.

"I'm still a little confused about how what happened at the fight club turned you into a werewolf," she said.

"I was born with the gene," Hale said, saying the words as if he was repeating something that he'd been told. "If a person who has it goes through a traumatic life-or-death event like the one I did, the body gets flooded with high levels of adrenaline and cortisol, flipping the gene and turning that person into a werewolf."

Karissa considered that for a moment before realizing it didn't help. She was never very good with science. "But what does that even mean? Do you grow fur and bay at the moon once a month or is that only in fairy tales, too?"

He chuckled, his face finally lighting up. "All fairy tales. There's no connection between the moon and werewolves. We shift whenever we want, but only some of us can go far enough to get fur."

"Can you turn into a real wolf?" Karissa asked, unable to hide the excitement in her voice.

Hale shook his head ruefully. "I wish. Several members of my pack can accomplish a full shift into wolf form, but I've never been able to pull it off. Apparently I'm not completely in tune with my inner werewolf...or something like that."

"Okay, so no to the fully wolf thing then," she said, not bothering to hide her disappointment. "I'm guessing you can shift at least some, right? I mean, you have claws."

That got her a nod. "Being a werewolf means I have enhanced physical strength, speed, and healing. My senses are better than a regular human's— well, except for my nose because of that fight with your brothers. And yeah, I have claws and fangs."

Fangs! You've got to be kidding me.

Karissa gazed at him, wide-eyed. "Cool! Can I see?"

Hale pulled back and stared at her in shock, like she'd just asked the most indelicate question ever.

"What? I showed you my sword." She smiled. "You're a little bit old to be acting all shy, aren't you?"

"That's what you're going with?" He snorted. "I showed you mine, now you show me yours?"

"Maybe. Will it work?" she asked with a laugh, glad to see that he wasn't really upset. "I never did get a chance to try that particular line on you when we were dating."

Hale regarded her appraisingly for a moment. And then, just that fast, his face changed. The tips of two fangs appeared, growing down over his lower lip, until they were at least an inch and a half long. She glanced down to check his hands to see sharp claws that were even longer.

But while the fangs and claws were definitely amazing, the most striking change with Hale's werewolf shift were his eyes. Normally a beautiful blue, they now glowed a vivid yellow-gold so bright they were practically humming with energy. It was the sexiest thing she'd ever seen.

And a confirmation that it hadn't been a trick of the light the other night at the hotel.

Hale sat on the couch beside her, motionless and barely breathing, as if he expected her to jump up and bolt from the apartment.

"Well, you're not running away screaming," Hale said, and Karissa realized his face and hands had shifted back so quickly that she hadn't even noticed. "That's a plus, I guess."

She reached out and grabbed his hand, holding on to it tightly. "I'm not running anywhere. Definitely not over something like claws and fangs. Did you really think I would?"

He shrugged. "People have been known to bail for less."

Like she'd walked away from him back in high school on nothing more than her parents' insistence that their relationship was over.

"I already agreed to try and fix what my family broke," she said softly, her fingers still interlaced with his. "Nothing I've seen or heard tonight changes any of that. Unless you want it to."

He continued to gaze at her, his expression impossible to read. But at the same time, he squeezed her hand a little tighter. It felt nice.

"I'm definitely still okay with that plan," he said, his voice equally soft. "I want to keep working on trying to see if we can get back to what we had all those years ago. I only thought I should give you a chance to change your mind now that you know how different I am. I know dealing with something like this is a big ask. I wouldn't blame you if you wanted to back off and reassess."

While Karissa understood the sentiment—even appreciated it to a degree—it was getting frustrating, both of them dancing around each other like this. "Hale, you can stop right there. I don't need to reassess anything. Okay?"

Karissa expected a word or two signifying that Hale understood, or maybe a nod. What she got instead was Hale leaning forward to kiss her. It was unexpected but certainly wanted.

Hale's fingers slid into her hair, tilting her head just so as his mouth closed over hers. She may have moaned, but she wasn't sure. Then his tongue was teasing its way along her lips, Karissa opening up to let him in. She moaned louder this time. She couldn't help it. He tasted so damn good.

Their tongues tangled together slowly, taking

their time, even as Karissa wondered if she might burst into flames at any second. Without thought, she wrapped a hand around his strong neck, pulling him in closer, refusing to let him get away. Never wanting this kiss to end.

It struck her then how long it had been since she'd had a real kiss—the kind that made her heart beat faster and heat pool in her core. Ten years, if she was being honest with herself.

She'd dated a few guys over the past decade. She was a Paladin, not a nun—Karissa had checked, and they weren't the same thing. But none of them had ever seemed to work out. In every case, there was something missing. In fact, most had been downright bland. Like kissing a tub of cold mashed potatoes—with congealed gravy on top.

Kissing Hale now reminded her exactly how much time she'd wasted.

When he finally pulled back, ending the kiss, Karissa had to fight the urge to chase after those absolutely perfect lips. It was almost scary how badly she wanted to climb onto his lap, especially after catching sight of the hungry yellow-gold tint of color now rimming his eyes.

"I think that settles any questions either of us might have had about where we want this thing between us to go," she whispered softly, leaning forward to kiss him again.

"I guess so," he said with a grin as she continued

to kiss him. "It seems like the only thing we need to figure out now is where we go from here."

Karissa took a deep breath and then answered in the most honest words she could think of. "Perhaps your bedroom. Together?"

Hale's eyes flared even brighter for a moment before dropping back down to a smolder. "I'm definitely open to the idea, but I want to make sure you're certain. We don't need to rush, you know."

"Who's rushing?" she said. "The way I see it, we've been waiting for this moment for ten years. Don't you think that's long enough?"

Hale gazed at her for a few seconds, then stood and held out his hand. "Ten years of waiting is more than long enough for me."

Chapter 17

AS SHE AND HALE WALKED DOWN THE SHORT hallway to the bedroom, it took a few moments for Karissa to realize that the tingling in her stomach was more than excitement.

She was *nervous*.

At first she couldn't understand why, since it wasn't like she didn't want this. She wanted to be with Hale more than anything. But then she realized that was the point. She'd been waiting so long for this moment—without even knowing it—that she was freaked out about messing it up.

"Karissa," Hale said, coming up behind her once they stepped into the bedroom to wrap his strong arms around her middle and pull her back against his equally strong chest. "Breathe. You're starting to spiral."

She did as he suggested, leaning back into his body and tugging his arms around her tighter. It felt amazing. "How did you know?"

"Your heart," he whispered against her ear. "I could hear it thumping like a drum, getting faster with every passing second. Will you tell me what has you so rattled? Like I said, we don't have to do this if you're not ready."

"It's not that. I promise." She turned in his arms to reach up and place her hands lightly against his powerful chest. "It's simply that after everything, I never allowed myself to imagine this happening. And now that it is, it's a little…"

"Overwhelming?" Hale finished softly.

"Yes, but not in a bad way," she said quickly, not wanting him to misunderstand. "I'm just really excited."

He slid his hands down to her waist, tugging her closer and bending his head until his mouth was only inches from hers. "I can work with excited."

The kiss was slow and gentle, like he was afraid of spooking her. That was never going to happen, of course, and as soon his fingers found their way into her hair again, the butterflies that had been barreling around in her stomach disappeared, replaced with a completely different tingling sensation, this one a bit farther south.

Getting a firm grip on Hale's shirtfront, Karissa twisted him around before giving him a little nudge toward the bed. Truthfully, she didn't push him all that hard, but Hale still toppled back onto the bed, taking her with him.

Karissa straddled Hale's hips as he lay there flat on his back, her palms once against resting on his nicely muscled chest. "You have a very comfortable lap," she murmured, leaning over so her long hair draped down over both of their faces. "Has anyone ever told you that?"

"Actually, no. I can't recall anyone mentioning that particular detail." He grinned up at her as his hands glided back and forth along her thighs, getting closer to her butt with every passing second. "But thanks for letting me know."

Leaning down, she kissed him again, her tongue darting inside to tease and tangle with his. There was still a hint of the salty, cheesy, buttery goodness from the popcorn, but mostly he tasted like...him. It was impossible to describe in any words other than intoxicating.

They kissed for long minutes, neither of them in a rush to take things any faster. But as Karissa felt Hale's hardening cock between her legs, she couldn't help but grind a little, sending wonderful pulses of pleasure through her core. It had been so long since she'd been this aroused.

Actually, Karissa realized, she'd never been this turned on before. And to think she still had all her clothes on. Of course, that part started to change soon enough when Hale slid his fingers under her shirt and gently pushed it up. She lifted up a bit, helping him slide it over her head. Reaching back, she unhooked her bra, pulling it off her shoulders and tossing it aside.

Then she sat there on Hale's lap as he lay gazing up at her, eyes beginning to glimmer with just the faintest trace of yellow-gold. To know it was the sight of her, sitting there half-naked on his lap, that drew the wolf out of him was an exhilarating thought.

She took her time undoing the buttons of his uniform top, pushing it open to slide her hands up his T-shirt–covered chest. Through the thin material, she could feel the muscles there bunching and flexing. It was fabulous.

Hale helped her, sitting up enough to get the uniform top off, followed by his T-shirt. Then it was Karissa's turn to gawk, taking in the view of what had to be the most scrumptious-looking body she'd ever seen.

His shoulders were even broader than she'd thought, the thick muscles to either side of his neck gracefully descending down to meet the top of his arms, rounded and powerful. She moved her gaze lower, taking in his drool-worthy pecs and lightly sculpted abs. The happy trail of dark-blond hair that ran along the center of those abs and disappeared into his pants was mesmerizing, and her fingers almost itched with the need to scratch there.

Hale had a tattoo on the upper left side of his chest, directly over his heart. It was a wolf's head, eyes flashing, jaws open to show off the animal's long fangs. The ink work was incredible, but considering his intimate connection to the wolf, she could understand why he chose it.

She was lightly tracing the outline of the wolf when she saw the scars. There was a thin one on the left side of his chest, about an inch and a half long, thicker at the top than at the bottom. While it looked at least a month old, she realized with surprise that it was the knife wound he'd gotten in the alley almost a week ago.

Moving lower, she immediately noticed a perfectly circular scar to the right side of his stomach, just above the belt line. It was fully closed but looked much fresher than the knife wound. Her mind jumped to the blood she'd seen earlier that day after the fight with the Balauri. It took a moment to figure out what she was looking at. Hale had been shot during that fight in the woods. And he'd never said a word.

"Are you okay?" she asked, gently touching the scar, her eyes searching his for any sign of pain.

He covered her hand with his. "It's fine. Werewolves heal quickly. It doesn't even hurt anymore."

Karissa found that difficult to believe as her lips came down to kiss the older knife wound higher on his chest before heading lower. Long before she got to the bullet wound, she discovered other scars to kiss—lots of them.

"Are you accident prone?" Karissa murmured, only realizing she'd spoken the question out loud when Hale started chuckling under her.

"No, but being a SWAT cop—and a werewolf—is a dangerous job," he said, making appreciative sounds as she continued to kiss and nibble her way south. "I've gotten a few bumps and bruises over the years."

Karissa wanted to point out that the bumps and bruises looked more like knife and gunshot wounds to her but decided to keep that to herself, even as she realized her stomach was quivering at the thought of him getting hurt so much. He might heal fast, but she still didn't like it.

After paying the appropriate amount of attention to Hale's most recent gunshot wound, she reached for his belt. Because it was there…and, well…really shouldn't be. The act of unbuckling it and yanking it out was so fun she almost laughed. But amusement turned to arousal as his eyes flared brighter.

Damn, that was sexy as hell.

Enjoying the idea of stripping Hale completely naked, Karissa went for the boots first, unlacing and tossing them aside with the most delightful thuds. His uniform pants and underwear soon followed, leaving him gloriously naked, exactly like she'd imagined.

Except he was nothing like she'd imagined.

But only because her imagination wasn't that good.

In a word, Hale was stunning.

His long legs were as muscular and sculpted as the rest of him, his waist was trim, and his cock was spectacular. Karissa wouldn't say she had a

particular type when it came to masculine hard-
ware, but if she did, it would be Hale's. Long and
thick, hard, and ready for what was coming next,
Karissa decided he was simply perfect for her.
Almost as if he'd been made for her.

Kicking off her own boots and pants, Karissa
paused for a second at the side of the bed with her
hands on her hips, gazing down at Hale. His eyes
were pulsing with that yellow-gold color now, and
she swore she could even make out the tips of his
upper fangs.

*Nothing like making a guy wolf out to get a woman
feel good about herself.*

Karissa slipped her fingers in the waistband of
her panties, watching Hale as she bent over a little
too slowly and slid them over her hips and down
her legs. He looked hungry enough now to eat her
up. Which actually sounded fun. Outside of the
whole fangs thing, of course.

Hale started to sit up as Karissa climbed back
onto the bed, but she quickly pushed him back
and threw a leg over his knees to pin him down.
A part of her wanted to sit right on that amazing
shaft of his. She was on long-term birth control so
that wasn't a problem and her Paladin instincts told
her that he was clean. But sitting here like she was,
her butt pressing against his lower legs, his hard-on
standing up straight and proud right in front of her
gave Karissa other ideas. And from the smoldering

expression on Hale's face, something told her that he was thinking about it, too.

Leaning forward, she wrapped her hand around him, her insides quivering a little at the realization that her fingers barely made it around his girth.

"Ka-ching," she whispered before closing her mouth over the head and covering every inch of it with quick little kitten licks.

She wasn't sure who groaned louder, Hale at the pleasure or her at the tantalizing flavor. In the end, it didn't matter. They were both obviously enjoying what she was doing, so she kept going. She took him deeper into her mouth, moving her hand in counterpoint to the motion of her lips. The act was hypnotic, and she found it extremely easy to get lost in the rhythm.

More than ready to keep going for the rest of the night, Karissa was caught off guard when Hale reached down and gently urged her upward, making her let go of his cock to maintain her balance.

"What's wrong?" Karissa asked, thinking she might sound a little dazed at the moment. "Didn't you like that?"

"That's an understatement." With a soft chuckle, he flipped her over on her back and settled himself between her legs. "But since I was planning for our first time together to last a little longer, I've decided to return the favor."

A bolt of excitement surged through Karissa,

even as she tried to mutter some inane crap about Hale not needing to do that. He didn't listen. Not that she was sure she'd even said the words out loud. A few seconds later her eyes were rolling back in her head and her hands were sliding down between her legs to get a grip on Hale's hair.

"Don't you dare stop doing that," she said, weaving her fingers into his hair and making sure that mouth stayed right where she wanted. He was so damn good at this!

Karissa closed her eyes and allowed herself to feel every caress of his talented tongue, from the slow movements up and down her wet folds to the little twirl he did around her clit every time he reached the top.

Heaven was several floors down from the level Karissa was currently occupying, but the pulsing sensations building up inside her only got better when Hale slipped a finger inside, finding every one of her most sensitive places like he had them marked on a map.

When Karissa orgasmed, her entire body seized up at once, every muscle locking tight and her vision going completely white. She was vaguely aware of a long keening sound coming from the general vicinity of her throat but wouldn't have been able to describe the noises she was making. She was far too busy falling apart.

When her awareness of the world around them

came back, Karissa found that Hale had climbed a little higher up her body. The pleased, bordering-on-smug expression on his face shouldn't have been so devastatingly charming, but it was.

"You okay?" he asked softly, gazing down at her warmly.

Yup, devastatingly charming.

"Understatement," she murmured, letting her head drop back to the bed, her body too gooey to hold it up any longer.

Hale slipped off the bed with another warm chuckle, and for a second, she thought he was going to turn out the lights—as in *turn out the lights…the party's over*—but then she heard rustling sounds coming from the direction of his bedside table.

If he came out of there with a Snickers bar, she was going to propose right on the spot.

But when she finally found the strength to lift her head again, it was to see Hale coming toward her with a familiar foil packet.

"Oh…condom…that's nice, too."

Hale gave her a curious look but didn't bother to ask for details. Watching him roll the latex protection down over his cock, she expected he was focused on something other than her frequent off-topic mutterings.

Karissa watched him move to the side of the bed, completely hypnotized by the hungry look on his face as he eyed her naked and languid body.

She was about to ask how he wanted her—because it was all good in her mind—when he casually reached down and wrapped his hands around her ankles, pulling her gently toward him until her butt was right there on the edge.

Oh, yeah. That definitely worked.

Hale settled between her wide-spread legs, sliding up and down her folds, making little bolts of lightning tingle through her every time he touched her clit.

"You can stop teasing me with the appetizers," she said with a moan. "I am *definitely* ready for the main course."

She was all set to keep complaining when Hale finally slid in.

"Oh yes, just like that," she moaned.

Damn, this was perfect.

Wrapping her legs around his waist, Karissa locked her ankles together behind his back, pulling him in as deep as she could. The growl Hale let out was the sexiest thing she'd ever heard. The fact that his eyes were glowing so brightly they were practically on fire only added to her arousal.

Holding the tops of each thigh firmly, Hale pounded into her, each hard thrust causing the base of his cock to thump against her clit, providing the perfect stimulation Karissa needed. She gasped out loud, already feeling the tremors beginning to build up again.

She was barely aware when Hale slipped his arms under her back and lifted her up, moving her higher on the bed so that he could join. The next second, he was above her, his mouth on her hers, kissing her as he continued to pound himself deep inside her.

Karissa kissed him hard, intoxicated by the feel of his fangs gliding over her tongue. "Just like that," she murmured against his lips. "Keep going. I'm close."

Hale didn't simply keep going—he started moving faster, every thrust making her gasp out loud. Kissing became impossible at that point, so she buried her face in the junction between his neck and shoulder and held on for dear life.

It was Hale's fangs grazing lightly across her own neck that sent Karissa over the edge. She screamed against his strong shoulders and wrapped her legs around his waist tighter, keeping him buried deep, refusing to let him move.

Hale ground against her, the friction between her thighs drawing her orgasm out longer and longer until Karissa was sure she'd pass out. Just as her climax peaked, he flipped them over, the move so smooth it took her a few moments to realize she was now on top of him, her body continuing to undulate on his, him buried so deep inside she had no idea where he stopped and she began.

He grabbed her butt, holding her tightly as he

thrust up into her, his growls almost a roar as he came with her. Knowing what he was feeling coaxed a few more spasms out of her depleted body, until there was absolutely nothing left inside her to give and she slumped against his muscular chest in an exhausted heap.

Karissa could feel the thudding of Hale's heart against hers, along with his warm breath against her hair. Their hearts were actually beating in time. Could it get any better than this? It was like they were meant to be together.

It had been ten long years, but right now, she almost had to think it had all been worth it.

Chapter 18

HALE GLANCED AT THE REARVIEW MIRROR AS HE parked his SUV in front of the diner, gazing at his reflection and wondering if his pack mates would be able to tell from his face that he'd spent nearly the entire night making love with his soul mate.

Because that's what he and Karissa had done—made love.

Yes, the sex had been incredible—beyond imagining—but the soul mate bond he'd formed with Karissa last night had been even more special. He could feel it in every fiber of his being. He only wished he could have told her that.

Had she felt the connection like he had? It was terrifying to think that she hadn't. For all he knew, Paladins couldn't form the soul mate bond. Karissa did already have a bond of sorts…with Athena.

Jumping out of the vehicle, Hale headed for the door of the restaurant, cursing as he realized he was almost fifteen minutes late for breakfast with the guys. Maybe they wouldn't notice.

They were supposed to brainstorm a plan on what to do about the Balauri. It would likely be a waste of time, since they had no new leads to even start with, but they had to try and come up with something.

The diner was reminiscent of something out of the 1950s, complete with black-and-white floor tile, parlor chairs, and red booths. There was even a retro jukebox and old-fashioned Coke machines. Overall, the nostalgia was pretty damn cool. More importantly, the food was outstanding.

Hale found Carter, Mike, and Connor waiting for him in a big booth at the back of the diner, mugs of coffee in front of them. He slid into the empty space beside Connor. The moment he was seated, their server immediately came over to pour coffee for him. He smiled at the gray-haired woman and thanked her.

"Everything okay?" Mike asked when she left, his tone more curious than concerned. "You seemed a little distracted when you walked in, and it's not like you to be even a few minutes late for work…or breakfast."

"Yeah, everything's fine," Hale said, taking a second to peruse the menu even though he already knew what was on it. "Karissa stayed at my place last night and it took a little while for both of us to get ready this morning. You know, with the one bathroom?"

He didn't bother to point out that the number of bathrooms in his apartment hadn't actually been the cause of his delay. Instead, it had been the fact that there was only one shower—and a rather small one at that. He and Karissa had barely fit, regardless of how close they'd gotten to each other. Which, he had to admit, was pretty damn close. But they'd made it work well enough—until they'd nearly run the apartment complex out of hot water.

His pack mates regarded him thoughtfully, looking as if they completely understood, which struck him as rather fishy. They couldn't possibly know about last night—or this morning.

"You know, if you were busy with Karissa this morning, you could have told us," Mike said, giving him that fatherly look he got sometimes whenever he talked to someone in the Pack, even if he wasn't that much older than the rest of them. "We could have handled this on our own and given you some more quality time with your soul mate this morning."

"Don't worry about it," Hale said, picking up his coffee and taking a sip. "Karissa had to go see Deven about some clues he found regarding the person he thinks hired Bagley."

He would have said more, but their server chose that moment to show up to take their orders. His pack mates opted for various combinations of bacon, eggs, toast, hash browns, and pancakes.

Hale went with the same, his mind preoccupied with other thoughts. Some of it was the stuff he'd been thinking about that morning in bed with Karissa and their soul mate bond. But mostly, he was worried about her being out and about on her own. He knew it was simply his inner wolf being overly protective of his soul mate, but the whole purpose of her staying at his place while Bagley was running around was so he could help keep her safe. How was he supposed to do that if he wasn't with her?

But Karissa had refused to let him go with her, telling him that while she appreciated the thought, she still had a job to do, and she was going to do it. She refused to let her concerns about Bagley affect how she did that. While Hale completely understood what she was saying, that didn't mean he wasn't still worried. After ten frigging years, he'd finally gotten her back. Just the mere thought of losing her again made it difficult to breathe.

"You okay?" Mike asked, jarring him from his thoughts. Hale looked up to see his pack mate studying him with that patented concerned-slash-curious look. "Your heart is beating a mile a minute all of a sudden."

Damn, sometimes he hated being on a team full of other werewolves.

Hale opened his mouth to answer, even if he wasn't quite sure what to say. Fortunately, he got a reprieve as two servers came over to the table with their breakfast food. The moment they left again, he immediately slathered creamy butter and maple syrup all over his perfectly cooked chocolate chip pancakes, then concentrated on adding salt and pepper to his fluffy-looking scrambled eggs, hoping Mike would forget his earlier question.

But when the silence began to stretch out and all three of his pack mates began glancing at him out of the corners of their eyes, he realized he was going to have to say something to steer this conversation in a safe direction or they'd be bombarding him with even more questions in another minute.

"So, what's the latest on our five Romanian gladiators?" he asked, pausing with a big forkful of syrup-covered pancake hovering above his plate. "Any tips come in yet through the hotline on a possible location?"

Carter snorted as he dug into his over-easy eggs. "Hundreds of them. Unfortunately, none of them are worth looking into."

"Which is difficult to believe," Connor added. "You'd think that five guys as scary-looking as the Balauri—who never seem to be far from their tactical gear and heavy weaponry—would stand out in a crowd. Somebody had to have seen them, right? Especially after yesterday's news coverage."

"Maybe the reason we haven't gotten any tips on them is because they've left town?" Hale suggested, nibbling on a piece of bacon, even if he didn't believe it himself.

"Somehow I don't think we're going to get that lucky," Mike muttered. "They're out there somewhere, waiting for the right time to make their move. If they continue to follow their established pattern, it will be soon and against a target they know will get our attention."

On the other side of the table, Carter frowned. "Do you honestly think they'll bother trying to lure us into a fight again?" He took a sip of coffee. "If Davina was right about these guys looking for a good battle, wouldn't they simply show up at the SWAT compound and come straight at us?"

"Considering that this Tamm guy seems to have a personal vendetta against Hale, I think we might have to worry about them coming straight after him," Conner said.

Hale couldn't disagree with that theory. He'd already written off the tussle in the alley as random chance. Tamm had run and Hale happened to be the werewolf who'd chased him. But that fight in the forest had felt different. Like Tamm had been looking for him specifically.

"Connor might be onto something," Hale murmured, taking another big bite of pancakes. They had just the right amount of chocolate chips in them. "Maybe we should use that to our advantage."

Even with his attention focused on his breakfast, Hale could still sense his three pack mates exchanging concerned looks.

"Meaning what, that you intend to put yourself up as bait or something?" Mike asked. "Try and lure the Balauri to come after you so we can, what, ambush them? Hopefully before they kill you."

Hale ate another strip of bacon, realizing his idea had sounded so much worse when Mike said it out loud. "Something like that," he finally said.

"Truthfully, I wouldn't necessarily be against the idea," Mike admitted. "Except for two major problems you seem to be ignoring."

"Just two?" Hale asked drily, surprised Mike hadn't gone into a complete rant about this admittedly not-very-well-thought-out scheme.

"Yeah." Mike gestured toward Hale with a slice of toast. "First, there's the issue of how we'd deal with those guys even if we're able to lure them into a trap. Or am I the only one who remembered that we still don't know if these things have a weakness we can exploit?"

"Good point," Connor muttered, polishing off the last of his eggs and then using his toast to wipe the plate clean. "It might be something we want to put some thought into."

Carter snorted. "You think?"

Hale chuckled, turning his attention back to Mike. "You said there are two problems. If not having a clue how we'll take down these guys is the first, what's the second?"

Mike frowned. "If you decide to purposely make yourself a target, you run the risk of Karissa becoming collateral damage. Since the two of you are sleeping together now, that's something you have to consider."

Hale almost choked on his pancakes. "How did you know we're sleeping together?"

Mike tapped his nose. "Her scent is all over you."

Hale should have known that, but he was so used to having a crappy sense of smell that he rarely thought about what it was like for everyone else in the Pack. "You're right, we are sleeping together, and yeah, I obviously wouldn't want her getting caught in the middle of things if the Balauri come after me. Karissa has enough problems to deal with. She doesn't need to get involved with mine."

"They aren't only your problems," Mike pointed out. "They're the whole pack's. And if Karissa needs an assist, let us know how we can help, and we will."

As they ate, they batted around ideas on how they might be able to defeat the Balauri, each suggestion worse than the last. They finally gave up half an hour later after realizing that they weren't going to stumble across an answer. The scariest part was that they'd almost certainly be facing the Balauri again soon, whether they came up with a way to deal with them or not.

It wasn't a comforting thought.

After their server refilled their coffee, the conversation shifted to Karissa, Hale giving the highlights of the threat she was facing. He kept Karissa's connection with Athena out of the discussion but was still able to get across exactly how dangerous Thomas Bagley was on the off chance that any of them ever had to face him.

"Okay, you can consider us suitably warned," Connor said. "Now, enough about the bad guys. Tell us what's going on with Karissa. How did you two finally end up getting together?"

Hale's first instinct was to tell them everything, to shout to the heavens how perfect Karissa was and how amazing it was to be with her. And about his worries. But there was a part of him—a small but very insistent part—hesitant to be quite that open. Still, these were his pack mates. If he couldn't talk to them, who could he talk to?

So he told them about how he'd asked Karissa to stay at his apartment and the lengthy conversation they'd had about how he'd become a werewolf.

"She handled it way better than I thought she would," he admitted. "After that, everything all seemed to fall into place."

Hale expected his pack mates to tease him since they all liked to rag on the other members of the Pack who'd found their soul mates. Instead, the three of them sat there looking...well...a little worried, he supposed was the best way to describe it.

"What?" he demanded.

"Nothing," Mike said, then frowned. "It's just that I can't shake the feeling you're holding back a little. I mean, it's clear you're crazy about Karissa, but I don't think it's a stretch to say that you're still not all in."

Hale wanted to say that wasn't true at all, but he simply couldn't get the words out. Once again, he couldn't help but replay the thoughts he'd had earlier that morning as Karissa lay there sleeping in his arms.

"Did you bring up the topic of soul mates yet?" Mike asked when he didn't say anything.

All Hale could do was shrug. "Karissa just learned about werewolves," he explained, playing absently with the handle of his coffee mug. "And while she's cool with it, I don't want to push my luck. One major hurdle at a time and all that."

"Hurdle?" Connor repeated, looking at him strangely. "I wouldn't call having a soul mate a hurdle to get over. What aren't you telling us?"

"It's…complicated," Hale said, knowing he'd have to reveal most of Karissa's secret for any of his concerns to make any sense. He wasn't too thrilled about doing that, even if they were his pack mates. He could only pray that she would forgive him.

His pack mates didn't rush him. Instead, they sat there sipping coffee and waiting patiently, which helped him get his thoughts straight. Well, at least as straight as he could get them at the moment.

"Karissa is a Paladin," he finally said. "That means she's basically an avatar—a soldier—for

Athena. That connection has her running around the world saving people. It's more than what she does. It's who she is now at her core. It's an instinct that can't be ignored."

"You know, you wouldn't be the only member of the SWAT Pack who has a mate with significant responsibilities," Mike pointed out. "Alyssa's work with STAT has her going all over the country to investigate supernatural creatures. Sometimes Zane goes with her, but most of the time he can't. They still make it work."

Hale sighed. He got what Mike was trying to say, but Zane and Alyssa's situation was completely different than his and Karissa's.

"Alyssa works for STAT," Hale softly pointed out. "If she ever decides to quit, all she has to do is turn in her gun, sign about a hundred nondisclosure agreements, and the job is done. Karissa has a lifetime commitment to a Greek goddess. The Paladin duties don't come with a retirement plan."

"Well, being a werewolf doesn't come with an opt-out date either," Carter pointed out. "If Karissa can accept that as part of you, then you need to ask yourself if you can accept those things that are unique about her, including her Paladin duties. I know it probably won't be easy, but coming from one of the two guys left in the Pack who doesn't have a soul mate, trust me, it's a small price to pay."

"I know all of that," Hale said, shoving his hand

through his hair in frustration. "But my biggest fear is that the soul mate bond won't work for Karissa and me because of her Paladin bond with Athena. How can the bond between us take when she's already bonded to another?"

On the other side of the table, Mike cursed. "What do you do, lie around all night and make up stuff to worry about? The bond has obviously already taken, or you wouldn't be able to smell her. Especially considering your crap nose."

Hale considered that. Maybe Mike was right, but still...

"What if it only goes in one direction?" Hale asked, finally saying out loud what had really been terrifying him all night and this morning. "What if I have a soul mate bond with her, but she can't reciprocate? Because of this thing with Athena."

"Dude, that's the most ridiculous thing I've ever heard," Connor said. "Clearly she's reciprocating already. Why else would she have slept with you? It's not like you're an amazing catch or anything."

"Well, thanks for that," Hale said drily. "I appreciate the unbiased assessment of the situation but forgive me if I need a little more evidence than one night together to convince me that Karissa has really accepted me as *The One* for her."

Mike leaned forward, pushing his empty mug aside and resting his arms on the table. "If you're so worried about this, maybe you should talk to her about the soul mate thing. Then you'll know what's going on instead of guessing."

Hale drank some of his coffee. "It's not as easy as it sounds."

"Actually, it is, but you're too damn stubborn to accept that," Mike said. "So by all means, you keep being you. I have no doubt that this thing will come to a head one way or another. Then you can explain to Karissa why you kept it to yourself."

Hale knew Mike was probably right, but he sure as hell wasn't going to admit that in front of the other guys.

Mike and Connor left a little while after that, saying something about getting back to the compound for a training exercise. Hale stayed behind with Carter so they could both finish their coffee, though that only took another couple of minutes.

"Is the meditation helping any?" Hale asked after they'd finished paying at the register. "You seem a little more chill than you were after the fight at the hunting preserve."

Carter snorted as he pushed open the front door of the diner and led the way outside. "That's only because I was a complete train wreck then. In comparison, anything seems better. But to answer your question, no, the meditation doesn't seem to help anymore. I can feel my control slipping a little more each day."

Hale opened his mouth to ask Carter what he

planned to try instead but closed it again when he realized that his pack mate had stopped in his tracks and was staring intently at the alley across the street from the diner. Two men stood there, both of them tall and fit, one blond and the other dark-haired. Hale didn't notice anything out of place about either of them.

"What's wrong?" Hale asked.

"I'm not sure what it is, but there's something off about those two guys," Carter said, gaze still locked on the men across the street. "My nose isn't the best in the Pack, and it's been getting worse lately thanks to these episodes I've been having, but they smell like werewolves. Just not like us."

Hale had no idea what any of that stuff about his nose getting worse meant and didn't have a chance to ask for clarification as Carter started across the street, dodging through the morning traffic as if it weren't even there. Cursing, Hale followed, albeit more cautiously.

The two men took off running down the alley the moment he and Carter headed their way. A few feet behind Carter, Hale prayed his pack mate didn't lose it again right there in the middle of the city as they gave chase.

Whoever these guys were, they moved fast—like unbelievably fast. Running full-out down the alley, he and Carter could still barely catch up to them. That more than anything else confirmed the fact they were dealing with some kind of supernaturals.

Hale still had no idea why the men were running—or why he and Carter were even chasing them—but as they darted across several more side streets and continued moving down the alley, he thought they were going to get those questions answered soon enough. Because he and Hale were close to catching them.

Then something happened.

And Hale nearly fell on his face.

One second, the two men were running ahead of them, the next they both leaped upward at the same time. And then there were two large gray wolves lightly touching down in their place.

What the hell?

He and Carter slid to a stop. Any thought of continuing the chase evaporated as the two wolves—who were larger than any in the wild but still slightly smaller than any of their pack mates—bolted at a pace they'd never be able to match. No werewolf Hale had ever heard of could have run that fast.

"What the hell just happened?" he asked.

Beside him, Carter crouched down to pick up a piece of material that belonged to one of the men's shirts. The edges were frayed, as if every thread had popped at once. The men had shifted so fast that their frigging clothes had exploded!

Hale didn't even know that was possible.

The ability to accomplish a full shift generally came with maturity and acceptance of their inner wolf. But even Gage—the most mature member of the Pack by far—took several seconds to pull off the transition from human form to wolf.

No one in the Pack could shift like those two men. It shouldn't even be possible.

"I'm not sure," Carter said, sniffing the piece of torn fabric in his hand. "But we'd better let Gage and the rest of the Pack know about it. Something tells me that whatever those wolves are here for, it can't be good."

Because of course.

They were already dealing with Romanian gladiators and a Greek god of dread. Why not add a pair of mysterious werewolves to their list of problems?

Chapter 19

KARISSA EASILY SPOTTED DEVEN SITTING AT A table in the back of the café when she walked in. The restaurant was only a few minutes from their extended-stay hotel and had quickly become their go-to for breakfast. Her brother already had a plate of scrambled eggs and bacon in front of him, fork in one hand, fingers of the other tapping on the keyboard of his laptop on the table.

Pulling back before he could see her, Karissa took out her phone and flipped through her contacts until she found the old number Nicos had given her ten years ago. She hadn't bothered calling him in years, mostly because she'd become tired of wasting her time. But after last night, Karissa knew she had to try again—for Hale. And for the future the two of them might be able to have.

As usual, the call went to voicemail, which was a mixed blessing. In those rare cases when she'd been able to talk to Nicos directly, the discussions had ended in failure and frustration. Not that leaving a message had ever worked any better.

But right then, after the night she'd spent with Hale, Karissa hoped a personal plea might get through this time. Because she was willing to beg if necessary. Then the voice on the other end of the line was telling her to leave her message and she had no more time to wonder what could have been different if Nicos had actually answered his damn phone.

"It's me," she said without bothering to introduce herself. "I know it's probably a waste of time, but I need your help. I've run into more trouble than I can deal with…more than a Paladin can deal with. The man I'm facing is an avatar of Deimos and is almost three hundred years old and too powerful for me to fight. If that weren't enough, there's also a band of creatures here in Dallas called the Balauri. Apparently, they're some kind of supernatural Romanian gladiators with dragon scales for skin and an uncontrollable urge to hunt and kill. My sword will barely scratch them, and they've become fixated on a group of my friends, including a man who's become very important to me. More important than I would ever have imagined. I need to know if there's any way a Paladin can defeat Deimos's avatar. But more than that, I need to know if these Balauri have a weakness that can be exploited. Please, Nicos. Anything you can tell me would be helpful. I'm—"

Karissa was about to start begging but was cut off by the beep. She considered calling the priest back so she could include the beseeching part but ultimately decided against it. If Nicos didn't want to help, he wouldn't, regardless of how much she implored him.

Deven caught sight of Karissa as she stepped back into view, throwing a wave her way as she wandered over to the buffet and perused the options. Normally, she'd just grab some avocado toast and a bowl of strawberries to go along with her coffee, but after this morning's vigorous shower, she needed something a little more filling.

As she scooped a generous helping of scrambled eggs onto a plate, she found herself replaying everything she and Hale had done that morning. It was a good thing no one else was at the buffet right then because she was pretty sure she was blushing.

This morning—and last night—had been nothing short of incredible. Beyond that, actually. But as amazing as the sex had been—and yes, it had been world-changing—it was the connection she'd felt between herself and Hale that had captivated her the most. It seemed silly to even think it, but she had no other word to describe what she'd experienced last night other than that. As she'd lain half-asleep on his chest after making love, it was like she could somehow sense his thoughts as well as feel what he felt for her.

She'd tried to write it off as the byproduct of all those mind-blowing orgasms, but that didn't explain why she'd still felt the same way this morning before their fun in the shower. Hell, she could still feel the connection now. Like she could close her eyes and simply know where Hale was at that exact moment.

It was amazing.

And mind-boggling.

Not to mention maybe a little bit scary, too.

Karissa carried her plate of eggs, bacon, and toast over to the table, taking a seat across from Deven to find a mug of coffee waiting for her. Deven must have asked their server for it while she'd been at the buffet.

"So, how was last night?" her brother asked casually.

Most of his attention was seemingly fixed on the screen of his laptop and the rest on his breakfast, but Karissa didn't miss the sneaky glance he threw her way out of the corner of his eye. She recognized that smirk. It was the one he wore whenever he thought he knew something. If it had been any of her other brothers, Karissa would have probably refused to even talk to them, but this was Deven asking, and they shared everything. They always had.

"It was amazing," she said, smiling as she loaded her fork with the fluffy yellow eggs. "But also kind of terrifying."

Deven glanced up from his plate of food. "Because you're worried about what comes next after sleeping with Hale."

Karissa blinked, pausing with her fork halfway to her mouth. "When did you become so wise?"

"Last week." He grinned. "But you were busy eating a Snickers bar, so I think you probably missed it."

Knowing she'd never keep up with her brother when it came to snarky comebacks, she turned her attention to her eggs, thinking about how perfectly Deven had synopsized her present conundrum.

"Being with Hale is unlike anything I've ever experienced," she admitted after a moment. "But it's more than the physical part. We spent one night together and I'm already thinking about what a future with him would look like."

"I'm happy for you. I'm even happier with the lack of details when it comes to what you and Hale got up to last night," Deven said, his smile like a ray of sunshine. "So, what has you concerned?"

She hesitated, taking the time to spread strawberry preserves on her whole wheat toast, then nibbling on it for a moment as she tried to put her doubts into words.

"Hale is incredible," she finally said, letting out a sigh. "Only I'm not sure what I'm supposed to do about it."

Deven snorted as he started in on his second piece of toast. "Forgive me for being crass, but I'm pretty sure you already did what you were supposed to do about it last night in Hale's bed."

If she hadn't finished her eggs already, Karissa would have thrown some at him. Instead, she threw a salty look his way. "Very funny. What I mean is how can I possibly have a relationship with a guy when I'm a Paladin?"

Her brother frowned in confusion. "I don't see the issue here. Is there some rule that says a Paladin can't have a committed relationship?"

"No, of course not," she said, letting out another sigh, of exasperation this time. "But my gift has me running all over the world to save people. How do I balance my life as a Paladin with what I want to have with Hale?"

"By being open and honest with him," Deven said simply, taking a bite of his toast and chewing thoughtfully. "Tell him everything you feel for him and ask for the same in return. I mean, it'll add an entirely new level to the long-distance relationship thing, but if you both really want it, you can make it work. Love conquers all and everything."

Karissa considered pointing out that love hadn't come into the conversation yet but decided it was unnecessary. The important thing was that her brother was right. If they wanted this, it was there for the taking. They simply needed to reach out for it.

She only hoped Hale felt the same.

"Once again, I can't help but wonder when you became this wise, but I'm glad you are," she said, giving her brother a smile as she picked up her mug of coffee. "Thank you."

"Happy to help. Now, don't go and waste all my wisdom by screwing up this second chance you have with Hale, okay?"

"I won't," she promised, sipping her coffee. "Okay, enough about my love life. Did you discover anything about who hired Bagley?"

Deven spun around his laptop so that Karissa could see the screen and began punching keys. Karissa had to admit she was impressed by her brother's display of nerd prowess.

"The analyst from STAT that Davina put me in contact with was dope when it came to digging up dirt on people," he said, glancing her way. "The woman's advice improved my intel-gathering techniques light years ahead of where I've been. Damn near all of it's illegal as hell, but I guess that's a given."

"Wait a second," Karissa said, confused. "Davina called you about new ways to dig up dirt on our list of suspects? How did she even know you existed?"

"I get the feeling they did a background check on you while checking out Bagley, which obviously led them to me," Deven explained. "Davina mentioned you were interested in finding out who hired him, and since digging into people's financial backgrounds wasn't her thing, she put me into contact with someone at STAT who's better at it."

Karissa wasn't sure what she thought of STAT knowing about her brother, not to mention contacting him directly. She didn't think STAT was dangerous, but still... Deven was her little brother. She felt an uncontrollable urge to protect him from anything even remotely scary. And that included a covert federal agency that basically didn't exist as far as the rest of the world knew.

Deven found what he was looking for, then showed her a plethora of screenshots of endless numbers that meant absolutely nothing to her.

"What am I looking at?" she asked. "And don't you dare say something snarky like a laptop screen."

Her brother stopped with his mouth halfway open, a disappointed expression on his face. "Bottom line, it's a money trail," he finally said. "It leads from a personal account in Glenn Patterson's name to a corporate shell account controlled by a Swiss real estate firm that specializes in laundering money for worldwide criminal enterprises. It was a messy and convoluted path to follow, routed through a dozen banks, a dark web funding maze, and at least three different crypto accounts, each in a different country. But the end result is an account associated with Thomas Bagley—the one he uses to launder the money he makes from murdering people."

Karissa wasn't sure if she was surprised or disappointed. "So that's it? Glenn hired a hit man to kill his father?" She shook her head. "I have to admit I didn't see this coming. Not once in all the times I've talked to the man did I ever get a killer vibe off him. I must be losing my touch."

Her brother didn't say anything but simply went back to the first page of evidence and walked her through every step of the money trail. She hated to believe it, but after Deven explained everything, it seemed obvious. She was convinced, not needing to see any more. Yet she sat there and watched as Deven went through the evidence trail a third time and then a fourth, his green eyes darting back and forth across the screen.

"What is it?" she asked, having spent enough time with her brother to know when something was bothering him. "I can tell there's something you're not saying."

"This stuff took a little while to dig up—don't get me wrong—but it wasn't that difficult to find," Deven said with a frustrated shake of his head. "In fact, it shouldn't have taken me talking to STAT to uncover it. Lorenzo and Dad have a dozen contacts in the FBI, CIA, and Interpol. Why didn't they come up with this info first? We should have known about this days ago."

Karissa didn't have an answer for that. Her parents—and Lorenzo to a certain degree these days—took care of all the background investigations. And they were good at their jobs. She had to believe that STAT had helped out Deven much more than he wanted to admit.

"We'll deal with that question later," she said. "Until then, I think it would be best if we go talk to Dominic Patterson. Maybe his son, too. Let's see what they have to say about all of this."

"You think Glenn will crack if we confront him with proof right in front of his father?" Deven asked, clearly excited at the prospect of confronting the younger Patterson.

Karissa wondered whether her brother would be as thrilled if Glenn went into panic mode and pulled a gun. Knowing Deven, the answer was probably yes.

The auto plant was complete bedlam when Karissa and Deven arrived, as construction workers, engineers, and public relations people ran around trying to get the place ready for the media event that was supposed to take place in less than a day. She wondered how the opening would go once the press found out that Dominic Patterson's son was in jail for conspiracy to commit murder.

Karissa cringed at the thought.

She and Deven found Jerome easily enough among the crowd of people running here and there, only to discover that Patterson senior wouldn't be available for the rest of the day.

"He's down at city hall dealing with zoning permits that were supposed to be done months ago," Jerome said, looking back and forth between her and Deven curiously. "He'll probably be there until late this afternoon, maybe this evening. But don't worry, he has four armed guards sticking to him like glue."

That announcement should have prompted some kind of professional thought one way or the other, but the truth was Karissa hadn't gotten a single inkling of danger concerning Dominic Patterson for three days. Not since the night she'd fought Bagley at the gala, now that she thought about it. Even today, with Patterson all the way on the other side of town with four guards who would barely slow Bagley down, she wasn't worried.

Karissa had no idea what the hell that was supposed to mean.

"Is something wrong?" Jerome finally asked when neither she nor Deven said anything after a few moments. "Should I call the security detail and get the boss into lockdown?"

Karissa shook her head, glancing at her brother, wondering if maybe it would be better to come back later or perhaps track Patterson down at city hall. Ultimately, she decided against both of those things.

"No, that won't be necessary," she said, thinking this might actually work to their advantage.

"If Glenn's here, we could talk with him instead. You might want to sit in on the conversation though."

Jerome frowned in obvious confusion, but instead of asking the question she was sure was on the tip of his tongue, he gave them a nod, then turned and led them upstairs to the same conference room she'd been in a few days ago.

Glenn was sitting at the long table in the center of the room, poring over plotter-sized printouts of the plant's floor plans, circling some areas in red, others in green and yellow. Karissa could only guess that he was outlining sections of the place that were ready for the grand opening and those that weren't quite ready for prime time.

There seemed to be a lot of red areas left. But hey, maybe she was wrong and red meant something good? Sure, that was possible.

"Glenn, you have a few minutes?" Jerome called out, getting the other man's attention. "Karissa and Deven are here. They have something for us."

The man glanced up, looking tired but curious. "Yeah, I have time." He surveyed the papers in front of him with a rueful snort. "It's not like staring at these floor plans longer is going to make the situation any better."

Karissa took a seat across the table from Glenn while Deven took one right beside him, already pulling out his laptop and setting it up. Jerome didn't sit, instead leaning against the nearest wall, apparently preferring to stand.

"We've identified the hit man hired to kill your father," she said without preamble, keeping her eyes locked on Glenn's face as Deven pulled up the most recent picture they had of the man trying to murder Patterson. "His name is Thomas Bagley."

Jerome moved over and leaned in closer, but Glenn didn't bat an eye at the mention of the name or Bagley's face on the screen. No even a twinge. Part of Karissa wondered if the man was simply that cold and calculating but couldn't square that image with the read she'd gotten off him during their first meeting. She glanced at Deven to see that he seemed just as surprised as she was.

Glenn Patterson definitely wasn't acting like a guilty man who'd just been caught.

"Bagley is a highly experienced killer," Karissa continued, her eyes locked on Glenn's face. "We have no idea how many murders the man is responsible for over the years, but it's a lot."

"It appears he doesn't come cheap either," Deven added smoothly, pulling a document up on his laptop screen. "In fact, for this particular job, Bagley was paid one hundred thousand dollars. In advance."

Glenn looked at Deven, then Karissa and Jerome. "I have to admit, I have no frame of reference for anything like this. Is a hundred thousand a lot?"

She shrugged. "In Chicago, if you're not too picky about how the job is done, you can hire a killer for fifteen hundred. So yeah, a hundred thousand is a lot. It buys you the best in the business."

"Okay, so we know who the hit man is," Glenn said, leaning back in his chair. "That's good. But have you figured out who hired him yet?"

"Yes," she said. "Deven was able to track down the money trail all the way back from Bagley to the person who paid him."

Karissa gave her brother a nod, then watched as he pulled up the most important document he'd discovered with STAT's assistance. "And that's where things get really interesting."

Glenn and Jerome moved closer, both appearing extremely interested in whatever Deven had to show them. As Karissa focused on Glenn, she started to think this man might be the best actor she'd ever seen.

"Interesting? How so?" Glenn repeated, leaning in even closer to the computer screen. "Who hired the hit man who's after my father?"

"You did," she said bluntly. "The money that paid Thomas Bagley came from an account under your name."

"What?" Jerome said, clearly startled.

Karissa didn't even glance his way. She was too busy watching Glenn, who merely sat there looking stunned.

"I didn't hire him," Glenn finally said, his voice barely above a whisper. "I would never do anything to hurt my father."

"The bank account information says differently," Karissa said, pointing to Deven's laptop even as she realized something didn't feel right. Glenn wasn't reacting like a bad guy backed into a corner. Her instincts were still telling her that he wasn't the guy. Which made no sense at all.

"I couldn't have used this account to pay someone a hundred thousand dollars," Glenn said firmly, leaning forward to tap the laptop screen. "It's the old college trust fund account my grandfather set up for me when I was a kid. It had a good chunk of change in there when I was eighteen, but it was drained down to almost nothing after I got my MBA from MIT. There's probably less than five thousand dollars in there now and there's no way to get it out without taking another college class. There's no way to put money in there either. Like I said, my grandfather opened the account, and he was the only one able to move money in or out. He passed away years ago."

Karissa hated how incredibly rational that all sounded, not to mention how completely truthful it seemed as well. She threw a look at Deven, who only shrugged his shoulders in that way that might mean *sounds plausible* but could also mean *why are you looking at me since I'm only eighteen, don't have a college trust fund, and likely never will.*

A glance at Jerome wasn't any more helpful. He shrugged in that way that probably meant *don't look at me, I'm just the security guy*.

"Okay, let's assume you're telling the truth and you didn't move money through this account," she said after a long moment, deciding to go with her instincts on this. "That would mean you're not the person who hired Bagley. Raising the question of if not you, then who? And why would they go through all this effort to make you look guilty?"

"The real guilty party?" Jerome proposed, and Karissa couldn't disagree with his logic. "They had to know that sooner or later someone would start looking for the person who hired the killer, so they made sure we'd have someone to find."

Once again, Karissa found herself agreeing with the man's logic, while Deven muttered something about Glenn maybe making himself look guilty so they wouldn't think he *was* guilty. She decided her brother needed to stop watching so many Agatha Christie movies.

"So if we assume that Glenn is telling the truth," Karissa said, giving her brother a pointed look, "I think the first question we should be asking is who else knows about Glenn's trust fund. And not merely that you had one but knew the details, too. Like the bank and the account number."

"That's actually a very small list," Glenn murmured softly, almost hesitantly. "Beyond my father, the only people who have access to that kind of information are Jolie Washington and Tristan Bond. Between the two of them, they know everything about my family there is to know."

"Wait a minute," Deven said with a frown. "I thought they only worked for the company, Washington as lead counsel and Bond as the CFO. How can they do that and still be involved in your personal stuff? Isn't that an inherent conflict of interest?"

"Probably," Glenn admitted. "But my father has never cared about stuff like that. Tristan has been my father's personal attorney for decades and Jolie has been handling the family's day-to-day financial dealings for maybe five years now."

"And just to make this clear," Karissa said, having a tough time believing they'd missed this, "you think both Tristan and Jolie know about this old college trust fund account?"

"I think so," Glenn said, then shrugged. "They maintain all of the family accounts, and there's no reason this one would be special." He looked back and forth between Karissa, Deven, and Jerome. "Do you honestly believe that one of my family's oldest friends would have something to do with hiring the man who's trying to kill my father? I have to admit it doesn't seem possible."

"We don't believe anything yet," Deven said, diplomatic as always. "But we'll be taking a closer look at the two of them and digging around enough to see if there's been any other activity with the account that you never noticed. Anyone who's savvy with money laundering techniques could have been using that account for years to move money around without you or your father ever knowing it."

Glenn nodded. "Should I talk to my father about this?"

Karissa shook her head. "Not yet."

She and Deven left a little while after that, feeling more confused and less enlightened than they had an hour ago. Karissa had thought they were close to wrapping this case up, but it seemed now they were back to square one.

Chapter 20

"I CAN TALK TO MY CONTACT AT STAT," DEVEN said as they took the elevator back up to their rooms half an hour later. "But with both Washington and Bond being so well versed in the financial world, I get the feeling that tracking their movements is going to be much more difficult than it was with Glenn's trail."

Karissa nodded with a sigh, having already figured that last part out on her own. In theory, she'd come back to the hotel with Deven so they could brainstorm some ideas on how to draw out Washington or Bond, assuming one of them was actually involved in this supernatural murder-for-hire scheme. But she already knew the effort was doomed to failure. They had no leverage on either of them so how could they possibly lure them anywhere?

"The door's been opened," Deven whispered softly when they got to his room, reaching a hand out to stop her before pointing toward the tooth-pick on the floor. "I always wedge one of those in between the door and the frame whenever I leave. And housekeeping never gets to this floor until later in the day."

Karissa frowned at the tiny sliver of wood on the floor, worried her brother was watching too many spy movies to go along with those mysteries. Maybe he was watching too much TV in general.

But before she had a chance to say anything, a tingling sensation ran up her spine. Someone was in Deven's room. And whoever it was, they were waiting for them. The hilt of her sword immediately appeared in her hand and she started moving even as her brother quietly tapped the key card to the door to unlock it.

Karissa threw herself into the room and straight into a roll that carried her all the way into the small living room. Then she came up, sword swinging toward the man to her right, Deven directly behind her with his handgun drawn.

She had just enough time to recognize the familiar face in front of her, halting the blade a fraction of a second before beheading her oldest brother, Lorenzo. Remembering what he'd done to Hale, there was a small part of her wondering if she should have stopped herself.

Lorenzo was a big man, probably only an inch or two shorter than Hale, with bulkier shoulders and arms than anyone else in her family, but the same dark hair, although his eyes were deeper green than either hers or Deven's. He leaned back as far as he could while sitting on the couch, trying his best not to look freaked out while she stood there with a sword to his neck.

"Lorenzo," Karissa said. "I see you're still showing up unannounced and letting yourself into other people's rooms."

"Other people's rooms?" he said with a short laugh, reaching out to push the blade of her sword to the side. She simply brought it back, ignoring his grimace. "Who do you think paid for this room?"

"That would be our family's security company, obviously," she said.

She realized with a certain sense of humor that Deven was still holding his weapon. He wasn't pointing it at Lorenzo anymore, which was a sign of good training, but he hadn't put it back in its holster. Instead, he was holding it down at his side, typing out a text on his phone with his other hand in between glaring at their older brother.

"And since damn near every penny the company makes is thanks to me, one might say that I paid for the room," she added coldly. "But let's skip the unlawful entry part and get right to the important stuff. What are you doing here?"

Without waiting for an answer, Karissa flicked her sword away, then headed for Deven's fridge, disappointed to find there wasn't a Snickers to be found.

"What am I doing here?" Lorenzo said in that irritating condescending tone of his. "Did you

really think none of us would see the news footage
of you fighting those supernaturals in the middle of
a hunting preserve with that moron Hale Delaney
at your side?"

Karissa was stunned at the burst of anger that
roiled through her at hearing her ass-clown of a
brother refer to Hale as a moron. The urge to pull
her sword and lop off his head—or at least an ear—
was difficult to resist.

"I'm still not hearing the part where you explain
why you're here," she said as she continued to look
for something to snack on. The only thing that
seemed even close to interesting was the box of
Fruit Loops, but she was hesitant to eat it, not sure
why Deven had put the box in the fridge in the first
place.

"Are you honestly that stupid?" Lorenzo
demanded, getting to his feet and stomping in her
direction. Once again she had to fight the desire to
pop her sword back into existence and poke him
in the chest with it. "I'm here to straighten you out
and get you focused on dealing with this job so you
can wrap it up and come home. Where you belong.
With family."

"Family?" Deven said with a derisive snort,
having put his weapon away at some point when
she wasn't looking. "Please. Like Karissa has ever
been anything more than a source of income for
the *family*."

"Keep out of this, Deven," Lorenzo said harshly, turning to confront him. "This has nothing to do with you."

"Of course it doesn't." Deven let out a sarcastic chuckle. "It's not like I pissed away the majority of my high school education running around helping my sister. Not that I ever regretted being there for her since the rest of you are always too busy sitting at home counting the money we earned to ever put your lives at risk."

Karissa was a little surprised at the anger in Deven's voice. She'd never thought about the baggage he'd been dragging around with him thanks to their parents. The truth was he'd given up as much for this life they both led as she had. In some ways, maybe more. At least she'd almost been an adult when her parents had thrown her into the deep end. Deven hadn't been more than ten or twelve when they'd expected him to start using his computer prowess and pulling his weight.

"Somebody has to stay focused on finding clientele and minding the bottom line," Lorenzo snapped, looking at the two of them like they were children. "The business would dry up and blow away if it wasn't for the constant flow of new clients I bring in. We can't all have fun gallivanting around the world playing with our swords and guns, fighting supernatural bogeymen."

"Fun?" Karissa slammed the fridge shut. "See

if you think it's fun the next time someone with a sword tries to cut you in half. Oh, wait, that's never going to happen. You never do field work anymore, do you? Which makes me wonder what you're doing here now, since you've never come out before regardless of what kind of bad guy we were facing."

"I don't think Lorenzo's visit has anything to do with us wrapping up this job—or helping us deal with the bad guy," Deven pointed out before their older brother could say anything. "Mom and Dad sent him here to make sure they don't lose control of their meal ticket."

Karissa stared, baffled for a moment, not sure what Deven was implying. Until she remembered that Lorenzo had made a point of mentioning that Hale had been in the woods with her at the hunting preserve. She could definitely see her parents freaking out at the thought of her and Hale getting together again. But did that mean they were genuinely worried she'd leave their security company for Hale?

She thought back to her conversation with Deven that morning about finding a way to make things work with Hale. Was quitting her job at her family's business really an option?

It took her a moment to realize that while she'd been lost in thought, Deven and Lorenzo had gotten in each other's faces, the volume of their arguing climbing higher by the second as it became clear that Lorenzo's visit was more about the family losing money than any concern for Karissa's health or safety.

"Do you have any idea how much money the company is set to make on this Patterson job?" Lorenzo shouted. "Half a million dollars! And it's like you're doing everything you can to blow it, all because our sister can't stay focused on what's important!"

Karissa ground her jaw. She'd always known that her parents were making a lot of money off the work she did for them, but she'd never actually thought of the amounts. She'd never imagined it was this much. Half a million was obscene. And the part that hurt the most was that she and Deven were making the same amount of money for this job as they'd made on all the previous ones, basically a field stipend, as her parents called it. It was sort of like a travel per diem to cover the cost of food and any incidentals they might incur while working. It didn't add up to much, and after ten years of working for them, she didn't have more than twenty thousand in her personal bank account. Deven probably had less. Their parents were raking in more on one job than she had made in her entire *career* as a Paladin.

And she was the one who had to fight a frigging Greek god!

A sudden commotion jerked Karissa out of

her musings, and she looked up to see that her brothers were close to a physical fight. Which would not end well. Deven might be scrappy, but Lorenzo outweighed him by at least seventy-five pounds and had a lot more experience in hand-to-hand combat. Cursing, she quickly moved to step between them.

"This is all that asshole's fault!" Lorenzo shouted as he attempted to push past Karissa like he didn't even see her. He was so focused on Deven, it was as if she wasn't even there. "Hale Delaney. He's gotten into our sister's head again, poisoning her against us. Making her turn against her own family!"

Karissa's sword was in her hand before she even realized it, the sharp tip pressed against Lorenzo's chest. She forced him across the small living room with it. Lorenzo scrambled back as fast as he could, having no choice if he wanted to avoid being skewered like a piece of meat. The far wall stopped his retreat.

"You lied to me," she hissed in a low voice laced with anger. "Hale never left me. You and our other two pieces-of-crap brothers ambushed him and beat the hell out of him. My three older brothers—all of you full-grown adults—beat a teenager so badly that he spent nearly a week in the hospital. You told him that I didn't want to see him ever again and then threatened to send his family to prison if he didn't disappear. So don't you dare talk about

Hale *poisoning* me against my family. You did that all on your own."

Lorenzo tried to push the blade aside with his hand like he'd done before, earning a nicked finger for his troubles. "Karissa," he pleaded with a wince. "We had to do that. For your own good. He wasn't right for you."

"And who the hell decided you were ever the arbitrator of what's right for me?" she demanded furiously, fighting the urge to shove the blade into him. To make him feel even a tiny smidgen of the pain he'd caused her. "I was in love with Hale and you went out of your way to destroy that."

"Love?" he scoffed. "You were sixteen! What the hell did you know about love? He was using you to try and clear his family name."

"Using me?" she repeated with a harsh laugh. "I think you, Mom, and Dad have already cornered the market on that concept. I'm not stupid. Once you all figured out how to make money off my gifts, you needed Hale gone so you could keep control of your—how did Deven put it?—oh yeah, your meal ticket."

Lorenzo stood with his back against the wall, his hands up in a placating gesture, not even trying to deny it, which only made it hurt all that much more.

"Are you going to stop this?" he asked, giving Deven an exasperated look. "I'm frigging bleeding here!"

"Stop her? Are you kidding me?" Deven asked with a laugh. "I'm not the kind of brother who would stop her from killing you. I'm the kind who's going to help her hide the body."

Lorenzo looked stunned for all of a second before a hard knock at the door interrupted whatever he was about to say next.

Deven smirked. "Then again, maybe I won't be the one helping to hide the body."

Turning, he walked over to the door, opening it without even checking at the peephole, revealing an angry-looking Hale standing there in his SWAT uniform.

Karissa had no clue how Hale could possibly know to be there—at this very specific place and time—until she remembered the text that Deven had sent the moment they'd walked in the door. He'd obviously let Hale know Lorenzo was here, but had he also told him that she'd been tempted to violence every time her damn brother opened his damn mouth?

"Lorenzo," Hale said, his voice calm as he walked into the room. "I can't say I'm thrilled to see you, but I also can't say I'm surprised. Having experienced your crap firsthand, I'm not shocked to see Karissa about to shove her sword through your chest. Though it does make me wish I'd waited in the hallway for a few more minutes."

Karissa had no clue how her asshat of a brother

would react, but she definitely didn't expect him to violently shove her sword aside—especially at the cost of his own skin—and then charge straight at the man she was falling in love with.

Love?

Wait. What?

She was distracted from that stunning revelation by the sound of her brother shouting something ridiculous about this whole thing being Hale's fault even as he was swinging a hard right hook at him, looking for all the world as if he intended to kill Hale.

The blow struck with a heavy thud, and Karissa took a quick step forward, prepared for the worst. But Hale barely rocked back on his heels, his head jerking to one side for a moment from the force of the impact before coming right back.

Seeing the complete lack of effect from his punch, Lorenzo tried again, this one heading straight for the center of Hale's face, right at his nose, which he had broken the first time ten years ago. She moved toward them, sword coming up high, already knowing she'd be too late to stop the strike from landing.

The blow never landed though as Hale caught Lorenzo's fist in midair, squeezing until Karissa could hear crunching. At the same time, Hale wrapped his other hand around Lorenzo's neck, jerking him off his feet and thumping him back against the nearest wall.

"Stop it," Hale said, bouncing Lorenzo off the wall again as he tried to punch him with his other hand. "I'm not a seventeen-year-old kid anymore and you don't have your other two brothers here to help. So stop trying to take a swing at me. You're only embarrassing yourself."

Lorenzo had given up the struggle by the time Karissa reached them. Hale glanced her way for a moment before dropping her older brother back to the floor. Lorenzo pushed Hale's arm away in a blatant attempt to recover his dignity, but it was pretty much a wasted effort.

"Okay, Lorenzo," Karissa said, stopping to stand beside Hale. "You've delivered the message you were sent here to deliver, so you can leave now. Deven and I have a job to finish. What happens after that is completely up to me."

Lorenzo opened his mouth to say something— that was almost assuredly asinine—but stopped himself at the look on her face. Not to mention the fact that Hale was still standing barely eighteen inches away from him and obviously ready to continue the fight if Lorenzo felt so inclined.

With a grunt of disgust and anger, Lorenzo shoved past both of them to yank open the door. Then he turned and glared at her.

"This isn't over, Karissa," he ground out, his eyes blazing with what almost looked like hatred. "You may think what happens is up to you, but that isn't true, especially after I tell our parents about this."

He stormed out before she had a chance to respond, leaving her, Hale, and Deven standing there listening to his footsteps retreat down the hallway. Karissa had to fight the urge to chase after her brother and smack the stupid out of him.

Until Deven started chuckling.

"Did our brother—he of the manly law enforcement background—just threaten to tell Mom and Dad on you?"

Karissa considered that for a moment before she started laughing too. "Yeah. I think that's exactly what he did."

Chapter 21

"I SHOULD HAVE SAID THIS EARLIER," KARISSA said, glancing over her shoulder at Hale as she led the way up the steps to the roof of the fancy hotel where Dominic Patterson was staying. "But I appreciate you not pounding my oldest brother into the ground like a fence post. I know firsthand how irritating he can be. Your restraint after getting punched in the jaw is commendable."

Hale chuckled, taking a moment to admire the amazing bottom moving ahead of him. Damn, Karissa really did have an absolutely irresistible butt.

"To be honest, it took everything I had not to break your brother's nose in repayment for ten years of not being able to smell bacon, cinnamon buns, or chocolate," he finally said, dragging his attention to the top of the staircase and the sign there saying they'd reached the twelfth floor. "I held back more out of concern for the effect it would have on this thing between us than any qualms about hurting Lorenzo."

Karissa threw another look over her shoulder at him. "If someone had kept me from smelling choc-olate for ten years, a broken nose would be the least of their problems. So again, I'm going to have to commend you for your restraint. And don't worry, we're good, regardless of what you do to my ass-clown of a brother."

Hale laughed again but kept any further thoughts to himself as they reached the top of the steps. Karissa pushed open the door without the alarm going off, which was only possible because she'd arranged this little visit to the roof with hotel security earlier. Apparently, the money that Patterson spent here gave the head of his personal protective detail a lot of leeway.

When they stepped out into the late-afternoon sun, Karissa stopped and glanced around like she was looking for something only she wasn't sure what it was.

He had to admit that he'd been a little surprised when Karissa announced out of the blue that she needed to go to Patterson's hotel barely five minutes after Lorenzo had walked out. When he'd asked if there was a problem, she'd merely shrugged and said, "Maybe." The fact that Deven hadn't even batted an eye at her peculiar behavior didn't do anything to make him feel any better. Thankfully, when he'd suggested going with her, Karissa hadn't put up a fuss.

Hale wasn't sure if that was a good sign or a bad one.

"So," he said casually as he continued to follow

her around the rooftop, watching as she circled the big HVAC units and then leaned out over the metal guardrail at the edge of the roof to glance at the ground far below them. "Is there anything in particular you're looking for? I could help search if I knew what it was."

"I'm not sure what I'm looking for," Karissa admitted, glancing at him as she wandered around. "I'm simply following my instincts. And right now, they're telling me I need to be on this roof."

Hale remembered Karissa telling him about her instincts and how she followed them without hesitation. The fact that she'd followed them across town in time to save his butt from Darijo Tamm told him everything he needed to know about trusting them.

"You think Bagley might be coming here to attack Patterson?" he asked, going with what seemed to be the most likely threat.

"Possibly. I thought Patterson was going to be at city hall all day, but he might have come back here for something," she said, then shrugged. "Though admittedly, the god of dread hasn't shown much interest in Patterson over the past few days. Then again, it's just as likely that a meteor will hit the building in the next fifteen minutes or that aliens will arrive to probe everyone on the even-numbered floors. My instincts aren't very specific. They give me general warnings about bad things happening and let me handle it from there."

Hale snorted. "As superpowers go, these spidey senses of yours leave a little to be desired."

"I won't disagree with you on that," Karissa said with a laugh. "But I've learned to work with them. Athena has a habit of putting me in the right place at the right time and then let's me worry about the details."

Hale only shook his head because in the end he couldn't really say much about it. How many times had he and his fellow werewolves run headlong into danger simply because their inner wolves had screamed at them to act first and ask questions later?

"You think Lorenzo will cause any more trouble?" he asked as they checked behind a squat brick structure that probably housed the equipment for the main elevator shaft. "Or that he'll really call your parents?"

"I have no doubt he's called them already." She sighed. "It's also extremely likely that my parents are either on a plane right now or at least headed to the airport this very minute. There's too much money involved for them to risk me walking away from the company."

Hale's heart began to thump harder at the admission that she was thinking about leaving her parents' security company. Would she really cut ties with her family to stay with him?

"What kind of money are we talking about?" he asked, not wanting her to know how incredibly off balance her words had put him.

"Patterson is paying my family half a million dollars for this job," she said, guiding them toward the far edge of the roof. "None of which Deven and I will likely ever see. It turns out I've never been anything more than a meal ticket to them…and they're keeping all the food."

There wasn't much he could say about that. It wasn't like he was going to tell her that she was wrong. He'd always thought her parents—and older brothers—were shitty human beings.

"Just once I wish I could have normal parents," she said after several moments of silence. "That they were a mom and a dad who were simply content to see their kid happy and healthy. But no, all my parents see when they look at me are dollar signs."

"Well, I'd offer you my parents as replacements, but I'm not sure you'd find them to be any kind of upgrade," he said with a soft chuckle, leaning against the metal guardrail to look out over the edge of the roof at the ground a dizzying distance away. "Plus one of them is still in prison."

Karissa laughed as they turned around and headed to the last side of the roof they'd yet to search. "I appreciate the offer, but I'm good."

"Would you do it?" Hale asked after another

few minutes of wandering around, unaware he was going to ask the question until the words were coming out of his mouth. "Walk away from your family, I mean? Not Deven, of course. But everyone else."

"If you had asked me that even a week ago, my answer would have been a resounding no," she said softly as she glanced across the roof toward the crisp blue sky. "But now, knowing that I'd be giving up my family to be with you, the idea doesn't sound so scary."

Hale had once read something about not realizing how heavy your burden was until you set it down. At that moment, he finally understood the concept because it seemed he was finally able to breathe for the first time in ten years. He'd always assumed that crushing weight on his chest was normal.

He didn't delude himself into thinking that everything was rainbows and unicorns now. There was still the soul mate issue to deal with, and talking about leaving her family to be with him wasn't the same thing as actually doing it. But still, right then, a future seemed possible.

"But, you know," Karissa added slowly, "just because I leave my family doesn't mean I'll stop being a Paladin. Would you be okay with me running out all the time to save the world?"

Hale almost snorted out loud, realizing that this

was the exact same conversation he'd had with the guys earlier. "I won't lie. When you go somewhere on your own, I'm probably going to worry my ass off. But I imagine you'll be worried too when I go off to do something dangerous with SWAT. So we'll both have to promise to be careful and always come back to one another."

"Deal," Karissa said with a smile. "By the way, Deven might have to live with us for a while. There's no way he'll go back to Chicago if I don't, and it's not like he can stay in a hotel forever."

Rational thought fled at that point, Hale's head spinning at the fact that Karissa had clearly already been thinking about moving in with him. He definitely wasn't against that idea, even if Deven came with the deal, but he had to admit he was starting to think this was too good to be true.

"Deven can stay with us as long as he needs to," Hale said before taking a deep breath, deciding it was time to get this soul mate thing over with, even if it ruined the good vibe they'd just established. "But before we get too far ahead of ourselves with this, there's one other subject we need to talk about. It's something I've been a little hesitant to bring up until now."

Karissa turned to look at him, her expression curious. But before he could even get started, she was reaching behind her and plucking her sword out of thin air.

A split second later, his inner wolf was screaming danger.

Hale turned to see an ink-black cloud billowing into existence a few feet away from where he and Karissa stood. He didn't need to ask what the hell it was. Or, more precisely, *who*.

"I guess this is why your instincts wanted you here," he said to Karissa as a tall, muscular man with broad shoulders and a mane of dark hair stepped out of the darkness, his shoes crunching on the roof's gravel coating.

"I guess so," she said, lifting her sword high. "I almost thought he'd forgotten about Patterson."

Hale took a few steps to the side and drew his handgun.

The dark-eyed man slowly came toward them, the suit he wore transforming into multiple layers of gleaming leather armor. Hale had to admit it looked kind of badass, even if the guy intended to try and kill them in the next couple of seconds.

Two curved, single-edged swords appeared in the man's hands, the blades whistling through the air as he began to swing them in a mesmerizing pattern in front of himself. Hale didn't know what the blades were called, but whatever they were, they looked incredibly sharp.

"I'm not here for Patterson," Bagley said in a soft voice that reminded Hale of a snake's hiss. Creepy. As. Hell. "Though I'm sure I'll get around to murdering him at some point, even if I'm not actually supposed to. I'm here for you, Paladin. Killing you comes first."

Hale was still attempting to figure out what Bagley meant about killing Patterson even though he wasn't actually supposed to when the part about the asshole being here for Karissa grabbed his attention.

Hale stepped in front of her without thought, the need to protect his soul mate overwhelming any other consideration. He ignored the sound of frustration Karissa let out behind him, focused entirely on the man in front of him and his spinning blades.

Until that moment, Bagley had acted like Hale wasn't even there. But now, the man turned his full attention on him, tilting his head sideways like he was eyeing a particularly interesting bug and trying to decide if he should step on it or not.

"And who might you be?" Bagley asked, stepping closer as that soft voice began to slide across Hale's body, oozing here and there like it was trying to find a way inside his soul. Hale took a deep breath, realizing his gut was starting to spasm in an attempt to get rid of everything he'd eaten in the past two weeks.

Oh, yeah. The god of dread. Now he understood what that meant.

"Now I recognize you," Bagley said, giving Hale

a smile so malevolent that he was tempted to take a step back to get away from him. "You're that police officer the media caught on camera, the one fighting with our sweet little Paladin in the woods. I have to admit I'm surprised you're up and about after the beating those Balauri put on you. They're more animal than human. Everyone knows that."

Hale found it disconcerting to realize that Bagley knew who he was, but he pushed that thought aside, fighting to control the sense of dread trying to overwhelm him.

Standing tall and straightening his spine, Hale lifted his weapon higher and snorted. "It's nice that you already know who I am. That means I won't have to waste time introducing myself before telling you to keep the fuck back or I'll drop you where you stand."

Bagley only laughed and moved toward him in a blur. Hale didn't think. He simply pulled the trigger.

The first round ricocheted off one of Bagley's swords, a chance event that defied the laws of probability. When the next three rounds did the same thing, Hale knew random chance had nothing to do with it.

He also knew he was screwed.

Hale ducked the sword coming at his head, taking a glancing blow on the left forearm from the second, and was completely surprised by the heavy boot that slammed into his chest. By the time he felt his ribs crack, he was flying backward, not aware of how close he was to the edge of the roof until he crashed into the metal guardrail.

The guardrail crushed under the force of his impact, and for a few frantic heartbeats, Hale thought he was going over the edge. More pain flared through him before he felt something solid under his flailing fingers and he latched on for dear life, praying it held.

Hale slid to a stop with more than half his body hanging over open air. A glance over his shoulder was enough to make him dizzy at the thought of what would have happened if he'd gone completely over. He didn't want to find out whether a werewolf could handle a fall that far.

Then he heard grunting and the clang of metal on metal, and he forced his mind to stop worrying about it.

This wasn't over.

Hale clawed his way back to solid ground, looking over to see Karissa and Bagley swinging swords at each other so fast they were nothing but a blur. His soul mate was holding her own, but Hale's first instinct was still to immediately charge right back into the fight, gun blazing. But since his weapon was nowhere in sight—and hadn't worked well the first time around—he realized he needed another tactic.

Pausing to scan the rooftop, his gaze came to rest on the crushed remnants of the guardrail he'd almost smashed through. The part that caught his attention the most was the vertical piece that had been attached to the edge of the roof. It had been ripped off its base, the end ragged and sharp.

That was all he needed to see.

With a growl, he grabbed at the length of metal, ripping it away from the horizontal pieces still hanging on to it by a thread. Then he turned and followed his original plan. He charged across the roof, letting out an echoing snarl to let Karissa know he was coming.

His muscles began to twist as he tried to run faster than his human form would let him, and he almost felt the urge to go over onto all fours. But he held back, not sure if that was the best way to fight right now. The next second, he was sliding to Karissa's left, attacking Bagley from that side.

As if she knew he was there, Karissa moved farther to the right, forcing Bagley to twist back and forth to defend himself from both of them at once. They didn't make it easy on him, attacking relentlessly, their timing so perfect it was like they'd fought together for months.

Metal clanged loudly on metal and Bagley was forced back step by step, his eyes beginning to widen in alarm. Then Hale caught one of the blades on his makeshift weapon, trapping it for a split second as he let his body shift further, claws and fangs coming out to their full extension.

Bagley tried to twist away but couldn't without opening himself up to Karissa's attack. He had no choice but to move back in an attempt to disengage. He didn't get it done in time, and Hale's claws tore into the magically reinforced leather of his chest piece, ripping out whole pieces and drawing blood.

Maybe he would have done better if he'd turned into a full wolf—if he could.

Finally able to break away, Bagley stumbled back, his attention focused completely on Hale as a black, inky cloud began to surround him.

"You're a werewolf!" he spat in disgust, visibly recoiling as the blackness continued to roil around him. His eyes went flat and emotionless as he turned to glare at Karissa, and then back at Hale, face going pale as he looked back and forth between them. "You two are together? Bonded?"

Hale was too stunned to answer. The werewolf stuff was obvious, but he couldn't imagine how Bagley could have possibly known about the soul mate stuff. And Hale had no doubt that he knew.

Then the Greek god disappeared into his black cloud, muttering something about coming after the two of them a different way.

And as fast as the fight had started, it was over. But Hale and Karissa were both still alive and unhurt. That was the important thing.

"What did he mean about a bond?" Karissa asked, pinning Hale with a curious look. "Is this what you were just about to tell me before?"

Well, he'd wanted to talk to Karissa about them being soul mates. Looks like that time had come.

Chapter 22

Karissa followed Hale back to his apartment in her car since she hadn't wanted to leave it at Patterson's hotel. She was getting more worried by the second about that *bond* thing Bagley had mentioned. Whatever it was, it had clearly rattled the otherwise stone-cold killer. Enough that he'd up and disappeared in the middle of the fight. It was also clear that the subject was sensitive to Hale. While he'd assured her it wasn't anything bad, he'd still wanted to wait until they got back to his place before discussing it in detail.

"Man, I'm starving," he said, closing the door of his apartment behind them, then heading straight for the kitchen.

"Yeah, I figured that out when you suggested stopping at Keller's to pick up dinner," she said drily.

While she could definitely eat—especially after the tussle with Bagley on the hotel rooftop followed by the tedious hour or so attempting to explain the guardrail damage to the hotel security staff—she would rather have Hale explain what the bond was. But after spending time with him and the other werewolves in his pack, she was coming to realize that food was an integral part of every conversation they had. It was like a werewolf couldn't think clearly without it.

Karissa followed Hale into the kitchen, unpacking the cheeseburgers and fries while he poured them glasses of iced tea.

"Do you plan on telling me what Bagley meant about the bond he mentioned?" she asked after they both sat down at the kitchen table. "I get the feeling that whatever it is, it's kind of a big deal to him."

Hale gazed at her for a moment, then shoved a big handful of fries in his mouth.

Real mature.

She didn't realize she'd said it out loud until Hale suddenly stopped mid-chew, looking like he was damn near ready to blush.

Picking up his glass, he took a big gulp of iced tea. "Sorry. This is a little difficult to talk about. In fact, I'll admit I've been putting it off because I've been trying to come up with the best way to tell you about it."

Karissa stared at him, her burger halfway to her mouth. "I know you said it wasn't anything bad, but the way you keep delaying makes me think it is."

Hale shook his head. "No, it's not bad at all. At least, I don't think it's bad. I hope you don't think it is."

She wanted to ask what the hell that meant but

forced herself to be patient, even going so far as to take another bite of her cheeseburger and a few fries. She could see why Hale raved about the burgers. They were as juicy and delicious as he'd said.

"Werewolves have this…urban legend…I guess you'd call it," Hale said slowly. Even though he was looking at her, his gaze was a little distant, like he was struggling to find the right words. "For a long time, the Pack all thought it was merely a fairy tale werewolves told each other to make themselves feel better about being…well…like we are."

Once again, she wanted to ask him what that meant—because it didn't sound good at all—but instead she bit her tongue and let him keep going.

"Then Gage found his, and a little while later, some of my other pack mates did, too," Hale murmured, not making any sense at all. "It was like dominoes. One after the other, each member of the Pack finding theirs."

"Their what?" Karissa finally asked, too baffled and frustrated to keep silent any longer. But she couldn't help it. Hale was completely crap at telling a story. Her birthday would come before he got to the important part. "What are you talking about?"

"Soul mates," he said, his voice soft. "Werewolves call it *The One*. As in the one person in the world who will truly and completely accept us for what we are—fur, claws, fangs, and all."

She considered that, her heart speeding up a

little. "What about the bond Bagley mentioned?" Part of her knew exactly where this conversation was going, but she needed to be sure. "He was trying to say that you and I are...?"

"Soul mates," Hale finished, his eyes locking with hers, and Karissa saw a hope there...and possibly concern. "You're my soul mate. I don't know how, but Bagley picked up on it. Maybe because of how well we teamed up to fight him."

Karissa was admittedly more focused on the concept of Hale being her soul mate. But now that she thought about what had happened on the hotel roof, she realized that the two of them had worked together to defeat Bagley like a well-oiled machine. Something told her that wasn't how Bagley knew she and Hale were soul mates, though.

"Okay, I'm your soul mate," she said after letting the idea sink in. "I guess that means you're mine, right?"

Hale nodded, which wasn't helpful at all. Crap, she had a hundred questions and no idea where to start.

"You said that werewolves get someone who can accept them for who they are," she said carefully. "The soul mate thing goes both ways, right?"

"Yeah, of course!" Hale looked like she'd just rapped him on the nose with a rolled-up newspaper. "Being your soul mate means that I'm the one person in the world who really gets you. The person you're destined to be with. Your perfect match in every way. I'd do anything to be with you and keep you safe and happy."

It was her turn to stare. "You love me?"

"Yeah." He gave her a lopsided grin. "It took me a little while to figure out, but it finally dawned on me that I've never stopped loving you, even after all these years."

Karissa was pretty sure she'd already known that. Just like she'd known that she'd never stopped loving him. For a long time, when she'd thought he'd dumped her, she told herself that she hated him. But now she knew that hadn't been true at all.

She picked up a fry and nibbled on it. "And the destined to be together part? Does that mean we were always meant to be together—that we were soul mates—even back in high school?"

Hale seemed to consider that for a long time before answering. "To be honest, I'm not sure how it works. My first thought is that we couldn't have been soul mates back then because I wasn't a were-wolf yet. But Mike believes he had his soul mate and lost her before he became a werewolf, so the official answer is…maybe."

"How long have you known we're soul mates?" Karissa asked, trying to wrap her head around the idea that they'd been destined for each other all the way back in high school. If she'd been furious at her family before for tearing them apart, that didn't come close to describing how she felt now.

"From the moment I saw you in that alley," he said with another smile. "You know, the night you saved my life? It took me a few more days to be sure, but yeah, that night was basically when I knew."

"How could you possibly know that fast?" she asked, replaying the events in the alley to see if there was something she'd missed. "We didn't even talk to each other that night."

"It was your scent," he said simply. "My nose hasn't worked since that day ten years ago when Lorenzo kicked me in the face. But the moment you appeared in that alley, the most mesmerizing scent of lilac blossoms filled the air, and I just knew."

She was tempted to lean over and sniff her own skin but decided against it. She got the feeling it was a scent only Hale could pick up or every werewolf in the state would have been chasing her around for a sniff.

"If you knew that soon, why didn't you tell me earlier?" she asked.

He gazed down at the two cheeseburgers still on his plate with a frown. "I didn't tell you because I was worried that you might not feel the same connection."

Hearing him say that hurt. Did he think she didn't love him in return?

"Not because you didn't want to," he added

quickly, looking at her. "It's just that...well...you're already bonded to Athena. I was worried that your connection with her would prevent a soul mate bond forming between the two of us."

Karissa opened her mouth to tell him that was impossible, but then realized Hale might have a point. How did she know that her bond with Athena wouldn't affect this one? "How do I know if you're my soul mate? I mean, you have the advantage of being able to smell my scent, but how am I supposed to know for sure?"

Hale gazed at her for a long time, his expression impossible to read. "Even if I couldn't pick up your unique scent, I like to think I'd still know you're my soul mate. When I'm around you, I can't stop myself from thinking about our future together. And the future I see is always happy. If that doesn't sound like we're soul mates, I'm not sure what does. But as far as how you'll know, I guess you need to ask yourself what you feel for me."

Karissa had hoped for something more definitive, like a test of some kind, but she supposed that what he was saying made sense. So...what did she feel for Hale? She loved him more than anything. She always had. But what did she feel about being *bonded* to him?

After a few moments of thinking about it and a couple bites of her burger, she realized she wasn't scared by the soul mate thing at all. Ever since she was sixteen years old, the course of her life had been laid out for her in neat, relatively fixed lines. Go here. Protect this person. Fight that person. Save these people. She'd never had a say in any of it, even without counting the interference of her family. She was surprisingly—or maybe *not* so surprisingly—comfortable with fate taking the wheel.

Finding out that her love life was being guided by an unseen force seemed sort of par for the course. The fact that her soul mate was Hale—that it had always been him—was comforting. And the idea that she'd been drawn here to Dallas to reconnect with him felt righter than anything had in a long time.

She took a sip of iced tea, then looked at Hale. "Ten years ago, when I thought you dumped me, my parents told me that I should be glad, that being with you would weaken the gifts Athena had given me. That you would have slowed me down and held me back."

Hale didn't say anything, but she could see the anguish in his eyes.

"They were wrong," Karissa said quickly, reaching across the table to take his hand and giving him a smile. "I love you, Hale. And when I think of having a bond with you that's similar but at the same time different from the one I have with Athena, I can't help but feel strong, wanted, and cherished. I could never imagine being with anyone else."

Hale was up and stepping around the table so fast Karissa didn't have a chance to move. Half a second later, he urged her to her feet, his mouth coming down to cover hers. They kissed so long and deep that Karissa actually started to get a little light-headed—but in the best possible way. When Hale finally broke the kiss, she was almost gasping for breath.

"I wasn't sure what you were going to say," he murmured, his breath warm on her hair as he held her close to his chest. "It's part of the reason I couldn't find the courage to say anything earlier. I was scared you'd walk away from me again. I know now that's not what happened before, but still…if you had walked away, it would have crushed me."

"I'm not going anywhere," she whispered, her whole body on fire at the thought of what her life with a soul mate would be like. "Except to bed with you."

And that's where they ended up, what was left of their burgers and fries forgotten as they made love long into the night. It was only after Karissa collapsed onto Hale's naked chest, worn out and completely satiated, that thoughts of anything else could fill her head.

"What does it mean that Bagley was somehow aware of our bond?" she murmured against his chest, his heart thumping hard under her lips. "Do you think we should be worried?"

"I have no idea," Hale answered, one arm behind his head, the other around her shoulders. "And yeah, we probably should."

They were both quiet for a little while, just enjoying the moment as Hale's heartbeat slowed further. Then her cell phone buzzed, forcing Karissa to push herself upright to reach it on the nightstand. Hale groaned in complaint, murmuring for her to ignore it. But much like it wasn't an option for him, that wasn't an option for her.

Karissa almost fell off Hale's chest when she realized the text was from Nicos. The number of responses she'd received from the Greek priest could be counted on one hand. Of course, considering the fact that most of those responses had been monosyllabic in nature, she wasn't exactly expecting much this time, either.

So Karissa was surprised when she discovered an extremely long text. Long enough that anyone else would probably have sent an email. But technology was not Nicos's friend.

"What is it?" Hale asked from his position under her, having clearly picked up on her surprise. "Is everything okay?"

She nodded, reading through the long text once again before answering. "Everything's fine. I called Nicos hoping he might know how to deal with Bagley or the Balauri. I didn't really expect a response, but he just texted me. Unfortunately, he didn't share any advice on Bagley," she admitted, more than a little disappointed. "According to him, I have everything at hand I need to deal with Deimos's avatar. But he did send a recipe for a potion that's supposed to help make the Balauri vulnerable. Though I have no idea what the hell we're supposed to do with it. I'm pretty sure we can't buy this stuff at the local Walgreens."

Sighing, she handed him the phone.

"Blooms of a smoke tree, blessed olive oil, hair of a snake?" Hale muttered, making a face. "No, we definitely won't be getting any of this at a pharmacy. Fortunately, I know just the person who might be able to help with this."

"Who?" Karissa asked. She had no idea who to turn to for ingredients like this.

"A witch," he said simply, already thumbing the buttons on her phone to forward the message to someone.

Karissa was sitting on Hale's couch, wearing a pair of shorts and one of his SWAT T-shirts, eating a bowl of Cheerios and catching up on the newest season of *Spy Racers* on his gigantic flat screen, when someone rang the doorbell. She seriously considered ignoring whoever it was. Deven would have texted first before coming over and Hale had left for work early this morning, saying something about the Pack having a solid lead on the location of the Balauri. He hadn't liked the idea of leaving her alone, but she'd convinced him that Bagley had no idea where she was staying.

The grand opening event of Patterson's automotive plant was scheduled for seven o'clock that night, and even though she needed to be there early, she still had another hour to relax and watch TV. A plan that someone was ruining by pounding on the door hard enough to practically rattle it in its frame, followed by the repeated ringing of the doorbell.

Karissa supposed it could be Kat Davenport, coming over to talk about Nicos's potion. Even if it had only been a few hours since Hale had sent the formula over to the woman.

When Hale had mentioned giving the potion recipe to a witch, Karissa had naturally assumed he was talking about Davina. But instead, the witch in question was Kat, the soul mate of one of Hale's teammates, Connor. To say Karissa was thrilled the woman had promised she could create the potion they'd sent her was an understatement. On the downside, Kat had no idea if it would work, but at least she could make it.

Maybe she was done with it already.

Sighing, Karissa set her bowl down on the coffee table, then paused the show she was watching. As she got up and padded barefoot to the door, her instincts weren't exactly singing the praises of whoever was out there, but she wasn't picking up any sense of danger either. Still, she stopped to take a quick look out the peephole anyway to see who it was. When she did, she almost turned around and headed straight back to the couch and her bowl of cereal.

"Oh, damn," she whispered. "I really don't need this."

Taking a deep breath, she opened the door.

"I wish I could say I'm surprised to see you here," she said, looking past her parents at Lorenzo, who was standing behind them with a self-satisfied smirk on his face. "But now that you have Mommy and Daddy to hold your hand, I suppose it's to be expected."

Karissa stood in the doorway of Hale's apartment, taking in her parents' angry expressions, wondering if she should slam the door in their faces. She was still trying to decide when her mother spoke.

"Are you going to let us in?" she demanded.

As tall as Karissa, her mother was an older version of her with the same dark hair and green eyes, which were glinting with fury at the moment.

"I wasn't planning on it," Karissa said casually, keeping herself firmly in the middle of the threshold, one hand on the frame, the other on the edge of the door. "I assume my turd of a brother told you about what I'm dealing with on this job, so unless you have something to add when it comes to handling Bagley, there's really nothing to talk about."

Her father's mouth tightened, his gray eyes flinty. "We know about Bagley. That's what we're here to talk about."

Having no doubt that Lorenzo had told them everything he knew—or suspected—about her current relationship with Hale, Karissa honestly doubted Bagley was the only thing her parents were there to talk about.

When her dad moved determinedly toward the door, Karissa had no choice but step aside or risk him stomping on her toes. Her mom and Lorenzo immediately followed him into the apartment. Cursing silently, Karissa closed the door behind them.

Her mom and brother looked around Hale's apartment, taking in the photos on the wall with distaste. Her dad, on the other hand, was more interested in the fact that Karissa was clearly wearing Hale's T-shirt. And from the scowl on his face, he knew exactly why—and he wasn't happy about it.

Karissa followed her family into the living room, waiting to see which of her parents was going to start yelling at her first. She didn't have to wait very long.

"I can't believe you let yourself get sucked back

into Hale Delaney's toxic orbit," her mother said with a shake of her head. "He almost destroyed your life ten years ago, and now he's trying to do it again."

Karissa had to admit this was exactly how she'd expected the conversation regarding Hale to go. In fact, she would have been disappointed if her mom hadn't badmouthed him. Even though she wanted to go off on her parents about everything they'd done to Hale, she bit her tongue and forced herself to stay calm.

"Mom, stop," she said. "Hale was never toxic, and he never did anything to destroy my life, and you know it. When I got my gifts from Athena, I was a confused, scared sixteen-year-old who had no idea what was happening to me. And when I needed my family to be there for me, all I got were manipulations and lies. Instead of you and Dad caring about what I needed, all both of you cared about was retaining control over me—and the potential money I could make for you."

Her dad snorted. "Delaney's entire family were criminals and he was no different. We saved you from that."

Karissa had to close her eyes and count to ten to keep from losing her cool. How could her father completely ignore every word she'd just said?

"You want to talk about criminal?" she shot back. "You mean like sending my three adult brothers to beat up a seventeen-year-old boy so badly that Hale ended up in the hospital? That seems pretty damn criminal to me."

Her mother, father, and Lorenzo all opened their mouths at once, but whether it was to deny what they did or justify it, Karissa didn't care. She was done listening to them talk crap about Hale.

"Enough!" she said firmly, holding up her hand. "You said you came here to talk about Bagley. If we're not going to do that, you might as well leave."

Lorenzo sulked at that, while her parents exchanged looks. She cut them off before they could say anything. She wasn't playing this game with them.

"Thomas Bagley is the most dangerous person I've ever faced," Karissa said. "If we don't come up with a way to stop him, he's going to kill our client—right after he kills me."

The blunt words seemed to finally shock her family out of their obsession with Hale and the fact that the two of them were back together.

"Are you certain Bagley is Deimos?" her mom asked. "When Deven called and told us about it, he failed to explain where he'd gotten his information."

Not really sure why the source of the information mattered, Karissa nevertheless knew she needed to tell them about STAT. She didn't like the idea of revealing the existence of the secretive organization, but her parents would be more likely to believe what she had to tell them if they knew it came from a federal agency.

So she told them how Hale's SWAT team had put her and Deven in contact with STAT while downplaying SWAT's involvement with the supernatural, knowing her family would only try and twist that around and use it against Hale. But she made sure they all understood how much information STAT had provided on Bagley, especially about how many other Paladins he'd already killed.

It was striking how differently each member of her family reacted to what she said. Her mother muttered something about Karissa and Deven using outside help of such a *dubious nature*, while her father got this weird look on his face, like he wasn't sure if he believed her. Only Lorenzo—of all people—seemed concerned about the fact that Bagley had killed Paladins before.

"So what these feds told you makes you think Bagley will be coming for you before he goes after Patterson?" Lorenzo asked.

"That certainly has a lot to do with it," Karissa said. "The man has killed at least five Paladins and he had no problem telling me that. But I have to admit that hearing Bagley tell me to my face that he's going to kill me first was more persuasive."

Her father crossed his arms over his chest with a frown. "Why didn't Deven say anything about Bagley threatening you when he talked to us?"

"Because he didn't know." Karissa sighed. "It happened yesterday when Bagley lured me to the roof of Patterson's hotel for the express purpose of trying to kill me. If Hale hadn't been there, he probably would have succeeded."

No one said anything. In fact, the silence stretched out for so long that Karissa started to think that her parents didn't believe her. At least Lorenzo seemed suitably alarmed.

Her mom glanced at her dad. "Is there any way we can save this situation? I mean, we could simply walk away, but there's still a lot of money on the table here."

Karissa looked back and forth between her parents, trying to understand what they were talking about. Lorenzo looked just as baffled.

"I could try calling him again," her father answered. "Offer an incentive to stick with the original plan. But I don't like the idea of giving in to blatant extortion. It doesn't sit right with me."

"What are the two of you talking about?" Karissa interrupted.

Her parents didn't answer, instead leaning closer to each other to whisper urgent words that Karissa couldn't make out. She threw a questioning glance at her brother, but he merely shrugged.

"It wasn't supposed to happen this way," her mom finally said, turning back to Karissa. "We hoped this job would catapult the company into the highest echelons of private security. No more small-time clients and their dangerous supernatural killers. No more risking your life for minimal payoff."

Karissa opened her mouth to tell her mother that she'd never done this job for the money, that it had always been her connection with Athena calling to her, urging her to protect those who needed her help. But her father interrupted before she had a chance to say anything.

"None of that matters now," he said, shooting her mother a sharp look. "I'll call Patterson and tell him that we're dropping him as a client. Walking away from a job is going to be damaging to our reputation, but we can't risk the alternative. You fighting Bagley was never part of the plan."

Karissa was so mixed up right now that she could barely tell up from down. And while she definitely didn't like the part about fighting Bagley never being "part of the plan," it was the part about walking away from the job that ultimately grabbed her attention. Because walking away meant leaving Dallas. And leaving Dallas meant leaving Hale—after realizing he was her soul mate not even twenty-four hours ago.

"Dad, I'm not walking away from this job," she said, refusing to give in to the panic that the mere thought of leaving Hale brought on. "First, my Paladin gifts won't let me leave an innocent person unprotected. They'll fight me every step of the way until I won't be able to take it. Second, leaving won't do anything to keep me safe. Bagley will just pop into the underworld and step out in Chicago, where he'll hunt me down. And third, I'm not leaving Dallas because I'm not leaving Hale here to deal with this crap on his own."

Her father immediately started saying something about Bagley being too powerful for her to fight, while her mother kept pushing that she shouldn't be risking her life if there wasn't enough money at the end of the job. Karissa would have liked to think that all of this meant they were worried about her safety, but she knew it probably wasn't that.

It was about the money.

It was *always* about the money.

"Dad, what did you mean when you said Karissa fighting Bagley was never part of the plan?" Lorenzo suddenly asked, his voice cutting across the babble. "And before that, Mom said it wasn't supposed to happen this way. There's something you aren't telling us. What the hell is it?"

Karissa was genuinely surprised to hear the angry tone in her brother's voice. Lorenzo was the dutiful son, the one who never asked questions. But he was definitely asking them now.

Furtive looks passed back and forth between her parents, the moment dragging out so long Karissa was close to screaming in frustration—right before pushing all of them out the door. She needed to change soon for the big opening anyway.

"We hired Thomas Bagley," her mother finally said.

Karissa did a double take, sure she'd heard wrong. "What do you mean, you hired him?"

"We hired him," her mom repeated. "We knew he was a hit man, but we didn't know he was tied to Deimos. Regardless, the deal we made with him was simple. He was to get close to Patterson and make it clear his life was in danger from a threat well beyond the abilities of his own security forces. Patterson would hire our firm and you'd sweep in to protect him from certain death, then Bagley would disappear. The reputation of our company would soar and billionaires around the world would clamor for our services. We'd be able to charge anything we wanted."

Karissa stared at her parents in disbelief, forcing air in and out of her lungs, wondering if she'd gone to bed and woken up in an alternate universe where cold, emotionless AI robots had replaced her mother and father. They'd always been greedy, but this went way beyond greed.

"Wait a minute," Lorenzo said. "Beyond the fact that you hired a hit man, how could you possibly know that Patterson would hire our firm? We might have a good reputation, but we're not *that* well-known. Not in Patterson's circles."

"We paid one of the people close to Patterson's chief of security to talk up our company," her dad explained. "After Bagley's first attack, everyone was so rattled, they hired us within a couple of hours."

Her father actually seemed to be proud of that fact, if the smile tipping up the corners of his mouth was any indication. Karissa couldn't help but wonder when her parents had so completely lost their way.

"This isn't some brilliant idea to pat yourselves on the back for," she snapped. "People died! Innocent people who never asked to be a part of your get-rich-quick scheme."

"That wasn't supposed to happen," her father said, having the grace to look at least somewhat guilty. "Bagley was only supposed to scare Patterson. No one was supposed to get hurt."

"You hired a man who has murdered hundreds of innocent people," she said, realizing she didn't know her parents at all. "And you're surprised that he didn't honor the terms of your *deal*? Bagley kills for pleasure."

"We didn't know that," her mom murmured softly, her face going slightly pale. "We told him after the first attack that no one else could die, but he ignored us. He hasn't responded to any of our attempts to contact him over the past three days— including when we told him that the contract terms have been fulfilled and that he could leave."

Karissa was beyond furious now. She was sickened. But one thing she wasn't was surprised.

"Three days?" she echoed. "That would have been the night I fought him at Patterson's gala when Bagley figured out I'm a Paladin, people he hates with every fiber of his being. He'll never stop coming after me—not until one of us is dead."

Her parents and Lorenzo all started talking at once, saying she had to leave town immediately, that she couldn't let herself be drawn into another fight with Bagley, that she needed to put her family first.

It was all too much to take.

"I have to get changed for the grand opening of Patterson's auto-assembly plant," she said coldly. "Deven is already waiting for me, so feel free to let yourselves out."

Then she turned and headed for Hale's bedroom, closing the door behind her without looking back.

Chapter 23

"Is it me or does this all seem a little too convenient?" Hale asked from where he stood in the back of the SWAT team's operations truck, staring at a computer-generated map showing the street layout around the Arlington South Industrial Park.

The space in the back of the renovated RV the team had converted into their ops vehicle was tight to say the least with nearly half the Pack jammed in there, but they made it work. Until that moment, every single eye in the place had been focused on the image of the recently closed warehouse in the center of the map, along with the half dozen cell phone pics their anonymous tipster had sent in to the police hotline, but at Hale's words, everyone turned to face him.

"What do you mean?" Gage asked with a frown, pausing the briefing he'd been giving on the main entry points to the warehouse the tipster had stated the Balauri were using as their hideout. The same warehouse the SWAT team was planning to raid in less than fifteen minutes.

"I'm not entirely sure," Hale admitted, wishing he could understand the unfamiliar sensation in his gut telling him this was a really bad idea. "I just can't escape the feeling that someone has been leading us around by the nose all day. That some- one wanted us here at this warehouse at this partic- ular time."

The whole pack had come into the compound early this morning to check out an anonymous lead that someone had called in to the hotline. It hadn't taken very long to confirm that the man in the blurry photo was Darijo Tamm. A little while later they'd tracked the location of the photo down to the White Rock farmers market, where the man had apparently been buying a large amount of food. There'd been other anonymous tips after the first one, pretty much dragging the SWAT team all over the city all frigging day. Now it was dark, and the last tip had brought them to a building the Balauri had apparently been hiding in the entire time.

"You don't think they're somewhere in that building?" Gage asked, lifting a brow. "Even after Mike got in close enough to confirm their scents?"

Hale glanced at Mike, then shook his head. "No, I definitely trust Mike's nose. It's only that the trail of crumbs that led us here seemed a little too easy to follow."

"He's not wrong," Mike murmured. "We spent weeks trying to get a lead on these guys and came up with nothing. Then, in the space of barely twelve hours, we get multiple anonymous tips leading us right to their front door. Hale's gut is trying to tell him the same thing we're all thinking, that this is a trap."

Gage nodded with a sigh. "I know. It's almost a certainty that the Balauri lured us out here so they could face us in a scenario heavily weighted to their advantage. I doubt they'd actually set up booby traps in there, especially since Davina said they want to fight us straight up, but I can see them using explosive devices to weaken us so they wouldn't have to fight us all at once."

"It doesn't help that we still don't have a way to actually hurt these guys," Carter said from the farthest corner of the ops van, holding up one of the small test tubes filled with thick pink liquid. "Other than an untested potion of dubious origin that Kat gave us at the last minute. If this pink crap doesn't work, we'll have a difficult time dealing with all five of these creatures, even with our greater numbers. And if they start setting off booby traps to weaken us, I'm not sure I like the way this is going to turn out."

Hale could understand why Carter was less than thrilled at the idea of putting their trust in a pink goo that Kat had whipped up in the kitchen she shared with Connor. The stuff didn't exactly look very impressive.

"If it helps, the potion Kat made for us includes the blooms off the same tree I used to thump Darijo Tamm with. That has to count for something, right?" Hale said.

"It would if I had any faith at all in your botany skills," Carter said with a snort. "Just because the tree branch you used to hit Tamm had pink flowers on it doesn't mean it was from a smoke tree."

"It also would have been nice if Karissa's mentor had sent some instructions along with the formula," Mike added, holding up another one of the glass tubes. "Do we have to feed this stuff to them or give them a massage?"

"Okay, so how are we going to handle this?" Connor asked from where he was standing right beside Hale, pointing toward the layout of the warehouse on the map. "Do we assume this potion stuff is going to work and just go charging in the front door?"

"I don't think I want to put all our eggs in one basket when it comes to Kat's potion," Gage said, motioning toward the sides of the target building where the Balauri were hiding. "We'll access the roof, then rappel down and use the upper windows for entry. That approach, along with the darkness and our enhanced senses, should give us the element of surprise and allow us to avoid any booby traps they may have set up on the main doors. From there, we'll see how it goes. If the potion works, great. If not, we'll have to depend on brute force to try and overwhelm the Balauri."

Hale grimaced at the thought of trying to take a creature like Tamm down by pure physical force.

If bullets couldn't penetrate the Balauri's skin, how hard would he and his pack mates have to punch for them to feel it?

Hale tried to focus on the rest of the briefing Gage was giving but found himself tuning out. While he was glad his pack mates had taken his warnings about the possibility of a trap seriously, he realized there was something else still bothering him. But no matter how long he stared at the map, he couldn't figure out what it was.

It wasn't until he realized the truck had fallen silent that Hale looked up and saw that the ops truck was nearly empty. Gage, Mike, Connor, and Carter were the only ones still there, and they were all regarding him with blatant concern.

"What's wrong?" Mike asked him. "And don't tell me *nothing* because I can see that something is screwing with your head."

"I don't know," he said softly.

He took a step closer to the big monitor mounted on the wall of the RV. He reached out and slowly glided his finger across the touch screen, sliding the view to the south. One mile, two, and then faster until he was at least five or six miles from the building they were about to raid. He stopped moving when he reached the northern perimeter of the Sentry Industrial Park and the blank space on the map he knew had only recently been filled by Patterson's auto assembly plant.

That was where he needed to be.

Now.

He could feel it.

"You think Karissa is in danger, don't you?" Mike asked softly, coming over to stand beside him.

Hale had no idea why Mike would ask a question like that even as he realized that was exactly what had been worrying him. The grand opening of Patterson's plant was happening as they spoke, and Karissa was there by herself.

Or at least without Hale.

"How could you know what I was worrying about before I did?" he asked Mike in confusion.

Mike's mouth curved into a small smile. "You aren't the first member of the Pack to have some level of precognition when it comes to your soul mate. Remember how Remy got when Triana was in danger? He tracked her down like she was wearing a GPS beacon when he had no idea where she was."

Hale had only heard about Remy's adventures in New Orleans secondhand, but he definitely remembered his pack mate saying he could simply *feel* when Triana was in danger. That he would do anything to find her when that happened.

Was that what was going on now with him? Was he so unsettled because Karissa was in danger?

Hale realized he'd felt this way before, when they'd both been on the roof of Patterson's hotel, right before Bagley had appeared. Was the asshole going after her at the auto plant opening?

"I need to leave," he said suddenly, his heart starting to pound at the thought that he might already be too late. "I know this is the absolute worst time, but there's something wrong."

"Don't worry about us," Gage said. "I trust your inner wolf even if you don't yet. Take Carter with you. If Bagley is there, you're going to need all the help you can get."

Hale glanced at Carter to see that his pack mate looked as stunned as he was. But underneath that surprise was another emotion. It was well hidden, but Hale had worked with Carter long enough to recognize that he was worried.

Maybe even scared.

Not of facing Bagley but of something else.

Hale was about to ask Carter if maybe he wanted to sit this one out, but before he could get the words out, Gage was tossing him two tubes of the pink goo. Hale caught them with a frown. He wasn't sure why his boss thought he would need it.

"In case we're wrong about all of the hunters being in that warehouse," Gage said. "And considering how much Tamm seems to hate you, it's a distinct possibility."

Hale had to admit that was probably true but decided he didn't have time to worry about any of it. He had to go. Without another word, he turned

PAIGE TYLER

and sprinted out of the ops truck, heading for the nearest SWAT SUV. Fortunately, Carter got ahead of him and jumped behind the wheel. Hale knew he was too rattled to drive himself.

He had his phone out and was pulling up Karissa's number before Carter even got them moving. The call went to voicemail. Cursing, Hale thumbed the red button and redialed as Carter took them around a corner so fast he felt them go up on two wheels for a moment. Hale barely paid attention, praying Karissa picked up this time.

She didn't.

He took a deep breath, damn near hyperventilating. Something was horribly wrong. What if Bagley had already gotten to her?

"You said the opening was at seven, right?" Carter interjected into the middle of Hale's total meltdown. "Karissa's a security professional. If she's on the job, she's not going to stop to pull out her phone. Leave a message and then text her."

Hale thought that might be the most logical collection of words ever grouped together in the history of the English language and he grabbed hold of them like they were a life jacket.

Calling Karissa again, he left a message on her voicemail asking her to call him, saying that he needed to know she was okay. Then he texted her the same thing. After that, he sat there and stared at his phone, waiting for something good to happen.

"We'll be there in less than five minutes," Carter announced calmly. "Karissa is fine."

Hale wanted to believe his pack mate, but then he hit the green button, fangs starting to extend as the call went to voicemail once again.

———

"Anything on the monitors or perimeter sensors?" Karissa asked softly into the lapel microphone of her carefully selected conservative dark pantsuit. "Because my instincts are screaming that Bagley will be making an appearance sometime soon."

There were a few agonizing moments of silence—long enough that Karissa was half a second from running straight for the security room at the back of the auto plant—before Deven finally answered.

"There's no sign of him anywhere," her brother said. "But that doesn't mean a whole hell of a lot when the guy we're worried about can appear out of thin air whenever and wherever he wants."

Karissa knew Deven was right, but that didn't keep her from hoping all the same. In her heart, she knew Bagley wouldn't be able to resist the opportunity to take out her and Patterson in one fell swoop. She wanted to think he wouldn't risk reporters and their cameras seeing him, but something told her he'd come up with a way to deal with that issue.

"Just make sure to keep every light in the plant turned on," she said. "Bagley will have a harder time materializing in a brightly lit room. Hopefully."

Half listening to the rest of what her brother was saying, Karissa continued moving around the crowded room, weaving around reporters as well as politicians and random rich people who seemed to be there simply to be seen. The primary focus of her attention was Dominic Patterson, of course, but she tried to keep an eye on Glenn, too, seeing a scenario where Bagley might want to grab the son as bait.

Unfortunately, it turned out keeping an eye on Patterson senior was a monumental task all in itself. The plant was a circus, with everyone roaming around the assembly-line equipment, and Dominic seemed in his element, flitting around like a pixie, glad-handing and ego-stroking. The man was a natural at it.

Karissa followed him from one assembly bay to the next, keeping close to him as best she could. As she moved, she caught the eye of Jerome and the other nearby security guards, making sure they were focusing their attention on their boss instead of all the expensive assembly robots that were being put through their paces by Patterson's engineers.

Jolie Washington and Tristan Bond were working the crowd as actively as their boss. It was funny how merely a few hours ago, Karissa would have been covertly watching them, trying to figure out which one had hired Bagley. After knowing they weren't involved at all, it changed everything about how she looked at them. Now, they seemed like nothing more than business executives, eager to help make sure Patterson's automotive plant was a success.

As Karissa moved through assembly bay 2, keeping pace with Patterson and his son without making it obvious, she found her mind repeatedly going back to her parents and everything they'd done. She realized there was still a part of her in denial, a part that wanted to believe the two people she'd loved her whole life—a mother and father who raised her to be honest, courageous, and compassionate—wouldn't do the things she'd heard them confess to earlier.

But there was another part of her that wondered if she'd ever known her parents at all. It had been bad enough when the worst thing she'd thought they'd done was to send her three oldest brothers to beat the hell out of her teenage boyfriend. And while that had been beyond awful, she had to admit it paled in comparison to hiring a known hit man to terrorize Dominic Patterson purely for the purposes of inflating their security company's public profile. A scheme that had resulted in multiple deaths that her parents had shrugged off as *not part of the plan*.

Karissa maneuvered around an impeccably

dressed server carrying a tray of champagne flutes, still keeping an eye on Patterson as she continued trying to square the mom and dad who'd read her bedtime stories as a child with the coldhearted people who existed now. But no matter how hard she tried, she simply couldn't get there. The distance was too great.

As crappy as she felt at that moment, Karissa knew this evening would only get worse because at some point she'd have to tell Deven what she'd learned. Her youngest brother liked to act as if he were worldly and tough, but she knew this was going to hit him hard. She worried how bad the fallout was going to be.

She was about to contact Deven on the radio, driven by the sudden urge to check in and make sure everything was still okay, when the lights flickered. Her stomach twisted in that familiar way it always did whenever bad things were about to happen.

No one else around her seemed to even notice the slight flutter in the long row of fluorescent bulbs mounted high up on the ceiling, but Karissa definitely did. She'd practically been holding her breath for the last twenty minutes, waiting for the other shoe to drop.

Karissa spun in a slow circle as the lights flickered again. Other people actually noticed this time, glancing up toward the ceiling curiously. As she'd tried to do many times before, she attempted to reach out with her instincts, hoping they would tell her which direction Bagley would be coming from. But it didn't work. It never did.

She was a Paladin, not a Jedi.

She was trying to convince herself that the flickering had been nothing more than her imagination getting away from her when every light in the plant went out at once. The place was brightly lit one second and pitch-black the next.

For a moment, there was total silence. It was that all-consuming lack of sound that almost made her believe the darkness had stolen everyone else around her away and that she was alone in the nothingness.

The soft popping sound of the laughingly dim emergency lights coming on finally triggered the first murmurs of panic as people started looking around nervously. Karissa could almost sense their need to run, like they could feel the bad thing coming toward them, too.

"The connection to the lower power grid has been severed," Deven said into her earpiece, his words barely audible through the commotion going on in the security room with him. "And the on-site backup generator must have been sabotaged because it's not kicking in like it should."

Her spidey sense started pinging before Karissa had a chance to respond. Someone screamed behind her, and she spun around in time to see an inky-black, billowing darkness beginning to form on the far side of the assembly line fifteen feet from where Dominic Patterson was standing. The billionaire, as well as the people in his small group, seemed immobilized at the sight. They simply stood there frozen solid as that familiar sense of dread she knew came with Bagley began to fill the space.

"Bagley is in assembly bay 3," she shouted over the radio, immediately heading toward the shimmering curtain, intending to put herself between her client and the person who was going to be coming out of the portal any second. "Get Patterson and everyone else out of the building. Now!"

There was a second of stunned silence as the armored hit man stepped through the portal, his swords already beginning to move casually in his hands when he smiled in Karissa's direction as he moved toward Patterson.

Despite the emergency lights, it was still incredibly dark in the assembly bay areas, and Karissa doubted more than a dozen people could even see Bagley. But then the wave of dread that had been riding that line between disconcerting and uncomfortable became far more powerful. It sent some people running away into the darkness, while others dropped to their knees right where they'd been standing and cowered into balls. The wailing and screaming quickly followed, building to a terrifying intensity. Then a group of Patterson's security guards ran into the assembly bay and started blindly shooting. That's when everything descended into total bedlam.

"Stop shooting!" she shouted, already knowing it wasn't going to do any good. There was so much fear being pumped into the air right then that even the trained security guards were on the edge of losing it. One dropped to the floor with a moan of despair while the other two ran off into the dark in terror.

That was when Karissa realized Bagley's sensation of dread wasn't affecting her as severely as it had the previous time. The night of the gala and then again on the roof of Patterson's hotel, it had felt like her stomach was being twisted into knots merely from being near Bagley. Now, it was nothing more than a few shivers running up and down her spine. It definitely wasn't pleasant, but she could deal with it. She had no idea what had changed, but she wasn't complaining.

Patterson and his son were standing alone in the middle of the assembly bay, rigid as statues, abandoned by all the people who'd been fawning over them moments earlier. They barely seemed to register Karissa's arrival, their eyes locked on the man approaching them from the darkness.

Karissa got her sword out in time to block one of Bagley's, then took a step back and twisted sideways to avoid the second. But that action brought her closer to the Patterson men, both of whom were still standing there watching like this was a frigging dinner show.

"Glenn, wake the hell up and get your father out of here!" she shouted, hoping to snap the man out of his paralysis.

It didn't work. The younger Patterson barely reacted to her voice. And the distraction damn near got her head taken off.

Turning her attention back to the man trying to kill her didn't take much effort. Karissa was fond of her head and would prefer if it remained attached.

Normally, Karissa would have been content to stay on the defensive, letting Bagley come to her. But with the two Patterson men only a few steps away, she didn't have that option. She needed to put some space between them and the hit man, who would gladly take a swipe at one or both if he happened to get close enough—even if he was obviously more interested in killing her at the moment.

She charged with her sword, swinging fast at his head, catching Bagley completely by surprise and driving him back at least a half dozen strides. But he recovered quickly, flashing her a self-satisfied smirk as he started twirling his twin blades too fast to even see, forcing her back step after step. She deflected the strikes that got close, saving her skin, but damn, he was fast. After a few moments of the back-and-forth dance, Karissa had to admit she was surprised to still be holding him off.

Somehow, it seemed like she was a little faster than normal. Maybe even a little stronger. Not that she'd be able to keep Bagley at bay forever, but the longer the better.

"Without your soul mate here, you aren't a match for me," Bagley said. "It's only a matter of time until I slip through your defenses, and then it's over."

Karissa knew that last part was probably true, but it was the first part that grabbed her attention. Was Bagley saying that having Hale as a soul mate made her stronger? Is that why she felt a little faster and stronger? Would it be even more noticeable if he were here?

That extraneous train of thought nearly got Karissa beheaded again, a quick jerk to the side the only thing preventing it. But even her Paladin reflexes couldn't save her completely, as the tip of one of Bagley's blades caught her left shoulder and dragged halfway across her back.

The stripe of white-hot pain across her body was enough to rip a gasp from her throat, and for a second, her vision went blurry as fire engulfed her back and arm. Bagley took advantage of the distraction, coming after her so fast that she stumbled backward, landing hard on her butt and then sliding a few more feet. She tried to breathe, desperate for oxygen, but her lungs simply refused to work.

Between the lack of air and the pain, she couldn't do anything but lie there on the floor even as Bagley strode toward her with his swords swinging high.

"That was almost disappointingly easy," the man said, looming over her. "Having a soul mate can make you strong, but without him, you are incomplete."

Karissa got her own sword up to try and defend herself, but on the floor like this, she knew she wouldn't last long. And she was just as sure that Hale was going to blame himself for not being there to fight alongside her.

But just as Bagley started to swing one of his blades down toward her, a loud snarl of rage rippled through the room, the low, rumbling sound echoing off the walls around them. Glenn and Dominic Patterson—as well as the rest of the people still in the assembly bay—looked around in pure panic, their minds clearly pushed beyond the limits of comprehension.

A blur of movement in the darkness caught Karissa's eye, drawing her attention to the side. She looked over in time to see something streaking toward them and slamming into Bagley so hard she could hear the sound of bones crunching. Bagley went flying across the assembly bay floor, sliding a good ten feet before coming to an abrupt stop against the base of one of the robots that was swinging a car bumper in its automated hands.

Karissa looked up, her heart hammering hard in

her chest at the sight of Hale standing in front of her, his fangs and claws fully extended, fury on his face.

Bagley got to his feet with his own snarl of anger but stopped when another large blur slid to a stop beside Hale. Even in the dim glow from the emergency lights, it was easy to recognize Carter. His fangs and claws weren't out, but his eyes were glowing a vivid yellow-gold, and he looked pissed.

Carter was carrying some kind of rifle, which he tossed to Hale before pulling his own off his back where it had been hanging by a long strap. Hale moved closer to stand protectively near Karissa and then he and Carter turned their attention to Bagley.

For a moment, Karissa thought Bagley was going to charge them, regardless of the automatic weapons he was facing. But he must have thought better of it because a second later, the familiar billowing cloud of darkness appeared. Bagley stepped backward into it with a muttered series of words in a language she didn't recognize. But she knew cursing when she heard it, regardless of the language.

Hale was at her side in a heartbeat, reaching for the wound in her shoulder, tracing it all the way across her back. "You're bleeding!" he said, his words coming out like someone had punched him in the gut. "We have to get you out of here."

"There's no time," she said urgently as the other people around them on the floor started moving.

"We have to get Patterson to safety before Bagley comes back."

"He won't come back," Hale said. "He knows there's no chance of him beating the three of us, not when we're this well-armed."

Karissa wasn't too sure of that but didn't get the chance to tell him that as her spidey sense began to clang even harder than it had a few minutes earlier. Ignoring the burning pain in her shoulder, she shoved herself to her feet and spun in a slow circle, stopping when she saw Bagley's signature wall of darkness reappearing on the far side of the bay. The sense of dread returned as the man stepped through the portal.

But this time he wasn't alone.

It took a moment for Karissa to recognize the two black-clad men with him as the two Balauri that she and Hale had gone up against in the woods of the hunting preserve.

"Crap," she muttered as the two men leveled their own assault weapons at Hale and Carter.

"Kill the werewolves," Bagley said. "But leave the woman for me."

Chapter 24

HALE HAD BEEN CLOSE TO LOSING HIS MIND when Carter finally turned the SUV into the parking lot of Patterson's new automotive plant, holding on tight as the tires squawked across the asphalt. They'd made good time, but when he'd seen all the people pouring out the front doors of the darkened main building in a blind panic, he knew they were too late. Thomas Bagley had come after Karissa while Hale had been busy messing around with the Balauri miles away.

He jumped out of the SUV before it had even come to a stop, shoving and pushing through the people who were crawling over the top of each other to get out of the building. He hated going through the crowd like that, but he refused to let anything keep him from getting to his soul mate.

It was easy to pick up her scent the moment he stepped into the lobby of the dimly lit building, even though the place was immense and strung out in a bewildering maze of rooms and assembly bays. He took off running, thankful that his nose worked properly now—at least as far as Karissa was concerned. Then, not five seconds later, his heart dropped into his stomach as another powerful scent hit him.

Blood.

Karissa's blood.

Hale lost control of his inner wolf then. He was only glad the place was so dark, because if all those panicking people had seen his claws and fangs, it would have terrified them even more.

When he'd finally found Karissa and realized that she was injured but thankfully alive, it was like the weight of the world dropped from his shoulders. Dominic and Glenn Patterson were cowering on the floor along with half a dozen other people. They were all nearly comatose with fear from the dread emanating from Bagley, but as soon as the hit man retreated back into one of those creepy damn portals and disappeared, everyone had started to stir.

Whatever relief Hale felt evaporated the moment Bagley stepped back into the room less than a minute after he'd left, this time with Darijo Tamm and the other Balaur who Hale had fought with at the hunting preserve.

Shit.

How the hell had Davina missed the part about Bagley being able to take other people with him through these underworld portals? More importantly, why hadn't they known that Thomas Bagley and the Balauri were working together?

"Get Patterson and everyone else out of here," Hale said to Karissa as he watched Tamm and the other Balauri move toward him and Carter with

WILD AS A WOLF

their weapons raised. "Once the shooting starts, we won't be able to protect all of them."

From the look on her face, it was clear that Karissa didn't want to leave him. And that meant everything in the world to Hale. But he could also tell she knew he was right. Someone needed to get the people out of this assembly bay, and she was the only one who could do it.

"There's no way I can get everyone out," Karissa said, glancing around. "There are too many."

She was right, Hale thought.

He spun at the sudden thud of running footsteps, lifting his M4 carbine toward whoever was attacking them from behind, only to pull up when he recognized Deven and Lorenzo. Their eyes went wide in panic at the dread that had filled the room once again, their hearts beating so hard it was a miracle they were still standing.

Karissa started to ask what the hell they were doing there, but Hale cut her off. Deven and Lorenzo could help. That was all that mattered.

"Help Karissa get Patterson and the others out of the building," Hale said, reaching out to put his hand on Deven's shoulder. "Hurry."

Karissa glanced at him. "Don't do anything stupid," she warned before giving him a quick kiss. Then she was up and running toward Dominic Patterson, grabbing his arm, and shoving him and his son toward the way out at the same time.

Deven and Lorenzo—where the hell had her oldest brother come from?—got the other people to their feet, cajoling them toward the exit as fast as they would move. It was in the nick of time, too, as Tamm and his buddy chose that moment to start shooting.

Hale dove one way, Carter going the other. But even as they both moved to avoid being shot, they still made sure to keep themselves between the Balauri and the direction Karissa and everyone else had fled. With all those scared and shaken people to herd toward the exit, Hale knew he had to give his soul mate more time to get away.

Training and instinct had Hale pulling his M4 up to return fire, even though he knew it would do little good against the Balauri's impenetrable scales. But until he had time to figure out how to use those two test tubes of pink goo, there wasn't much else he could do. Bagley was still standing in the same place he'd been since arriving back in the bay, watching the scene in front of him play out with an amused expression on his face. But Hale had no time to worry about what the asshole of dread might be up to as Tamm charged straight at him, rifle chattering away on full automatic. Hale dove and rolled across the floor, closing the distance between himself and his attacker.

A rage-filled snarl came from Hale's left and he chanced a glance in that direction to see that Carter had completely lost control—again. His pack mate's eyes had changed from their normal yellow-gold to vivid blue. His claws and fangs had extended farther than Hale had ever seen, and somewhere along the way he'd lost his weapon. He'd shoved the other Balaur twenty feet across the floor, pinning him up against one of the assembly robots, and was going at the guy ferociously with his claws and fangs. The Balaur barely had a chance to get his arms up to defend himself.

Hearing Tamm reloading, Hale turned his attention back to the threat in front of him. Cursing, he lunged forward as the man fired at him on full automatic. Several of the rounds sliced across his back as he tackled Tamm to the floor, but he barely felt them.

Even though he'd fought the guy twice before, Hale was still stunned at how strong the Balaur was. The two of them rolled across the floor, exchanging kicks and punches as they both tried to get their weapons pointed at the other.

Hale got lucky, knocking the Balaur's assault rifle aside long enough to get the barrel of his own weapon twisted around so he could fire half his magazine into the guy's chest. Tamm slid back a few feet, grunting in pain, but as expected, the bullets failed to penetrate his skin.

Still, it gave Hale time to dig one of the tubes of goo out of a pocket on his tactical vest. Praying he wasn't making a huge mistake, he lunged forward and smashed the glass vial against Tamm's face, slicing the palm and fingers of his own hand but succeeding in smearing the pink potion all over the supernatural's face. The Balaur stumbled backward, free hand swiping at his eyes, growling as he tried to get the oily mess off.

Hale had no idea if the stuff was working, but before he could even try and make a guess, he heard another loud snarl from Carter's direction.

Carter was still upright and fighting, but from the rage twisting his face, Hale doubted his pack mate even remembered his own name, much less anything else. The Carter he knew was gone and in his place was someone Hale didn't even recognize. He'd heard of omega werewolves losing themselves in a rage, but he'd never personally seen it before. Simply put, it was terrifying as hell.

Carter was holding a length of metal wrapped in some kind of shiny plastic, and it took Hale a moment to realize it was the arm off the assembly robot that was now spinning slowly around in circles with nothing but a ragged composite-covered-stub sticking out. His pack mate was using what used to be the robot's arm to batter his opponent over and over, growling and snarling the whole time. But no matter how ferocious his friend fought or how hard he struck, the results were still the same. The Balaur's scale-covered skin was simply too tough to get through.

Unfortunately, Carter's skin wasn't the same, and even though he fought with an intensity the likes of which Hale had never seen, he was still taking one injury after another, blood running everywhere from multiple gunshot wounds. But sooner or later, one of those bullets would hit Carter in the head or heart, and it would all be over.

Hale couldn't let that happen.

Being too far away for anything else, Hale had no choice but to reach in his vest for the last tube of potion that would hopefully weaken the Balaur's invulnerable skin and sent it flying across the room.

The tube impacted exactly where Hale had aimed it, the glass shattering against the side of the Balaur's head, pink oily goo splattering everywhere.

The Balaur staggered back a few steps, reaching up to run his fingers through the liquid running down his neck and into the back of his shirt. From the way the Balaur's eyes widened, Hale suspected the creature wasn't enjoying the feel of the stuff on his skin.

Then Carter was wading back into the fray, swinging that makeshift metal club again, but this time the results were drastically different. This time Carter was actually causing damage.

A lot of damage.

Hale's mind refused to comprehend what he was seeing. The Pack had been fighting the Balauri for weeks, unable to do much—if any—damage to a supernatural creature impervious to any weapon they could name. Yet here was Carter, with a simple piece of metal, doing more damage than he would have ever thought possible.

The potion had worked. The Balauri were no longer invulnerable.

He looked over to see Tamm glancing back and forth between him and Carter, his dark eyes wide in alarm. A split second later, the Balaur let out a roar of anger and charged at Hale again, weapon coming up on full automatic. Hale met the other man halfway, wincing as bullets punched through his torso. Ignoring the instinct that told him to pull the trigger on his M4, he spun it around instead, slamming the butt into Tamm's forehead as hard as he could, hoping to replicate the effects of that tree branch at the hunting preserve.

Hale was actually surprised when Tamm flew backward and dropped like a rock. He took a cautious step forward to make sure the guy was actually out, but movement from the corner of his eye had him snapping his head up to look that way. He expected to see Bagley coming his way with those damn swords of his twirling. Instead, the armor-clad hit man was disappearing once again into one of those inky-black portals.

It wasn't hard to figure out that the asshole was going after Karissa again and that he'd only been waiting around to see the Balauri kill him and

Carter. He turned to Carter, praying his pack mate had regained enough control to be able to help go after Karissa and the others.

The chances of that seemed good. The second Balaur was lying on the floor in front of the still-spinning robot, apparently out cold. Carter walked slowly toward Hale, his hands empty. While his eyes were still glowing slightly blue, they were growing more tranquil by the second.

Then the Balaur that Carter had knocked out was moving again. Before Hale could shout a warning, the guy grabbed his weapon and fired at least half a dozen rounds right into Carter's back at near point-blank range. Carter stumbled forward as the bullets tore through him. In a single heartbeat, his eyes went from almost calm to filled with rage, the blue glow flaring so bright that people probably would have been able to see it two rooms away.

With a vicious snarl, Carter spun and charged at the Balaur, who was already trying to aim for another shot. Carter ignored the weapon completely, slamming into the man and shoving him back so hard he would have flown twenty feet through the air if there hadn't been a heavily damaged assembly line robot in the way.

The Balaur smacked into what was left of the robot's tattered arm, a length of steel support beam going right through his midsection. Hale stared, shocked. Carter seemed stunned as well. For a moment, he simply stood there looking at the carnage he'd caused. When he finally turned to Hale, his eyes were no longer blue. But before Hale could say anything, Carter took off, running away from him, into the darkened building.

Hale was torn. He wanted to go after Carter, but he had to find Karissa before Bagley did. He paused long enough to slap some cuffs on the still-unconscious Tamm, shoot a superfast text to Mike about the potion, and then ran in the same direction Karissa and her brothers had taken.

But he'd barely gone a dozen strides when his nose told him that Karissa was too far away for him to reach her fast enough this way. He needed speed—a lot of speed.

He needed to shift into his wolf form.

Only he'd never done it before.

He'd seen his pack mates do it though. Well, the ones who *could* do it.

His inner wolf was already howling to be free.

He had to try.

For Karissa.

Sliding to a stop, Hale reached down and quickly untied his boots, kicking them off at the same time he unbuckled his belt. Pulling his top over his head without slowing to unbutton it, he tossed it aside, then took a long, deep breath, reaching for his inner wolf.

Hale gritted his teeth as his body began to reshape

and take on his four-legged form. He remembered Gage telling him that it got easier and less painful the more often a werewolf fully shifted. And that the first time hurt like hell. But he had no other choice. His soul mate needed him, and he would do whatever he had to if it meant reaching her in time.

Karissa had thought she and her brothers would be able to get everyone out of the plant in minutes. Unfortunately, with having to focus so much of her attention on simply keeping their terrified group together—not to mention watching out for Bagley—they'd gotten turned around somewhere along the way. It didn't help that they ended up wandering into a part of the plant clearly not ready for the press or general public—an area where very few of the emergency lights had been wired up yet. On top of that, Patterson and son were damn near useless, both of them so rattled they could do little more than follow where they were led.

She'd hoped that her Paladin instincts would guide her to the nearest exit, but the only ones screaming at her right now were those connected to her soul mate. And all they wanted was for her to turn around and find Hale.

Karissa prayed she'd done the right thing leaving him in the first place. Yes, there was a part of her that knew getting Patterson and everyone else out of the building was the responsible thing to do, but that didn't make her worry any less. Her soul mate was in danger and the connection between them didn't give two ducks about being responsible.

"We're lost, aren't we?" Deven suddenly said from behind her, where he'd been riding rear guard to make sure they didn't lose any stragglers. "I'm sure we've been through this room before."

"Maybe," she admitted. "But on the bright side, if we don't know where we are, then I doubt Bagley will be able to find us."

"I'm not sure if I agree with that logic," Lorenzo said, looking around worriedly into the darkness. "How hard can it be to find a group this large in an empty building? We're making more noise than a herd of elephants."

Karissa realized her oldest brother was right, but there wasn't much they could do about it. Patterson and the others were only now starting to come out of the mental fog they'd been put under by Bagley's presence. Getting them to move quietly was a bit much to ask at the moment.

"I know," she said. "But there's no other choice than to keep going until we find a way out of here. We have to hope Bagley doesn't hear us."

Karissa probably shouldn't have said that last part out loud because thirty seconds later, that familiar inky cloud appeared right in front of them, so dark it was clearly visible even in the dimly lit section of the plant.

"Take everyone and go back the way we came," she told her brothers without looking away from the portal, pulling her sword out of the air at the same time. "Don't worry about being quiet. Run as fast as you can. I'll hold him off."

Both Deven and Lorenzo looked ready to argue with that. Karissa understood their concerns since she'd had the same ones not ten minutes ago when Hale had given her the same instructions. But then Lorenzo grabbed Deven's arm and dragged him away, shoving the two Patterson men and everyone else in front of them.

"You didn't think I'd forgotten you, did you?" Bagley asked as he stepped out of the portal with that ever-present shiver-inducing sneer on his face. "I apologize for making you wait, but I was entranced watching your soul mate try to deal with the Balauri."

Karissa's heart lurched at the thought of Hale being hurt, but a second later, a little whisper in the back of her mind told her that her soul mate was fine. It was impossible to explain, but if he'd been seriously hurt, she would have known it in her heart.

"So you and the Balauri are working together now?" Karissa countered, moving slowly to the right, forcing Bagley to move to keep in front of her. "I never thought of you as the teamwork type."

His eyes narrowed, like he'd expected more of a reaction about Hale. She was glad she hadn't given it to him.

Bagley stepped forward quickly, swinging one of his blades toward her. Karissa parried and then quickly backed away to avoid the second blade coming her way. If nothing else, she was giving Deven and Lorenzo more time to get everyone clear of the building.

Hopefully.

"We're not really working together," Bagley said, suddenly reversing the direction of the swords' rotation, forcing her to move and parry as he jabbed the point of one blade straight at her heart.

He seemed a little stunned at how fast she'd reacted. She had only a moment to wonder if her speed was part of the soul mate bond before Bagley recovered, once again reversing course, his blades weaving together in a blur of motion.

He was fast.

Faster than her, soul mate connection or not.

"When I realized you were developing a bond with your pet werewolf," Bagley added, his smile broadening, as if he'd somehow read her mind and knew she was aware of the disparity, "I knew I needed a distraction to separate the two of you long enough to let me get close to you alone. So I tracked down the Balauri and made them an offer they couldn't refuse—easy access to the very people they wanted to fight. I didn't have to even pay them. All I had to do was put them and your soul mate's pack in the same location."

"Yet my soul mate showed up all the same," Karissa said, stepping forward to knock one of his swords aside, the tip of her blade missing him by mere millimeters. "So it doesn't seem like your plan has worked."

"I don't know about that," Bagley said, stopping his predatory movements and squaring up to face her. "I have you here alone, which is what I was looking for all along."

The words were barely out of Bagley's mouth before he was attacking again, dual swords coming in so fast that Karissa knew she'd never stop them both. But she threw up her blade anyway, ready to defend herself as long as possible.

Karissa was surprised when she ended up blocking the attack, and the one that followed, and then the one after that. Bagley looked absolutely amazed himself—and maybe even a bit worried. She couldn't blame him. She'd never moved this fast or been this precise and sure of herself. Maybe this was why Bagley had been worried about her and Hale getting together.

She landed a few strikes, some getting through his hardened leather armor and drawing blood. Bagley landed a couple of shots of his own, too, but none of that mattered. The important thing was that he was beginning to get nervous.

That's when she knew she had him on the ropes.

That was also when everything went horribly wrong.

She heard the thud of rapidly approaching footsteps, then someone yelling, immediately followed by gunfire. Bagley stepped away from her far enough to turn and block the incoming rounds with his blades. Karissa had half a heartbeat to wonder if she could use the distraction to her advantage when Bagley darted toward whoever had interrupted them.

There was a clang of metal on metal and something bounced off into the darkness. Then one of Bagley's blades disappeared into thin air and he was wrapping an arm around the man's neck, choking so hard that Karissa was sure she could hear him crushing his victim's throat.

Karissa nearly screamed when she realized it was Lorenzo. Her doofus brother had come back to help, running headlong into the situation without even checking to see if she needed that help. And he'd gotten caught.

"Toss your sword across the room," Bagley instructed, that infuriating smirk back on his smug face as her brother attempted and failed to get himself free. The hit man barely seemed to notice. It was like her big brother was nothing more than a weak kitten. "Or I'll snap his neck."

Karissa instinctively took a half step forward but

stopped when Lorenzo winced in pain, gasping for air.

"Across the room," Bagley repeated, applying a little more pressure around Lorenzo's neck. "Don't make it disappear like you normally do. I want it physically across the room."

Karissa hesitated, especially when her brother looked at her with eyes pleading her not to do it. But another squeeze of Bagley's arm around Lorenzo's neck made her send the blade spinning off into the darkness.

Bagley laughed, and it had to be the most menacing sound Karissa had ever heard.

He pulled her brother closer to his chest, the arm around Lorenzo's neck tightening even more. "You really shouldn't have done that. Now you can't do anything but watch as I kill him...and then you."

She opened her mouth to beg for her brother's life, knowing she'd never get to him in time to save him. Then a blur suddenly streaked across her line of sight and something huge slammed into both Bagley and her brother.

A low snarl echoed around the room like thunder, practically making the walls tremble. A split second later, Bagley was stumbling back and shouting in pain as Lorenzo slid across the floor on his back. It took a second for Karissa to make sense of what she was seeing. When the fast-moving, fur-covered shape finally resolved itself into an absolutely enormous wolf, there wasn't a doubt in her mind.

It was Hale.

She simply knew it.

Bagley was still standing upright even though Hale had his jaws locked down firmly on the man's right shoulder and was shaking his head viciously side to side. Cursing, Bagley swung his sword. There were several sickening thuds as the blade came down on Hale's back, shoulder, and flank. Bagley spun in a circle, and all Karissa could do was watch helplessly as Hale went flying off into the darkness with a howl of pain, disappearing in the same direction her sword had gone. The crashing sound as his body hit the floor and slid even farther into the blackness crushed her heart.

Karissa didn't have time to think about how badly injured Hale might be. Bagley was already coming straight toward her, murder in his eyes. His right shoulder and arm were bleeding heavily, but his left hand was wrapped firmly around his sword.

Reaching behind her back, Karissa pulled out the only weapon she had left—the one lone throwing knife she'd been able to conceal in her pantsuit. She stepped forward to meet Bagley, not sure if holding on to the blade would be any better than throwing it. Either way, a small lightweight knife against a sword wasn't good odds.

"I'm going to kill you quickly," Bagley promised.

"But rest assured that I'll enjoy myself when it comes to finishing off your soul mate. And whoever the other man is over there, too."

Karissa swallowed the rage that filled her heart at those casual announcements of the murders of people she held dear and lunged with her knife.

Bagley knocked the blade aside, almost taking part of her hand with it. Fingers bleeding from the glancing blow, Karissa kept attacking, knowing that she had no other choice. But her efforts got her nowhere, and within moments, she was bleeding from multiple wounds while doing little more than carving a few gouges in Bagley's leather armor.

Karissa kept fighting until he knocked the knife from her grasp and it bounced off into the darkness, her hand and forearm numb from a heavy strike. Bagley had backed her up against a wall and as he lifted his blade high, she knew it was over.

Movement from the corner of her eye caught her attention, and Karissa risked a quick glance that way to see Hale walking toward her—on two legs this time—blood running down his naked body, her sword in one of his hands.

Her sword in one of his hands.

Before she could even attempt to question how he could possibly be holding her sword—a sword that disappeared when anyone other than her attempted to hold it—the blade was flying through the air toward her.

Bagley charged, swinging his blade. When the hilt of her sword slammed into the palm of her hand, his eyes widened, but he was moving too fast by then to stop his momentum. Knowing she'd never be able to avoid the blow coming her way, Karissa lunged forward instead.

And Bagley impaled himself on her blade.

Stunned, his sword tumbled slowly from his grasp, clattering loudly to the floor. As he looked down at the blade in his chest in disbelief, Karissa found it impossible to read all the emotions she saw on his face, but panic was definitely one of them.

Karissa felt Hale move over to stand beside her as Bagley collapsed to the floor in a heap. Before she could even wonder if there was any chance he might get back up, the man's body began disintegrating right in front of them, his skin aging and wrinkling until he looked every day of his two-hundred-and-seventy-years, hair going gray and then pure white. In less than a minute, Thomas Bagley—the human personification of a Greek god—was a desiccated shell of a man who looked like he'd been dead for a very long time.

Karissa let her sword fade away and then turned to pull Hale into her arms, terrified at how much he was bleeding but needing to hold him anyway.

"I thought you were…when he stabbed you and you didn't get up…I thought…" Karissa knew she was babbling incomprehensibly but couldn't stop.

"I'm okay. The wounds are already healing," he whispered, pulling her closer and pressing a gentle kiss to the top of her head. "I'm sorry for taking so long to get to you but changing back into my human form while I'm injured is more difficult than I thought it would be."

She pulled back to look at him, only then remembering the whole big furry wolf thing. "You turned into a wolf. I thought you said you've never been able to do that."

"I was worried I wouldn't reach you in time, so I took a risk and tried a full shift," he said softly, one of his hands coming up to cup her face, thumb caressing her lower lip. "It worked."

"That sounds incredibly foolish," she murmured, going up on her toes to kiss him, her hands resting on his warm chest. "But it did work and you're okay. That's all that matters."

She leaned in to kiss Hale again when she heard the soft tread of approaching footsteps. She looked over to see Lorenzo coming toward them. He was walking with a slight limp, holding one hand to his back in obvious discomfort.

"Yeah, I'm okay, too," Lorenzo said as he stopped a few feet away, clearly hesitant to get too close to Hale. "In case anyone was wondering."

"I'm really glad you aren't hurt," Karissa said, realizing that she genuinely meant it. "So don't take this the wrong way, but what are you even still doing in Dallas? I figured you'd be on a plane back to Chicago with Mom and Dad by now."

Her brother had the decency to look embarrassed as he shook his head. "I'll admit, when I left Hale's apartment after that argument, I had every intention of going straight home. But halfway to the airport, I realized there was no way I could leave my little brother and sister to handle someone like Bagley on their own, so I came to help. I didn't end up doing much, but I knew I had to try."

Karissa took a breath to point out that maybe he should have thought about helping a long time ago, but before she could get the words out, the sound of approaching sirens interrupted her.

She turned back to Hale, still amazed he'd shifted into a wolf to save her life. "It sounds like this place is going to get crowded in a minute, so maybe you should go find your clothes."

Hale kissed her, a smile tugging up the corners of his lips. "That's probably a good idea. I'm not sure how I'd be able to explain why I'm naked and covered in blood."

Taking her hand, he started in the direction he'd come. She and Hale had barely gone more than a few feet when the sound of Lorenzo clearing his throat had them turning around.

"Um, speaking of explaining things," her oldest brother said. "What are we going to say about the two-hundred-year-old corpse on the floor?"

Karissa looked questioningly at Hale.

He shrugged, then glanced at Lorenzo. "Well, you said you came to help, so we'll leave it up to you to figure out."

Her brother seemed less than thrilled with that idea but didn't say anything.

Still holding Hale's hand, Karissa turned and walked away with her soul mate.

Chapter 25

THERE WAS A TOUCH OF COOLNESS TO THE LATE-October air as Karissa and Hale walked into the back of the SWAT compound to drop off the extra bags of burger and hot dog buns that Mike had asked them to pick up on the way to the cookout. They'd just started walking across the compound, waving at all the people already gathered there—including Deven, who was playing volleyball with some of Hale's pack mates—when Tuffie came running across the grass to greet them with a big grin on her cute little doggy face.

Tuffie was the SWAT team's official mascot. Hale had told her the tear-inducing story of how several of his pack mates had found the pit bull mix barely alive at a crime scene almost two years ago. They'd rescued the lovable pooch from death's door and had been taking care of her ever since. The whole pack took turns taking Tuffie home with them, making sure she knew exactly how much she was loved. Tonight was Karissa and Hale's turn to host the little cutie, and Karissa couldn't wait.

Tuffie ran around them a few times, stopping to give the bags of buns a good sniff, then waited for pats from each of them before turning and running at full speed across the compound to join all the other pets gathered around the grills begging for food.

Karissa was surprised that Carter was manning the row of grills by himself. Hale had said that the Pack took turns cooking at these little parties, but she couldn't help thinking that he seemed so... alone. Except for all the cats and dogs sitting at his feet begging for scraps, of course.

She and Hale dropped the bags of buns off at one of the buffet tables, then grabbed two bottles of iced tea before heading over to one of the picnic tables near the volleyball game.

"Is Carter doing okay?" she asked, whispering as softly as she could. She knew that werewolves had exceptionally good hearing and hoped that the cheers and laughter around them would help keep Carter from overhearing. "I know it's only been a little while since what happened at Patterson's auto plant, but he seems so withdrawn."

Truthfully, that was an understatement. And after what happened when Carter had gone up against that Balaur, she supposed she couldn't blame him. But Carter seemed to be so detached. In the several times Karissa had stopped by the compound, she hadn't seen him say a single word to anyone. She knew that Hale and his pack mates were all worried about him. She was, too.

"Mike didn't want to talk about it, but when I

pressed, he admitted that Carter is having a hard time holding it together," Hale said quietly, taking a sip of iced tea. "Mike and Gage are afraid that he might actually leave the Pack."

Karissa did a double take at that. She might be new to this whole werewolf-pack thing, but Hale had said that the connection between them was stronger than family. He'd told her about that night at the auto plant and how, in the midst of the fight, Carter's inner werewolf had taken over so completely that he'd no longer been in control and that he'd ended up killing the Balaur he'd fought. Carter hadn't even realized what he'd done until after the fact. It might have been justified, but doing something like that with no memory of it happening had to be difficult.

It had taken Mike until sunrise to track Carter down afterward. He'd run nearly twenty miles in that time, collapsing in a recently harvested corn field with half a dozen bullets still buried in his body. Getting him back home had supposedly taken a minor miracle.

"Isn't there anything we can do to help?" she asked, glancing in Carter's direction to see him with another SWAT officer she'd only met briefly. The guy was helping Carter flip the burgers, hot dogs, and steaks, unsuccessfully trying to get his pack mate to talk. "I hate the thought of him going through this alone."

"Carter will never be alone," Mike said, appearing at their side suddenly and sliding onto the bench across from them. "In fact, Cooper is over there talking to him right now about someone we know who can help him."

"Who?" Karissa asked curiously. "I mean, are there werewolf therapists out there or something?"

The corner of Mike's mouth curved. "Actually, there is one. She just doesn't know it yet."

Karissa waited impatiently for him to elaborate, but before Mike could continue, Cooper shouted that the food on the grill was ready. Mike immediately jumped up. Hale was right behind him.

"You stay here and hold our seats," he said, leaning back down to give her a quick kiss. "I'll get our food. I know exactly how you like your burger."

She smiled as Hale got in line with everyone else collecting in front of the grills. He probably *did* know how she liked her burger. Then again, considering how much time they'd spent together over the past week, there likely wasn't much he didn't know about her.

Karissa had officially moved in with Hale the same night she'd defeated Bagley, and had never looked back. Not that there had been much to move in. She'd always traveled light and there'd been very little left behind in her hotel room to bother with. She didn't have much in the way of stuff back at her parents' home outside of Chicago either, so shopping was one of the first things on her to-do list.

"How's my favorite sister?" Deven asked as he sat down on the bench across the table from her, carrying a paper plate piled high with a hot dog, cheeseburger, barbecue beans, and coleslaw. "Life with your soul mate as blissful as you expected it to be?"

"First, I'm your only sister," Karissa pointed out with a laugh. "And second, no, life with my soul mate isn't as blissful as I expected. It's better."

There'd never really been any doubt about Hale and her being soul mates, but if there had been, they were washed away when Karissa saw him carrying her sword. They'd spent a lot of time talking about it since then, even conducting a few experiments. While he couldn't summon the blade, he could easily handle it. Their conclusion was that it was the soul mate bond that allowed Hale to use her weapon, as if the sword now viewed them as one instead of two separate people.

And yeah, Karissa couldn't help but think about how much that all sounded like a marriage vow... two becoming one. She found herself extremely comfortable with that idea.

Her brother chuckled as he picked up his burger. "I'm glad. If anyone deserves some happiness out of this screwed-up situation, it's you."

Karissa knew exactly what her brother meant by

screwed-up situation, so she didn't bother asking for clarification.

The morning after the fight at the auto plant, Lorenzo had shown up at Hale's place to convince her and Deven to go back to Chicago with him so they could try and repair the *misunderstanding* they had with their parents. Karissa had immediately refused, saying that her place was with Hale now. Lorenzo hadn't seemed surprised to hear that, but he'd genuinely been shocked when Deven announced he wasn't leaving, either.

"I'm staying with Karissa," he'd announced firmly. "She's family. Or at least the only family I trust."

Lorenzo had been speechless and left for the airport less than thirty minutes later. Neither of them had heard anything from him or any other member of their family since. In all honesty, Karissa wasn't that torn up about it. Maybe she'd attempt to reconnect with her parents and other brothers in the future. Lorenzo had risked his life to try and save her, so she owed him that much at least. But even with that in mind, it might be a long time before she was ready to forgive any of them. Even a little.

Hale came back to the table then, carefully balancing two plates full of food. Mike and Connor were right behind him, followed by Carter. The latter didn't say anything, instead sitting at the end of the table and focusing his attention on his barely cooked steak and generous helping of potato salad. Though when Tuffie came over and sat down near the bench beside him, he quickly reached out and gently ran his hand over her fur.

"What were you two talking about?" Hale asked curiously, picking up his burger as he looked back and forth between Karissa and Deven.

She lifted the top bun and checked her cheeseburger, confirming that it had dill pickles and extra mayo, then threw a pointed look at her little brother. "Actually, I was just about to ask Deven how his college search has been going. He mentioned a couple of days ago that going to school was something he was interested in, but he hasn't picked one yet. If he gets all the paperwork done, he can start classes next semester."

Everyone at the table turned to look at her brother, putting him on the spot to answer. Which was what Karissa had intended. The moment Deven had mentioned going to school, she'd been behind it one hundred percent, even saying she'd find a way to help pay for it. She wanted her brother to have a chance to do something she never had. But since their initial conversation, Deven had blown her off every time she'd brought up any of the local colleges. It was starting to get irritating. Mostly because it felt like she was momming him. And she was definitely *not* a mom.

Deven took a big bite of his hot dog, clearly to

give himself more time to fabricate a lie to cover up his procrastination. She was surprised when he looked up with a smile on his face after he finished chewing.

"Turns out," he said slowly, and Karissa got a quiver of concern in her stomach when her brother's expression suggested he was worried about something, "I've already applied at the college of my choice and been accepted. I start right after New Year's."

Everyone at the table, and at those nearby, cheered and offered their congratulations. But while Karissa was certainly thrilled at the idea of Deven going to college, she couldn't shake the sense of hurt filling her at the fact that he hadn't let her be part of the process.

"That's great," she said, hoping her smile was believable. "What kind of program are you going into? Which college did you pick? How much is it going to cost?"

"It's a computer science degree, majoring in cyber-security and information assurance," her brother answered, still grinning. "Working with my contact at STAT got me really interested in the subject."

Karissa was waiting for him to answer the rest of her questions but was forced to sit there stewing as Deven hid behind another big bite of hot dog. And then a forkful of beans. Okay, he was seriously pushing his luck now.

"So...computer science?" Hale asked, looking like he was about to laugh at how impatient she was being. "You going to North Texas? A&M maybe?"

"Neither, actually." Deven's smile slipped a little as he looked at Karissa. "I've been accepted at DC University in Washington. They have one of the best cybersecurity programs in the country. My contact at STAT recommended the school."

Karissa's mind went blank. Washington, DC? That was half a country away. She'd never see her brother. At least not often.

"And if you're worrying about paying for me to go to college, don't," her brother added, almost like he'd been rehearsing what he'd been going to say. Which he probably had. "I've already taken care of it. I'm covered for the whole four years, plus a little extra just in case."

Her head was swimming at that, and she paused with a forkful of coleslaw halfway to her mouth. "What do you mean, you've already taken care of it?"

Her brother shrugged and dug into his barbecue beans. "I know you don't want anything to do with Mom and Dad—or their money—but I'm not so forgiving. I missed out on most of high school because I was working for them. The way I look at it, they owe me for four years of education. I'm just making sure they pay for it."

Karissa could feel Hale and everyone else

around the table looking at them and knew without glancing over that they were smiling. She kept her attention on her brother, knowing he'd crack.

"Fine," he said with a long sigh. "I hacked into the company accounts and transferred an appropriate amount into an education trust fund to pay for college. I got the idea from that account Glenn Patterson had, and my contact at STAT helped me set it up. It's not like Mom and Dad have room to complain. Not after all the crap they pulled."

Karissa was starting to think that getting Deven and this person from STAT together was going to lead to a lot of trouble in the long run. But before she could point that out, Hale nudged her shoulder, obviously trying to get her attention.

"Now that we know what Deven has been doing behind your back, maybe you should let him know what you've been up to?" Hale said. "I'm sure he's been worried about what you're going to do with your life now that you're not working for your parents."

From the corner of her eye, she saw Deven looking at her with confusion. "I thought you'd just keep doing what you've been doing, saving innocents and stuff, but on your own."

On your own.

The mere sound of those words was painful to hear, even though Karissa knew she'd never be on her own again. Not since she'd found her soul mate.

But it appeared that she *would* be without her little brother. For at least a while. That was painful, too.

"I considered going into the personal security business on my own, but in the end, I had to admit I didn't have the kind of contacts necessary to find clients. That was Mom and Dad's part of the gig and I never really worried about it."

"So what are you going to do?" Deven asked, and Karissa realized he was actually a little worried about her. That concern felt nice.

"You know Hale's pack mate Rachel, right?" Karissa asked, looking around the compound until she saw the woman at another table. "She was at the auto plant after everything went down, helping to clean up."

Her brother glanced over at Rachel, who was sitting at the table beside theirs, then slowly nodded, clearly having no idea where this was going.

"Yeah," he said.

"Well, her mate, Knox, runs a private security company here in Dallas," Karissa said. "I was a little hesitant about working for someone I don't know—especially after what Mom and Dad did to us—but Hale promises that I can trust Knox. That he's part of the extended SWAT Pack, like you and me now. So I'm going to work for him."

Deven considered that for a moment. "Won't you miss running all over the world saving people?"

"Maybe," she admitted, sipping her iced tea. "But

after ten years of being separated from Hale, I'm actually looking forward to staying in one place."

Her brother seemed to take that answer in stride, and the two of them spent the next few minutes talking about their most recent plans. The conversation was interrupted by Gage slipping onto the bench beside Deven.

Karissa couldn't help noticing how tired Hale's pack alpha seemed. Well, as tired as a werewolf could look, she guessed. According to Hale, his commander had been run ragged over the past week trying to tie up all the loose ends from Bagley's assault on the auto plant, not to mention the involvement of the Gang of Five.

"Everything sorted with the Balauri and the district attorney?" Mike asked, looking up from his plate of steak and macaroni salad.

Gage nodded. "Officially, Darijo Tamm and the other three Balauri were handed over today to Interpol and the International Criminal Court, where they're facing several dozen lifetimes in prison for crimes against humanity. Unofficially, they've been taken into custody by STAT and are being held at wherever it is they take all their supernatural prisoners."

"So it's over?" Carter asked quietly from the end of the table. He'd been so quiet that Karissa had almost forgotten he was there. "There won't be anyone else asking questions about what happened that night?"

"It's over," Gage said. "As far as the DA and the chief are concerned, the Gang of Five was hired to kill Dominic Patterson and his son as part of a plot to steal secrets relating to the plant's high-tech robotic manufacturing equipment. Everything they'd done before that was merely to distract the police and keep us off balance."

"And the dried-up two-hundred-and-seventy-year-old corpse that Bagley turned into?" Connor asked in between bites of burger. "How did you explain that one?"

"I didn't," Gage said. "STAT showed up and took the body before anyone saw it."

Karissa looked around the table, having a difficult time believing it could be that easy, even though everyone else seemed to accept Gage's explanation—even Hale.

"That's it?" she asked. "People are going to buy a story about a convoluted murder plot by a team of international fugitives and a little industrial espionage? What about everyone who saw us fighting Bagley and the Balauri? Didn't their account of the events mess up your narrative?"

Gage shook his head. "It was dark and chaotic in the building and witness accounts were all over the place, with most of them admitting they couldn't see much of anything. The only thing that Patterson and his son could say for sure was that you, Hale, and Carter saved their lives."

"And all of this is going to fly with the press?" she asked.

There had to be someone out there looking closer at such a dramatic event. Especially with all the rich people who'd been in attendance.

"It was big news for a few days," Gage admitted with a shrug. "But news cycles fast in this country. The attempted murder will be back-page news soon and the only thing people will care about is when the plant will be fully operational and when they'll start hiring."

A part of her wanted to think that people couldn't possibly be that unaware of what was going on around them, but in her heart, she knew it wasn't true. She'd spent ten years fighting monsters— supernatural and otherwise—and in all that time, regardless of the unexplainable things that people had witnessed, nobody had ever said a word, much less asked a single question.

Maybe because people simply didn't want to know the answers.

The conversation around the table turned to more mundane subjects, like what training the team would be conducting over the next few weeks and where everyone was taking their soul mates for a special night out. In between, she and Hale talked about when she'd start working for Knox and how they'd sync up their schedules. It might be silly, but it felt nice to plan simple things, like grabbing lunch together and how they'd always make time for each other.

"What happens with Deimos?" Connor asked. "Now that Thomas Bagley is dead, is Deimos no longer a threat?"

Karissa looked at Connor. "I suppose Deimos will start looking for a new avatar to possess. Based on how Davina described the lopsided relationship he requires, it will take him a while to find the right person. And even then, it will take years before he's anywhere near as dangerous as he was with Bagley."

"I guess that's as much as we can ask for," Mike remarked. "It's still something we need to have STAT keep an eye out for though."

"Speaking of having STAT keep an eye out for stuff," Carter said. "Has anyone talked to them about those strange wolves Hale and I saw? Is there a chance they were involved with the Balauri—or Bagley?"

"I spoke to Davina about them and even brought the subject up with Tamm before STAT took custody of him," Gage answered. "Davina never heard of a werewolf who could transform as fast as you described, and while Tamm wasn't exactly talkative, he didn't react with anything but confusion when I asked him. I don't think these new werewolves have anything to do with the Balauri."

"And there's no way of knowing if they were helping Bagley since he's not around to ask," Karissa added. "But I have to admit I don't see him working that closely with anyone. The deal he made with the Balauri seemed to offend his sensibilities as it was. He was only using them to distract the Pack."

Mike sighed. "I guess we'll have to see if the first run-in with them was a random thing or a sign of some kind of future problem."

Karissa silently agreed. Her instincts were telling her that something really scary was coming their way and it was all tied to those new werewolves. But now wasn't the time to bring it up. She'd tell them later. For now, she forced herself to stop worrying. Whatever was headed their way, they'd all deal with it together. Like a family.

Because the Pack was as much her family now as Deven.

Another round of burgers, hot dogs, and steak followed the first—for the werewolves in attendance at least. Karissa nibbled little bites off Hale's plate now and then until they got around to dessert. She definitely made room for the brownies that Rachel had baked.

Volleyball followed the food, which seemed like a bizarre idea to Karissa. She was too full to jump around, much less throw herself on the sand to try and save a spike. But it was clear the SWAT wolves loved playing the game, and having a chance to be out there with Hale as he laughed and joked made it worth it.

While the Pack was obviously a competitive bunch, the games quickly turned into an excuse to run around and act like kids. Karissa couldn't remember having this much fun in a long time.

A decade, to be precise.

But when Karissa looked around, she realized there was one person missing out on the party. Carter was cleaning the grill and clearly lost in his own head again, Tuffie at his side. Any humor she'd felt disappeared, to be replaced by compassion for her newfound pack brother.

Hale must have sensed her change in emotion because he was immediately at her side, concern clear on his face. He started to ask what was wrong but then followed the direction of her gaze and saw his pack mate standing by himself.

"I know Cooper convinced him to talk to a therapist, but I still wish we could do something to help him right now," she said softly. "I mean, it feels wrong that the two of us get to be so incredibly happy while someone we care about seems so lost."

"The therapist Cooper mentioned is good at what she does. She'll help him. I'm sure of it," Hale said, squeezing her hand. "Carter just needs to hold on until all this turns around. Whatever *all this* happens to be."

"Maybe it would help if he found his soul mate," Karissa said, suddenly wishing Carter and Mike, the only two remaining werewolves in the Pack who didn't have one, could feel the same connection that she and Hale felt.

"I'm sure it would," Hale said, moving behind her and wrapping his arms around her middle, pulling her close. "But unfortunately, there's no way we can rush something like that. When it's time for Carter to find *The One* for him, it'll happen. Until then, all we can do is be there for him and hope that's enough."

Karissa thought that answer sucked. It also played hell with her need to save the innocent. But she supposed Hale was right. It wasn't like Carter was going to be able to sit down with this therapist and she'd be able to tell him who his soul mate was or something.

So she and Hale stood there watching as Carter finished cleaning the grill, then headed toward the parking lot without saying a word to anyone. Tuffie threw the two of them a quick almost-apologetic look and then hurried after Carter, jumping in his yellow Hummer when he opened the door. Karissa guessed the amazing dog knew who needed her the most right then.

Tears welled in Karissa's eyes, and she reached up to brush one away as it rolled down her face.

"Hey, it'll be okay," Hale said, squeezing her even tighter. "It took ten years for us to find each other again, but in the end, we did it. It will happen for Carter, too. I'm sure of it. We have to believe that."

Karissa turned in Hale's arms and pulled his head down for a kiss. Hearing him say the words out loud made her realize exactly how lucky she was. So many events and people had gotten in their way, but fate had pulled them back together against all those obstacles. They'd wasted ten years, but right then Karissa decided she'd never waste another second.

"Let's go home," she said, taking his hand. "And start making up for lost time."

Acknowledgments

I hope you had as much fun reading Karissa and Hale's story as we had writing it! We knew since the very first book in the series that Hale didn't have a keen sense of smell because his nose had gotten broken in a fight, courtesy of his girlfriend's brother, but we weren't quite sure what his story was then because he was kind of secretive about it. The moment he told us, though, we knew we had to get Karissa back in his life, especially when it was clear she was *The One* for him!

This whole series wouldn't be possible without some very incredible people. In addition to another big thank-you to my hubby for all his help with the action scenes and military and tactical jargon, thanks to the editors at Sourcebooks (who are always a phone call, text, or email away whenever we need something) and all the other amazing people there, including my fantastic publicist and the crazy-talented art department. The covers they make for me are seriously drool-worthy! Because I could never leave out my readers, a huge thank-you to everyone who reads my books and Snoopy danced right along with me with every new release. That includes the fantastic people on my amazing

Review Team as well as my assistant, Janet. You rock!

I also want to give a big thank-you to the men, women, and working dogs who protect and serve in police departments everywhere as well as their families. And a very special shout-out to our favorite restaurant, P.F. Chang's, where hubby and I bat story lines back and forth and come up with all our best ideas, as well as a thank-you to our fantastic waiter-turned-manager, Andrew, who makes sure our order is ready the moment we walk in the door! Hope you enjoy the next book in the SWAT: Special Wolf Alpha Team series coming soon and look forward to reading the rest of the series as much as I look forward to sharing it with you. Also, don't forget to look for our other series from Sourcebooks, STAT: Special Threat Assessment Team, a spin-off from SWAT! If you love a man in uniform as much as I do, make sure you check out X-Ops, our other action-packed paranormal/romantic-suspense series from Sourcebooks.

Happy Reading!

About the Author

Paige Tyler is the *New York Times* and *USA Today* bestselling author of sexy, romantic fiction, including the SWAT: Special Wolf Alpha Team Series, the STAT: Special Threat Assessment Team Series, the X-OPS Series, the SEALs of Coronado Series, and the Alaskan Werewolves Series. She and her very own military hero (also known as her husband) live on the beautiful Florida coast with their dog

Website: paigetylertheauthor.com
Facebook: PaigeTylerAuthor
Instagram: @authorpaigetyler
Twitter: @PaigeTyler

Also By Paige Tyler